"What if you wed a [...] **murmured, his lips against hers. "Would that be so terrible?"**

With that, he claimed her mouth. He kissed her gently, not wanting to frighten her. At first, her lips didn't move, so startled was she. But as he learned the shape of her mouth, teasing her, gradually she began to respond.

She twined her arms around his neck and tentatively moved her mouth against his. He stroked back her hair, encouraging her without words. His wife-to-be *did* have a more sensual side to her, and when he drew her body against his, she clung to him.

"I shouldn't do this," she whispered. "I am betrothed to another man."

"And what if that man were me?" he asked, sliding his hands down her spine. "Would you be so reluctant to wed?"

"No," she whispered.

Author Note

Forbidden Night with the Highlander is the second book in the Warriors of the Night series.

In this book, the Scottish heroine, Lianna MacKinnon, has OCD tendencies, and I wanted to pair her up with a man who would love and accept her for who she is. All her life she has been betrothed to Rhys de Laurent. Despite every effort to avoid the marriage, she has no choice but to wed her Norman enemy. And yet, she discovers that beneath his strong, serious ways, Rhys is a warrior with a kind heart, a man who appreciates her and respects her.

Look for the third book in this series, *Forbidden Night with the Prince*, which tells the story of Joan de Laurent and her Irish prince. Book one in the series is *Forbidden Night with the Warrior*, the story of Warrick de Laurent and Rosamund de Courcy. If you'd like me to email you when I have a new book out, please visit my website at www.michellewillingham.com to sign up for my newsletter. As a bonus, you'll receive a free story, just for subscribing!

MICHELLE WILLINGHAM

Forbidden Night with the Highlander

HARLEQUIN® HISTORICAL

ISBN-13: 978-1-335-52260-3

Forbidden Night with the Highlander

This edition published by arrangement with Harlequin Books S.A.

For questions and comments about the quality of this book, please contact us at CustomerService@Harlequin.com.

Printed in U.S.A.

RITA® Award finalist **Michelle Willingham** has written over twenty historical romances, novellas and short stories. Currently she lives in southeastern Virginia with her husband and children. When she's not writing, Michelle enjoys reading, baking and avoiding exercise at all costs. Visit her website at michellewillingham.com.

Books by Michelle Willingham

Harlequin Historical
and Harlequin Historical *Undone!* ebooks

Warriors of the Night

Forbidden Night with the Warrior
Forbidden Night with the Highlander

Warriors of Ireland
(linked to *The MacEgan Brothers*)

Warrior of Ice
Warrior of Fire

The MacKinloch Clan

Claimed by the Highland Warrior
Seduced by Her Highland Warrior
Craving the Highlander's Touch (Undone!)
Tempted by the Highland Warrior

The MacEgan Brothers

Her Warrior Slave (prequel)
Her Warrior King
Her Irish Warrior
The Warrior's Touch
Taming Her Irish Warrior
Surrender to an Irish Warrior
Warriors in Winter

Visit the Author Profile page
at Harlequin.com for more titles.

To Jamie Coldsnow, a friend who has made me laugh over the years and who has always been there for me when life got crazy.
Thanks for all that you do for me and my family.

Chapter One

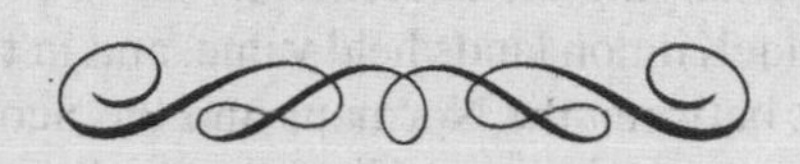

Scotland—1171

'My daughter is…not like other women.'

Rhys de Laurent eyed the Scottish chief, Alastair MacKinnon, wondering what the man meant by that statement.

There was a pained look upon the MacKinnon's face, but Rhys waited for the chief to continue. When there came nothing further, he prompted, 'Is she shrewish or is her face marked by pox?'

Alastair shook his head. 'Nay, she is fair of face. But you'll ken what I mean when you marry her. She is *different*.'

Rhys was not eager to claim the Scottish bride promised to him since her birth. He had travelled north for nearly a fortnight to Eiloch, Scotland, and he had no desire to live in this godforsaken land, half a world away from his family.

But he had come here for the sake of duty and obligation. He was a man who honoured promises, though he was not certain he would go through with the marriage as of yet.

Truthfully, he was here for his younger brother's sake. Warrick had no land of his own, due to an estrangement with their father. These lands in Scotland would give his brother a place to live in peace, and Warrick could help to defend the fortress when it was necessary. It might be that his brother could marry the bride, if he could coerce the young woman's father into changing the agreement.

The MacKinnon lands held value, and in the midst of unrest between the Normans and the Scots, Rhys knew his responsibilities. His father had made an alliance that depended on this marriage.

But he was uneasy about wedding a woman he had never seen before.

'I want to meet with my bride before I agree to the formal betrothal,' he told the chief. 'Both of us deserve that much.'

A tight expression crossed Alastair's face. 'That would no' be wise. Lianna has said she willna marry a Norman.'

Rhys wasn't surprised to hear it. 'Which is why we should meet and get to know one another. She may change her mind, once we are acquainted.' And he could discover if his brother might be a more suitable match.

But the chief was already shaking his head. 'Nay, if she sees you as a Norman, she'll do everything she can to avoid the marriage. Better if you should dress like a Highlander and let her ken who you are as a man. You would find her more appealing.' The Scot eyed him carefully. 'Unless you are too proud to wear our clothing.'

Rhys considered the matter. The chief was right

that Lianna MacKinnon would judge him as an outsider, no matter what he said or did. Fear would govern her opinion, and that was no foundation for a marriage. But he was uneasy about the deception. 'I don't like the idea of lying to my bride.'

'You need not give your name,' Alastair said. 'Trust me when I say that Lianna will soften at kindness. And then you may see her warm heart.' The Scot studied him carefully. 'I've heard a great deal about you, Rhys de Laurent. Most say you are a fair man, respected as a leader. I would never give my daughter into your hands, did I not believe it.'

He gave no reaction to the flattery, for he knew Alastair had no choice but to uphold the arrangement. If Rhys did not accept Lianna as his bride, then he had the right to take Eiloch back again and place Norman soldiers in command of the fortress. His own father, Edward de Laurent, could have done so a generation earlier, but out of respect for his mother, Margaret, he had not. Although she was Norman, she had loved her second husband, Fergus MacKinnon, and had spent many happy years in Scotland, as if it were her sanctuary.

Alastair motioned for one of his men to come forward, and murmured an order in Gaelic. Rhys understood every word, for he had learned the Scottish tongue at a young age. His grandmother had insisted upon it, for the MacKinnons would never accept him as their leader otherwise.

The servant disappeared to obey, and then Alastair turned back. 'I think you will be pleased with my daughter as your bride, once you ken the sort of woman she is and understand her ways.'

Rhys met the man's gaze. 'I will judge her for myself.'

Alastair nodded. 'She rides out to the coast every day for her noontide meal. You will meet her at the dolmen, but I caution you not to let her ken who you are. At least, not yet.'

His servant returned with a shirt and trews similar to those the chief wore. Alastair held out the garments and said, 'Wear this. And I'll bid you luck with Lianna.'

Rhys took the clothing and asked, 'How do I know she will be there?'

Alastair sighed. 'My daughter is a woman with ingrained habits. She has taken her meal by the dolmen every day for the past year. Believe me when I have no doubt you will see her.'

Rhys wasn't certain what to make of that, but he inclined his head. 'So be it.'

Lianna MacKinnon prided herself on order, keeping everything in its place. Her bedchamber had not a speck of dust upon the wooden floor, and every corner of the coverlet was tucked beneath the mattress. She ran a finger along the edge of a small table and found that it was spotless, just as it should be. The sight of the chamber filled her with satisfaction, and she felt a sense of contentment knowing that, at least within this place, she could control the life she lived.

A knock sounded at the door, and her maid Orna opened it without waiting to be invited inside. 'I've news for you, Lady Lianna. The Norman and his men are meeting with your father this morn.'

A cold sweat broke out upon Lianna's brow. Though

the men had sent word of their impending arrival at Eiloch, she could not bear to think of it. The idea of marrying a stranger was a disruption she didn't want to face. Though she had been promised to Rhys de Laurent since birth, she would do anything to avoid the marriage. And now, that moment was here.

Lianna's gaze flickered to the dirt tracks the older woman had brought into the chamber. She moved towards the broom resting on the opposite wall, feeling the desperate urge to clean the floor.

'He will not be my husband, Orna.' Lianna began sweeping up the dirt her maid had tracked in, forming a small pile as she moved towards the door. The older woman likely hadn't noticed it at all, given her failing eyesight. 'I will find a way out of this betrothal.'

She refused to believe that anything else would happen. Over the years, she had saved every spare silver coin, planning to bribe Rhys de Laurent into abandoning this marriage. She had never bought gowns or ribbons, preferring to keep herself plain and save the coins for something far more valuable—her freedom.

Her maid frowned. 'It may not be possible, my lady.'

Lianna found a rag and knelt down to wipe up the mud, cleaning the floor until it was spotless. 'It will be.' It had to be. For the idea of surrendering herself to a strange man was impossible. Rhys had been born and raised in England and knew nothing of their ways. He would not even be able to speak their language.

Her insides twisted up in knots at the thought of wedding a stranger—or worse, sharing his bed and bearing him children. Fear gripped her at the thought.

Her father had accepted it as a necessary arrangement, but she would not give up so easily.

'When Rhys de Laurent hears my proposal, he will gladly return to England without me. My father will remain the chief of Eiloch, and everything will return to the way it was.' Lianna clung to that idea, for it was the only future she wanted to imagine. She wanted her life to remain steady, in an ordered pattern, without straying from its path.

Then she squared her shoulders and informed Orna, 'It is time for my daily ride.'

Today, more than ever, she needed to travel along the coast. The speed of the horse and the wind upon her face would help her to forget about the future pressing her into a corner.

'And what if the chief summons you to meet your husband?' Orna asked. 'You must be here if he does.'

Lianna shuddered at the thought of being displayed before the Norman like a prized sheep. 'I am not married yet.' She reached for her shoes that lay against the far wall, walking barefoot across her clean floor. 'I must go.'

'Please, don't be making trouble for your father, Lianna. You *must* marry Rhys de Laurent and bear a son. Only then can we stay here, God willing.' Her maid risked a glance at the door. 'If you make him angry, the Norman lord will send us away, and we'll have nowhere to live.'

Lianna opened the door and paused. 'Don't be afraid, Orna. I will find a way to avoid this marriage and keep Eiloch in my father's hands. No one will take over our lands, I promise you.' Even if it took every last coin she possessed, she would bribe the man.

Her maid eyed Lianna as if she were uncertain. 'Should you not try to be the wife he wants?'

No. She would not even consider such a thing. With a half-smile, she admitted, 'Orna, I ken what I am. No man finds me appealing, and if my own kinsmen do not care for me, why should this one be any different?'

She adjusted her woollen *brat* to cover her fiery red hair. It was difficult to tame, but she combed it seventy-seven times every morn. And she would do the same when she returned from her ride. 'I will be back by this afternoon.'

Her maid's expression held doubt, but she said nothing. Lianna strode past the woman, carrying her shoes. She walked barefoot through the large gathering space, past her older brother and his men. Sían's face curved in a knowing smile, and he lifted his hand in greeting. She nodded to her brother, feeling her cheeks redden as she overheard one of the men mutter, *Thanks be, none of us has to wed her now.*

She didn't know which of them had spoken but pretended that she hadn't heard the barb. Holding her shoulders back, she glanced up at her brother, only to see him cuff Eachann MacKinnon. Though she appreciated his defence, Lianna was well aware that the men were laughing at her. She ignored them and put on her shoes before she walked down the stairs outside and stepped into the mud.

They thought it strange that she kept to her habits, leaving every day at the same hour to go riding. Each day, always the same. But she *liked* having the same pattern. It was comforting to know what she would do every day.

Sían lived his life from one hour to the next, never

thinking beyond what happened today. His confident manner sometimes bordered on arrogance, but Lianna found that it was easier to quietly clean up the disorder her brother left behind than to defy him.

Her father's house was larger than the others, a tower fortification built of wood and stone. The dwelling could hold twenty men, with three smaller chambers on the second floor. Beyond that, several crofters lived in thatched homes set in a semicircle.

Lianna spied her horse already waiting for her near the stables, and a kitchen boy hurried out to meet her. He held out the wrapped bundle of food, and she took it, knowing what was inside. One piece of bread, one hunk of cheese, and a small jug of ale—just as always. She thanked him and secured the bundle beside her saddle before mounting her mare.

As she rode past the crofters' homes, she studied each one carefully for signs of neglect. Though Sían did not want her to interfere in the people's lives, it was a necessary means of occupying her time. She knew which families had enough food stored for the winter and which crofters would face hardship. She prided herself in knowing the women who would give birth to new babies, and the names of the elderly folk who had died. Then she told Sían, and her brother made arrangements for the families. It gave her a sense of pride to know that she could take care of the others—even if they believed Sían was responsible for their welfare. She needed no accolades for her work, so it mattered not what others thought.

Once she reached the open valley, Lianna urged her horse to go faster. The wind tore through her red hair, and she lifted her face high, revelling in the sensation. She gloried in the freedom, feeling the joy in having this moment alone.

As they drew closer to the coast, she slowed the pace of her mare, turning in the direction of the dolmen. The stone altar had been there for hundreds of years—perhaps even a thousand—and she often wondered about the Druids who had placed it there.

Each day, she took her noon meal at the dolmen, so she would not have to dine with the others and hear their talk. She preferred the solitude and welcomed it.

But this morning, she saw a man standing beside the stone. Her smile faded, and a sense of unrest thrummed within her veins, for he was not supposed to be here. Who was he? For a moment, she wondered if he was Norman, but then dismissed the idea, given his attire.

Although she knew every member of her own clan and of the MacKinloch clan who dwelled nearby, she had never seen this man before. And yet…it almost seemed that he had been waiting for her.

She slowed her horse to a walk, wondering what to do. The man's brown hair was cut short, and his beard held stubble, as if he had shaved it a sennight ago. But it was his eyes that drew her in. They were the dark blue of the sea, with an almost savage beauty in them.

She nodded to him and was startled when he raised a hand in greeting. Every instinct warned her to leave, to abandon the dolmen and go back home. But instead, she drew her horse to a halt and stared at the man.

Keep riding, her instincts warned. *He is a stranger.*

'A good afternoon to you, lass. It's a beautiful place here.' Though he spoke Gaelic, his voice held an unfamiliar accent. Was he from Aberdeen or even Oban? It was difficult to tell. She frowned, wondering who he was. It bothered her so deeply, she drew her horse closer, to see if she could determine his identity from his features.

Her heartbeat quickened at the sight of him, and her mouth grew dry. His face captivated her attention, drawing her closer. There was a faint scar upon his throat, and his expression was hardened, like a man accustomed to battle. Everything about the man spoke of a leader, for he carried his confidence like a weapon.

He wore a saffron *léine*, trews, and a *brat* woven in the MacKinloch colours of blue and green. And yet, she knew he was not of that neighbouring clan. Curiosity roiled up within her, and she was torn about whether to return to her father's house. That would be the sensible thing to do.

But she didn't dare move. The long shirt was ill-fitting, straining against his muscular chest. Beneath it, she spied powerful thighs clad in the trews.

She couldn't think of one single word to say. Her brain could have been filled up with straw, so empty it was.

'You needn't be afraid of me,' he said. 'I came at your father's invitation.'

Only then did she realise that she was gripping the hilt of her dagger. She eyed the Highlander, wondering if he was any threat to her. Her brother had taught her to defend herself, and she would not hesitate, if it were necessary. Yet somehow, she believed this man when he'd said she shouldn't be afraid. He hadn't moved at all, treating her like a wild horse, ready to bolt.

She shook away her idle thoughts. 'Are you a visitor, then?'

He inclined his head. 'I've come for the wedding.'

With effort, she concealed her dismay. He was one of the MacKinloch guests, then. Perhaps distant kin to her mother. Lianna studied him a moment, feeling as if she ought to know who he was. But he looked like none of the clansmen.

She could almost imagine what her brother would say to her. *Ride back to our home at once. You cannot speak to a stranger alone.* If he were here, Sían would seize the reins of her horse and force her to go back.

Was it wrong to steal just another look at the man before she left? She hesitated, but before she could turn back, he smiled at her. Without understanding why, the very breath in her lungs seemed to catch.

Men didn't smile at her. Not ever. More often they rolled their eyes at her or let out an exasperated sigh while her brother made excuses.

Lianna glanced behind her, in case there was someone else approaching. But no, she was alone.

He was easily the most handsome man she'd ever seen. And he was smiling at her, wasn't he? That was something indeed. But only because he did not realise that *she* was the bride.

Lianna knew she should leave, but it bothered her to abandon her plans. Every day at this time, she took her meal at the dolmen. It gave her an hour to sit by the sea and dream. Her life formed a pattern with each day ordered into precise pieces. She knew when she would awaken, when she would work, when she would eat, and when she would sleep.

But it felt as if someone had shaken her life into pieces just now, shattering it with the impending presence of the Norman she was meant to wed. And now with this man.

His very presence had interrupted her noon meal. This was *her* place, not his. *He* ought to be the one to leave. And perhaps if she could convince him to go, she could return to her moments of peace.

'If you have come in search of the MacKinnon chief, he is back at Eiloch.' She pointed towards the road by which she had travelled. 'Follow the path, and you will find our house. My father will grant you hospitality.'

She expected him to nod and obey her command. Instead, he appeared to have little interest in departing. She noticed then that he had no horse. Had he stabled it elsewhere?

'You seem eager to be rid of me,' he remarked.

Lianna stopped herself before she nodded in agreement. Instead, she asked, 'What is your name?'

The Highlander leaned against the dolmen, staring out at the clear sky and the blue sea. A thin mist of clouds rimmed the horizon in the distance, and the sun lit the ripples of water in a pool of fire. 'You may call me Gavin MacAllister.'

A MacAllister? That didn't seem right at all. 'Then why are you wearing the MacKinloch colours?'

His mouth twisted. 'I had to borrow clothing when my daft horse tossed me into the mud.' His gaze fixed upon her face. 'I suppose you must be Lianna MacKinnon, the bride.'

'I am. Unfortunately.' She made no effort to hide her reluctance and patted her horse's back. Likely he had guessed her identity after she'd revealed that her father was the chief.

'Then you do not look forward to your wedding?'

She made a face. 'Not at all. How would you like to be forced into marriage with a stranger? He could be cruel. Nay, I've no wish to be married.'

'And what if he is a good man?' Gavin prompted.

'He is a Norman. And he will want me to change everything—my home, my clothing…everything about myself.' She shuddered at the thought. 'I want to stay here with my family. And…they need me here.'

She didn't know why she was confiding all of this to a stranger and changed the subject. 'What of you? You said you came to Eiloch for the wedding?' Lianna unfastened her bundle of food and spread it upon the stone dolmen between them. Though she had only a little to share, she would not eat without offering him what she had. She broke off a piece of the bread and held it out to him. He reached for it and caught her palm in his.

Lianna froze when his thumb grazed her skin. Heat swelled up inside her, and she could not understand how this man could have such an effect upon her.

'I came because my family wanted to build an alliance with your clan.'

Her mind began reeling through the names of all the MacAllisters she knew. There was a clan to the south, and it might be that he was kin to Rourke MacAllister. She was about to ask him when he interrupted.

'I am sorry you are being forced into this marriage,' he said, still holding her palm. 'I ken what it is to live a life where others make decisions and there is naught you can do.'

'But there is something I can do,' she said, pulling her hand back. With effort, she steadied her breathing and forced herself to eat a bite of bread. 'I have been saving coins for years. I will offer Rhys de Laurent all that I have in return for my freedom. We can go on as we did before.'

He gave her a sidelong look. 'Is he not wealthy, this Norman suitor of yours?'

She didn't like to think of that. 'I suppose. But surely, he would rather have the silver than an unwilling bride. And I doubt he would want me, either.'

'You are a beautiful woman,' he countered. 'Of course he would want you.'

Though his words were kind, she did not believe them. 'The Norman will see what everyone else sees. A plain woman who would make a terrible wife to any man.'

He surprised her when he laughed. 'Why would you say that, Lianna?'

The use of her name felt intimate, and she suddenly grew more aware of this man. Why did he tangle her emotions into such knots? Was it because she had never held a conversation with such a handsome Highlander? Or was it because he actually seemed to listen to her?

'I ken the sort of woman I am,' she said. To distract him from the question, she shared half her cheese with him. Then when they had finished, she folded up the cloth into perfect lines.

'If you're wanting to go and see my father, follow

the road as it leads west.' She pointed out the direction in which she had come. 'He will find a place for you to stay.'

Rhys had no intention of leaving Lianna MacKinnon behind. She was a complicated woman, and he was beginning to see what her father had meant. Everything about her spoke of an ordered life. Even the way she folded the linen cloth was precise.

It was clear that she despised change in any form, and the urge came over him to ruffle her calm exterior and find out if more lay beneath the surface.

A light rain began to fall, and she raised her green and brown *brat* to cover her hair, clearly waiting for him to go. The rain did not appear to bother her at all.

'It's raining,' he pointed out. 'Do you not wish to take shelter?'

'I am used to it.' Nodding towards the road, she prompted him again, 'Take the path, and you will see our home. It isn't far.'

There was no denying that she wanted him to depart. But he answered, 'Where I am from, we do not leave women unprotected.'

Lianna revealed the dagger tucked into her waist. 'I am not unprotected. And if you had threatened me in any way, I would have gutted you.' She spoke the words quietly and was startled to see him smile.

'Good.' He stared at her a moment and then said, 'I suppose if you do not wish to go, then I will stand guard over you.'

'There's no one here,' she pointed out. 'What would you guard me from? If there were any danger, I could scream, and half my clan would come running.'

He ignored her claim and pointed to the dolmen. 'You could take shelter beneath the stone. It will keep you dry for a little while.'

She laughed at his claim. 'I would not fit inside such a small space.' The humour in her brown eyes warmed him, and he liked her. She kept a tight control over her life, and it might be interesting to loosen those bonds. Rhys could not deny that this woman intrigued him.

He understood now, why her father had warned him not to reveal his true identity. In this moment, he could learn more about her without his Norman heritage overshadowing him. They could get acquainted as man and woman.

'Are you certain you do not wish to find another shelter?' he offered.

She shook her head. 'There isn't time. I usually visit with the crofters after I finish my meal. I should go now.'

But he caught her hand again and held it a moment. The rain spattered on her skin, and he stared at the droplets upon her lips. He wanted to know if she felt any sort of attraction towards him. The need was strong, and he wanted to unravel this woman, to see what lay beneath the surface.

And so, he decided to give her pieces of the truth. Let her make of them what she would.

'I didn't only come here to make an alliance,' he murmured. 'Or as a wedding guest.'

She closed her eyes but did not pull her hand away. Instead, it seemed that she was spellbound in the same way he was. 'Why did you come?'

'I came for you, Lianna MacKinnon. Because my father wanted me to wed you.'

Her eyes flew open at that, and she did try to pull away. 'But—I—I cannot. I am already promised.'

Her face flushed scarlet, and he moved in closer, placing both hands on either side of her waist upon the stone dolmen. He waited, giving her every opportunity to push past him. If she even attempted to escape his embrace, he would not hesitate to let her go.

'If you were not betrothed to the Norman, would you consider a different marriage?'

Her eyes were wild with fear, but she placed her hands upon his shoulders as if to ward him off. 'I—I don't think I—'

He leaned in, brushing his mouth against her temple. Her skin was soft, her red hair turning darker beneath the rain. But he could not deny his interest in her. He found himself wanting to coax this woman into yielding to him.

'What if you wed a man like me?' he murmured, his lips against hers. 'Would that be so terrible?' With that, he claimed her mouth. He kissed her gently, not wanting to frighten her. At first, her lips didn't move, so startled was she. But as he learned the shape of her mouth, teasing her, gradually she began to respond.

She twined her arms around his neck, and tentatively moved her mouth against his. He stroked back her hair, encouraging her without words. His wife-to-be *did* have a more sensual side to her, and when he drew her body against his, she clung to him.

'I shouldn't do this,' she whispered. 'I am betrothed to another man.'

'And what if that man were me?' he asked, sliding his hands down her spine. 'Would you be so reluctant to wed?'

'No,' she whispered. 'But that man isn't you.' This time, she did pull back, her cheeks reddening. 'I can do nothing until the Norman agrees to let me go. And that might not happen.'

She closed her eyes with guilt, and her mind was already forming plans, he could tell. But he wanted more from this woman. He wanted to tempt her into forgetting about the boundaries between them, offering her the chance to have a very different sort of marriage, like the one his grandmother had enjoyed.

Ever since adolescence, Rhys had been stifled by responsibilities. His father had taken full command over Rhys's life, demanding that he learn every skill necessary for governing Montbrooke. And his stepmother had seized her own control, trying to bend him to her will. He closed off the darker vision, for he would never again be at a woman's mercy. If he chose to wed Lianna MacKinnon, it would be on his terms.

He wanted to know if she found him desirable, if there was any hope for a true marriage between them. Rhys framed her face with his hands, and her eyes softened. The rain slid over her cheeks, and he kissed the water droplets, claiming her mouth again. This time, he would not allow her to think of anything else, save him. He needed to push away her doubts, and when he revealed the truth to her, she would no longer regret the match.

'Gavin—'

'Shh.' He silenced her and kissed her with more intensity, hoping to drive her towards madness. He pressed his leg between hers, and lifted her hips until she was straddling his thigh. The kiss turned hotter, and when he stroked her tongue with his, he lost sight of his own plans. She emitted a slight moan, shuddering as she rocked against him.

Her innocent reaction caused him to lose control. This woman was his and had been promised to him since birth. She gripped his shoulders, her nails digging into his skin when he kissed her. Her sensitivity made him reckless, and he could voice only one thought in his brain: *Mine.*

No longer would he consider giving her to Warrick. She belonged to him, and one day soon, this Scottish beauty would be naked in his bed, and he would enjoy pleasuring her. She shuddered, and he imagined how it would be to bring her to fulfilment.

But abruptly, she shoved him back, her face stricken. 'I cannot,' she whispered. 'I'm sorry.' Her face held shame and guilt, and she hurried past him to her horse.

'Lianna, wait.' It was better to admit the truth to her now, to reveal his name and let her know that there was no harm in what they had done.

But she had already mounted her mare. She urged the animal back towards the settlement, without looking at him. The rain had soaked through his borrowed clothing, but he hardly felt the chill at all. His body was raging for Lianna MacKinnon.

And he would stop at nothing to claim his promised bride.

Chapter Two

Lianna was on her hands and knees, cleaning a small pile of dirt from the floor when her brother Sían strode into the gathering space. He smiled warmly at her. 'You needn't kneel on my behalf, Sister.'

His teasing was meant to make her laugh, but she could not bring herself to do so. Inwardly, she was still shaken by the encounter with Gavin MacAllister. The Highlander had struck her speechless with his handsome face, and God help her, the kiss had made her into a trembling mess. It wasn't her first, but it was so very different from the dry peck upon her mouth, only given because one boy had dared another. No, Gavin's kiss had unravelled her senses. She had hardly been able to ride back to their fortress, for her face was burning with startled embarrassment.

Men didn't pay attention to her. They didn't even like her. As she rose from the floor, folding the cloth into a rectangle, she didn't miss the smirk from one of their kinsmen standing nearby.

'You missed a grain of sand,' Robbie mocked her. 'Just there.'

She glanced in the direction he pointed but saw nothing. The arrogant look in his eyes bothered her, and she looked to Sían to say something. But her brother ignored it, pulling out a chair before he sat.

'What have you seen this day?' he asked. 'Did any of the crofters' homes have cobwebs, or God forbid, a rat?'

Robbie snickered, but she ignored the man. The truth was, she'd forgotten to inspect the homes at all. She ought to confess to her brother the truth, that she had encountered Gavin MacAllister. And yet, a part of her wanted to hold that memory to herself.

Instead, she repeated what she had already told him in the past. 'Hamish and Maire lost two of their cattle to raiders. Their daughter, Lara, will give birth in the spring. And Orna is growing old and is suffering from aching of her hands and feet. Most of our people lack enough supplies to last through the winter. We need to be prepared.'

A part of her knew she ought to use her precious hoard of coins to buy supplies for her kinsmen, but she hoped that the Norman would take her exchange and give her freedom from the marriage. If he refused, she would use the silver to help her clan.

Sían sighed. 'Then everything with our clan is the same as always. What would I do without your observations?' He winked at his men, and Lianna decided to broach the subject she feared the most.

'Father has told me that the Norman has arrived with his men. He still wants me to marry Rhys de Laurent.' She gripped her hands together, waiting to hear his response. Sían had the most to lose, for once de Laurent married her, he would take command of the clan.

At that, her brother's expression turned cold. 'Is that so?' There was a cruel air within his voice, and he stood, resting his hand upon the dagger at his waist.

Lianna raised her eyes to his, pleading, 'Will you speak to Father on my behalf?' She knew her best hope was to flatter her brother's ego. '*You* should be the clan chief, not a stranger.' She steeled herself and said, 'If you can stop this marriage, I would be so grateful.'

Her brother did appear irritated by the idea of losing command. 'You are right that *I* should be the leader of our people. Father is sick, and we must be prepared for the worst.'

'Thank you,' she murmured. Her heart did worry over Alastair, for even during these past summer months, he had struggled to overcome a hacking cough. Sían had offered to take over his duties, but their father had refused. His pride prevented him from accepting help.

Sían took her hand and patted it as if she were a child. 'Does this Norman truly think he can trespass upon our land, plant a babe within you, and steal all that we have worked for?' He met the gazes of their kinsmen, who appeared as angry as he did. 'It will not happen.'

'Perhaps it could be avoided,' Lianna suggested. 'Give him another bride, if he wants an alliance with us.' Surely there was a young maid who would not mind living with a wealthy Norman.

'He can have your maid, Orna,' Sían remarked with a hearty laugh. 'As old as she is, she won't mind at all.'

But Lianna did not share in his laughter. She stood and walked away from the men, knowing that Sían would not be serious until they were alone. As she hoped, he started to follow. 'Peace, my sister. We will walk awhile and talk about this.'

Which meant he would discuss nothing in front of their kinsmen. She understood his need to remain a respected leader among them.

They walked in silence for half a mile before Sían turned serious. 'You are frightened of this marriage.'

'I am,' she admitted. 'I hope that the Norman will turn me down, that he will not want a woman like me.' No one did, for she knew most of the men made fun of her behind her back. They didn't understand her, and she didn't expect them to.

'It matters not if he wants someone like you. He would not willingly surrender command of Eiloch,' her brother answered. 'Our lands hold value, and he will want to gain favour in the sight of the English king by claiming them.'

'It doesn't have to be me,' she whispered. 'Why can we not ask him to go back? If we pay him, he may consider it. I have saved some silver over the years.'

Sían's eyes clouded a moment. 'Indeed.' Then he let out a sigh and dropped his arm across her shoulders. 'I will not let any man hurt you, Lianna. I promise you that. Especially not a Norman bastard.'

She wanted to believe her brother could defend her, but this agreement had been made before she was born. Not only that, but she knew the strength of the Norman warriors. They could tear the clan apart, leaving the crofters' homes in ashes.

Fear sank its claws into her, and she tried to steady

herself. Right now, she needed a mindless activity to help occupy her time. The winter stores could be reorganised, and she decided it would be a good distraction.

'Is there someone else you would rather wed?' her brother asked. With a light teasing tone, he added, 'Someone you have your eye on?'

The image of Gavin MacAllister suddenly invaded her mind. His body had filled out the MacKinloch clothing he wore, and she had welcomed the feeling of his arms around her. Even his kiss had captivated her senses.

Her face flushed, and her brother's expression gleamed. 'Who is he, Lianna?'

She covered her cheeks and shook her head. 'No one.' To avoid answering questions, she turned her back.

Sían laughed quietly. 'You will not tell me, I see.' He only ruffled her hair and said, 'Don't fear, Lianna. I will handle everything. You need not wed this man.'

'What will you do if the Normans will not listen to reason?' she asked. She knew better than to think it would be an easy escape.

A sly smile came over her brother's face. 'Don't worry your head over that. Trust that I ken what is best.'

She wanted to trust in him, but could not quite bring herself to do so. Sían never prepared for the future, but made decisions depending on his moods—and his decisions changed by the hour. Although she might love him as her brother, he was utterly unreliable. But she wanted to believe that he would intervene on her behalf, if she asked it of him. She had to hold on to her faith.

Worry gripped her with the fear of her father dying. After her mother's death in childbirth when Lianna was eight years old, he was all she had left. Although she had never understood Alastair's fierce desire for a Norman alliance, he had been a kind and loving father. More than once, he had confessed that he wished *she* had been the firstborn son.

'I know that you care for our people,' he'd said. 'You see what they truly need, instead of what they tell others to salvage their pride.'

His praise had warmed her heart, and because of it, she'd tried to fill the emptiness left behind by her mother. Davina had kept their house immaculate, and Lianna had tried to do the same. By holding on to her mother's ways, it was a means of remembering her.

Sían walked back with her to the fortress, and Lianna parted ways from him, moving towards the thatched shelter that housed the entrance to the underground storage chamber. She climbed down the ladder, adjusting her woollen *brat* against her shoulders. All along the stone walls, she had organised food stores by grains and fruits. Now, she wondered if it might be better to sort them according to the month the foods had been harvested. It was nearly autumn, but she was well aware that there was a dire lack of supplies.

After an hour of sorting, she had regained command of her fear. It was frigid below the ground, and she climbed back up the ladder, only to see her brother on horseback with several men. They were gathering weapons, and she overheard one of the men jeering about the Normans. Her brother had a bow and quiver of arrows strapped across his shoulder.

Had Rhys de Laurent arrived, then? A sudden uneasiness caught her heart, and she picked up her skirts, hurrying towards them. 'Sían, where are you going? Why do you have weapons?'

He wasn't planning an attack, was he?

Her brother only smiled. 'We're going hunting, Lianna. You said yourself that we've a lack of food.'

She wished she could feel a sense of relief, but one of his kinsmen had an axe strapped to his waist. It was not a weapon meant for hunting animals, and she could not relinquish her suspicions, despite his words.

Sían smiled at her and added, 'Don't you want fresh venison or pheasant?'

His tone bothered her, for she was deeply afraid that he meant to attack the Norman travelling party. If he did, it would bring war among them, and she had no doubt the soldiers would slaughter any man who raised weapons.

In a low voice, she warned, 'Sían, don't do anything foolish.' She didn't want to outwardly accuse him in front of his men, but she sensed his lies.

His thin smile transformed into a sneer. 'I am doing what is best for all of us, Lianna.' With a mocking smile, he added, 'We wouldn't want any predators threatening our people.'

She needed to speak with Alastair, in the hopes that someone could deter her brother. He might be able to reason with Sían, to make him see that violence would only beget more fighting. And if he threatened the Normans, it would undermine her own chance at freedom.

Her brother was already striding towards the others, and she called out, 'Sían, wait!'

He only raised his dagger in a mock salute, while his kinsmen laughed and mounted their horses. A flock of crows flew over their heads, and a premonition passed over her. *If they attack, they're going to die.*

She knew better than to think that she could stop them from whatever they planned, but perhaps her father could. Lianna hurried back to the house, not knowing what would happen.

But Sían had to be stopped.

Rhys de Laurent sat among his men by the fire, watching the golden flames flare amid the peat. Although the clan chief, Alastair MacKinnon, had offered them shelter at his home, he'd wanted to bide his time a little longer. He knew better than to think the Highlanders would welcome Norman soldiers among their clan. But now that he had decided to go through with the betrothal, they would travel to Eiloch in the morning.

He was glad to have these last few hours to clear his head. His mind was caught up with a thousand questions he could not answer. He had gone to meet with Lianna MacKinnon to see what sort of woman she was. He'd predicted that she would be soft-spoken and timid, obeying her father's bidding. Instead, she had met his gaze with her own courage. There was something about her that intrigued him—and now that he'd had a taste of her, he wanted more.

Once, he'd thought about switching places with his brother, allowing Warrick to wed Lianna in his stead.

Yet, now that he'd tasted her lips, he wouldn't even consider it. He had kissed her to satisfy a curiosity, to see if there was a woman of fiery spirit to match her red hair. Instead, he had found that she was innocent, confused and scared. Her kiss had been sweetly unknowing, as if it were her first. But in time, she had warmed to his touch, and he now believed that she would make a good wife for him.

God in Heaven, it had aroused him beyond all imaginings. Her palms had rested upon his chest, and she had opened to him, offering him her own yearning. When she had straddled his leg, allowing him to stroke her mouth with his tongue, he'd nearly lost himself. He had become a different man, one caught up beneath her spell.

He would indeed accept this woman as his bride. And although he had once imagined leaving her behind in Scotland, now he was reconsidering. It might be best to take her back to England with him.

And more than all else, he was looking forward to claiming her as his own.

'You look besotted,' his friend Ailric remarked. 'Was she fair of face?'

If fair of face meant hair like a sunset, and skin that resembled the petals of a rose, then yes.

'She was,' Rhys agreed. 'In the morning, we will go to Eiloch and you can see her for yourself.'

Ailric poked at the fire until a shower of sparks scattered across the air. 'I hope that your marriage will be as good as mine is, my friend.' There was a fleeting glimpse of longing on his face. His friend had been wedded for only a year, but already his wife Elia was expecting their first child.

'You shouldn't have come with us,' Rhys said. 'Better to have stayed home with your wife. This journey to Scotland is too far. What if Elia gives birth while you are away?'

'With another mouth to feed, I will do what I must. Better that I can earn silver from service to you, my lord. We will need more, soon enough.' He leaned back against a log, a gleam of joy in his eyes. 'I hope that one day you will know the happiness I've known. To see love in your wife's eyes and know that hers is the first face you'll see in the morning. To touch her belly and feel the faint kick of your son beneath her skin.' He shook his head as if he could not believe his good fortune. ''Tis a wonder, indeed.'

'You will see her soon,' Rhys promised. 'God willing, I hope to return to England within a fortnight. I must bring Lianna back to Montbrooke so that the betrothal document may be signed and witnessed.'

'Was that not already done when she was born?'

'It was, but our fathers demanded that both of us must give our consent to the marriage.' Rhys shrugged. 'It will not take long, and we will be wedded after that.'

He wondered if Lianna would be glad to marry him, once she learned the truth. It didn't sit well with him to lie to her, but perhaps she would understand his reasons. He hadn't wanted her to judge him on his Norman heritage before she had known him as a man. And he had found her more desirable than he'd imagined.

'God grant that you both are happy,' Ailric said. He stood in the darkness, and there came the sound of horses approaching.

They were not expecting visitors at this hour, and Rhys signalled for his men to be on alert. Instinctively, he reached for his sword. It might be Alastair and his kinsmen, or it might be a threat.

The hoofbeats ceased, and silence descended over their camp. Footsteps approached, and Rhys turned towards the sound, his hand upon his sword hilt.

Only seconds later, he heard a cry from his friend. Horror washed over him when he turned back and saw an arrow embedded in Ailric's chest. His friend crumpled to the ground, and God help him, Rhys knew it was over.

He seized Ailric's shield, releasing a battle roar of anguish. Then he charged into the darkness, his rage and grief swelling like a tide. He didn't know who had dared to attack, but their assailants would pay the price with their lives.

A tightness filled up his chest as Rhys kept his shield up, barking commands at his men to raise their shields and form a circle. It was difficult to see more than shadows in the night sky, but he caught a blur of motion and used the moment to attack. Fury poured through him with the need for vengeance.

As he slashed out at a faceless enemy, his rage mingled with grief. No longer would Ailric see his wife's smile in the morning, and his friend would never hold his newborn son.

Rhys's sword cut through human flesh, and he heard a man cry out as he was struck down. He ended his enemy's life, and his men held their positions, waiting for the Highland raiders to approach.

So, they had asked him to wed the chief's daughter, only to attempt a slaughter in the middle of the night? They would soon learn the strength and power of his forces.

One stepped into the light, clearly one of the MacKinnons, given his clothing. Damn them for this. Rhys had deliberately stayed back from the clan, not wanting to bring fear and war among them. But now that they had attacked like cowards in the night, they would see no mercy.

In the Norman tongue, he ordered his men to keep their shields up and pursue the Highlanders. His heart hardened, his emotions turning to stone. He had no idea how many there were, but any man who dared to attack would feel the edge of his blade.

For Ailric.

Another raider emerged, but he was no match for six trained Norman warriors. One by one, they defended themselves against the remaining raiders—but there was still the unknown archer. None of these men had a bow among them.

Rhys sent out three men to scout the number of horses. 'How many are left?' he asked, when they returned.

'There were four horses,' one answered. 'So at least one raider is still out there.'

The archer, Rhys guessed. And if his horse was still here, then so was the man. 'Spread out,' he ordered them, in the Norman language. 'Keep your shields raised and find that archer.' He would not rest until they had found them all. And if Alastair MacKinnon was responsible for ordering this raid, then Rhys would see every last member of the clan driven out of Eiloch.

His men obeyed the command, leaving Rhys by

the fire. He deliberately remained behind, wanting the light to guide him. He kept his shield raised, listening for the sound of the last Highlander.

'I know you're there,' he called out to the man, using the Gaelic language. 'And I know you have to hide in the shadows. Because you know that you are no match for Norman fighters.'

He sensed a ripple of motion and lifted his shield, just as an arrow struck the wood. It came from the opposite direction, but Rhys held his position.

'Arrogant Scot,' he jeered. 'Was this your chief's idea? To kill us all, before I claim his daughter as my bride?'

One man did step into the light, and he held another arrow nocked to the bow. 'You think I would let you claim what rightfully belongs to me? I should be the leader, not you.'

'These are my lands by birthright,' Rhys contradicted. 'You hold no claim to them.' He stared at the young man, noting the overconfidence in his bearing.

'I'm going to kill you, Norman. And your head will be displayed at our gates.' He released another arrow, but Rhys blocked it again.

'Your aim is poor.' He kept his shield up, circling the man. Footsteps approached, and one by one, his men returned to join him. 'Was it your idea to kill us in our sleep?'

'It was,' the man taunted. 'And you're still going to die. Norman bastards.'

As are you, Rhys thought. Because of this man, one of his most trusted soldiers was dead. If he lunged forward, he might be able to strike the archer's bow away, leaving him defenceless. But he would have to lower his shield.

'You cannot kill me,' the archer said with a sly smile. 'Do you know who I am?'

With that, Rhys dropped his sword and unsheathed the knife at his waist. He threw the knife at the man's heart and saw the look of shock in the Highlander's eyes as the blade struck true. His enemy dropped to his knees, the bow falling from his hands.

'I know exactly who you are,' Rhys said softly. 'The man who killed my friend.'

Lianna heard the outcry at dawn when the Norman soldiers arrived. She hurried outside and saw them leading horses…with the bodies of Highlanders draped across the saddles. Her throat closed up with terror, her hands shaking.

Last night, she had begged her father to send men after her brother, but Alastair had refused. He'd said that Sían would listen to no man's counsel, save his own. If he dared to attack, then that lay upon his shoulders.

And though she knew Alastair was right, her father should have tried. For now, she dreaded the worst.

The blood drained from her face, and Lianna stepped back against the outer wall of the house, trying to hold back the wave of fear. She knew, without asking, that Sían was dead. He hadn't been hunting deer or game at all. He'd been hunting the Norman soldiers. And from the looks of it, none had survived.

Alastair hobbled from his house, his complexion grey. The grief in his bearing made her fearful of what he would do now. Without thinking, Lianna rushed forward to his side.

'Father,' she whispered.

But he did not answer. Instead, he walked towards one of the bodies concealed by a wool covering. He lifted the edge and revealed Sían's face.

There came an uproar from the Highlanders gathered around, and God help her, Lianna feared they would rise up in rebellion. But they did not need more bloodshed, not now.

Her father raised his voice. 'I did not order this raid. It was never my intent to start a war.'

His words cast silence over the clan, and he continued. 'Lianna, make the arrangements for the burial of these men. I will meet with my council and with the Normans.'

Her eyes flooded with hot tears, and her stomach clenched. The Normans could burn in hell for all she cared. She stared at the horses bearing the bodies, and nausea twisted her stomach. Her maid Orna approached and said, 'I will help, Lianna.' The older woman motioned to several of the others, and she took the reins of one of the horses.

Lianna wanted to follow, but her legs would not move. With a fleeting glance towards the Normans, she wondered which one was Rhys de Laurent. All wore conical helms and chainmail armour. They appeared fully prepared for battle.

There was only one consolation that distracted her now—her father could not possibly demand that she marry the Norman. Not when these men had killed Sían. With a leaden heart, she followed Orna and reached for the reins of a second horse.

'Hear me,' her father called out to the clan members, and Lianna turned back to listen to him. 'I will not risk our clan's survival based on the lack of judgement from my son. I did not order this attack, and Sían's defiance resulted in tragedy. No one here will raise a hand against our Norman guests—or you will be exiled from us.' His grey eyes were the colour of iron, cold and unforgiving. He met the gazes of his men, who looked ready to engage in fighting.

Lianna saw murder brewing in the eyes of Eachann and Ross. The fierce Highlanders were among the strongest fighters remaining. They needed a means of releasing their anger, and she stepped towards them. 'Will you help dig the graves of your kinsmen?'

They didn't move, until Alastair said, 'Do as my daughter bids you.'

She stepped up, facing each of them. Tension stretched thin until finally Ross muttered, 'We will bide our time.' Then they stepped back to fetch shovels to begin digging the graves. Lianna chose two more men to help them, and then sent for the priest.

She was grateful for the many tasks that had to be done. It occupied her time, allowing her to push back the wave of emotion threatening to drown her. Sían had been her only brother, the laughing young man who had believed himself invincible. Tears pricked at her eyes, but she could not cry now. Several women were openly weeping at the loss of their sons and husbands. Lianna busied herself with helping them, asking them to gather linen for the burial shrouds.

But as the Normans departed with her father, she could only think that her freedom had been won at a terrible cost.

She led the horse bearing her brother's body, taking him back towards the stone kirk. There, she would prepare him for burial, and perhaps indulge in a moment of grief.

But, without warning, the hair on the back of her neck stood on end. She froze in place, wondering what had disturbed her so suddenly.

She turned and saw that one of the Normans was staring at her, his expression intent. There was a hint of familiarity around him, though she could not place it. From this distance, she could barely see his face and his hair was hidden beneath his helm.

It must be Rhys de Laurent.

Lianna lifted her chin in defiance, staring boldly back at him. Let him look. For he would never have her as his bride.

Rhys followed the clan chief into a private gathering space, accompanied by his men. Two other Scots joined them, and there was no denying the cold fury that permeated the demeanour of every man here.

He said nothing but waited for Alastair to speak. His own anger was raging, that they had come here in peace to fulfil the bargain, and the man's own son had dared to attack.

'Sían acted of his own accord,' Alastair said quietly. 'I gave no orders for a raid.'

Rhys stared back at the man in disbelief. Did he honestly think that he would believe such a statement? His gaze was hard and unyielding, but there was melancholy in the man's eyes.

'I am old, and my time here grows short,' Alastair said. 'My son coveted my position as chief, and time and again, he was wanting me to step down and let him lead.' He glanced at his companions. 'But such was impossible. Sían was too impulsive, believing he was always right. He often acted without thinking, and more than once, I've had to atone for his reckless actions.' He met Rhys's gaze evenly. 'As I am prepared to do now.'

'You broke our bargain of peace,' Rhys said coolly. 'I have the right to drive every man, woman, and child from Eiloch. These are Norman lands now, inherited by my father from the chief before you. And now they belong to me, as his heir.'

'They belong to both the Normans and the Scots,' Alastair corrected. 'Your grandfather saw that he would be needing protection for Eiloch one day. When he married your Norman grandmother, he made that bargain to guard us from outside threats.'

'You forfeited our treaty when your son tried to kill us,' Rhys said. 'I will not marry your daughter now. But I *will* seize command of Eiloch.'

Alastair closed his eyes and fell silent for a long moment. Then, after a long pause, he continued, 'I grieve the death of my son. Sían was my flesh and blood, and no father should outlive his child.' His hand closed in a fist. 'But Lianna is no' like her brother. She has the heart and the intelligence to lead this clan. Had she been a boy, I would have made her the leader, for she is a good woman who puts the needs of others before her own.'

Alastair poured mead into a silver mazer cup and lifted it high. 'I don't want war between the Normans and my people. They will struggle to survive this winter, and we need Norman aid to provide enough food for them.' He drank from the cup. 'I offer you this cup of peace. I will forgive you for killing my son, if you do not bring vengeance against our people.' He passed the cup to his advisors, who drank in turn, and then the cup was given to Rhys.

He hesitated, for he was uncertain whether to accept this offering. Sían MacKinnon might well have acted without his father's permission. Given the haggard expression on Alastair's face, he did appear to regret his son's actions.

This was a man who valued peace, above his own personal tragedy. And that was something to be respected.

'I will not drive your people out of Eiloch yet,' Rhys said quietly. 'For now, I will wait and use my own judgement. If they dare to raise a hand against any of us, they will die for it.' He drank the mead and passed it back.

'If any of my people strike back at you or your men,' Alastair answered, 'I will order their deaths myself.' He set down the mazer cup and leaned back in his chair. 'Lianna will not want to wed you—I must be honest about this. But she does understand the needs of our clan. She knows how dire our circumstances are, and if I command it of her, she will obey.'

Rhys wasn't certain *he* wanted to wed under these circumstances. But he did need to be honest with Lianna MacKinnon and tell her of his true identity. She deserved that much.

'I will speak with her this evening,' he said. 'In the meantime, I will inspect your crofters' homes and learn more about Eiloch.'

Alastair nodded. 'My men will accompany you to

ensure your safety.' He rose from his chair and said, 'Under most circumstances, I would join you and Lianna on your journey back to Montbrooke for the formal betrothal. But I think it best if I remain behind, to ensure that my people do not rise up in rebellion.'

'You assume that I will wed her,' Rhys said. 'I will not claim her if she displeases me.' Unbidden came the memory of her mouth beneath his, the softness of her kiss. But once she learned who he was, she would despise him.

Alastair's expression tightened with firm resolution. 'She will do as I command.'

Lianna stared at her father in shock. 'I will not.'

How could he even imagine she would wed the Norman who had murdered her brother? The very thought was monstrous. Her heart pounded, and she gripped her hands together so tightly, her knuckles turned white. 'The men are digging Sían's grave as we speak. How can you ask me to wed the man who put him there?' She rose from her place, panic gnawing inside her.

'Because if you do not make this alliance, he will drive our people out of Eiloch.' Her father's pallor was grey, and he sat down, resting his hand on his forehead. 'Lianna, you don't ken what lies ahead. Our people cannot survive if he drives us out.'

'Then fight back,' she insisted. 'We have more men than he does!'

'If we slaughter the heir of Montbrooke, his father will send Norman troops by the hundreds. They would kill every last one of us, and you ken this.' He swallowed hard. 'Sían made a terrible mistake, and I should have listened to you. I regret not sending men after him, but I never thought he would do something like this.'

'And yet, you ask me to marry his murderer.' Her voice broke away, and terror poured over her in a wave. 'I cannot do it. I *will* not do it.'

'He is coming to dine with us this evening after the burials. You will meet with him then,' her father said.

'I would rather die than wed Rhys de Laurent,' she shot back. Her rage poured over her, and she stood from the table. Right now, she needed to be on horseback, to ride hard and release the storm of tears building inside. She started to back away from the table, but her father raised a hand, and two of her kinsmen blocked her path.

'You will not leave, Lianna,' he said. 'It is not safe now. With all that has happened, you must stay here.'

And be his prisoner, she realised. A blinding anger overcame her, and she tried to shove her way past the men. But Eachann gripped her arm, staring back at her father for his orders.

'Go to your bedchamber,' Alastair warned. 'You may bide there until we bury Sían and the others. And you will meet with Rhys de Laurent later tonight.' Though he spoke calmly, she didn't miss the tremor of emotion in his voice. It seemed that he was holding back his own grief by a single thread.

'I will not meet with him.' Not now or ever. If he meant for her to stay in her room, stay she would. He could not force her to wed the Norman.

'Take her,' Alastair said.

Eachann was not gentle, but pulled her towards the stairs and marched her up each tread. When she reached her room, he opened the door and shoved her inside. She had no time to speak, but heard the telltale click of the key turning in the lock.

Lianna drew her knuckles into a fist and slammed her hand into the door, not even caring if it bruised. Her life was falling to pieces all around her, and she could not gather control of it. Anger roared through her, and she dropped to her knees on the floor. There was a stiff brush and a bucket of water in the corner, and she reached for them. She scrubbed the floor over and over, obliterating all traces of dirt. Her shoulders shook with rage and grief, and she wept for the loss of her brother…but most of all, for the loss of her freedom. She scrubbed until her fingers were raw from the effort, and her knees were damp from the water.

Then, a sudden thought took root in her mind. What of the coins she had saved to buy her freedom? Would the Norman consider the bribe? It was still a fragile glimmer of hope that she clung to.

She ran to the opposite side of the room and dropped to her knees again. With the blade of her dagger, she pried up the floorboard and reached for the sack of coins she had saved over the years.

It was gone. With horror, she reached her hand into the darkness, trying to see if it had somehow been pushed aside. But there was nothing at all, save something tiny, a scrap of fabric she could not see. When she pulled it from the hiding place, the tears sprang up again. It was a handkerchief she had embroidered for Sían.

He had taken her coins and used them for God only knew what. When had he done this? She had told him only a day ago, but it was clear that he had seized the coins long before that.

Where were they now? She recalled that he had gone 'hunting' with his men, but that was during the afternoon. They had not attacked the Norman camp until nightfall. Where had he been all that time?

She knew he had not kept the coins with him during the attack, for she had spent the past hour preparing his body for burial. A queasy feeling passed over her, and she sat against the wall, drawing her knees up. There was truly nothing left for her now. No silver, no means of convincing the Norman to leave her alone.

Her father wanted her to meet with the man this evening, but she could not fathom doing so. Her heart was ravaged with grief and frustration. If she laid eyes upon his face, it would only bring back her anger.

She lowered her face against her knees. Nothing would ever force her to wed the Norman—not after what he'd done.

She swore, with every breath in her body, that she would not let her enemy claim her.

Chapter Three

Rhys spent the remainder of the day inspecting the crofters' homes, surveying every inch of occupied property. He continued to wear his conical helm and chainmail armour, for he wanted the Highlanders to realise that he was indeed a threat if they dared to assault him or his men.

He saw four graves dug in the clearing beside the kirk. Inside, he knew that they had prepared the bodies, and the burial would happen within an hour or two. The people were gathering flowers, and he saw another woman enter the stone kirk, carrying a length of linen.

Earlier this morning, he and his men had already buried Ailric beside the forest, saying a prayer for the man's soul. It seemed impossible that they had broken bread with him last night, speaking of his wife and unborn child. Life was fleeting, and Rhys promised himself that they would somehow provide for Ailric's widow, Elia.

The priest stepped outside by the graves, wearing a long brown robe knotted with a cord. His expression was sombre, and he approached Rhys and his men with a lowered head.

'I offer you the peace of Christ,' he said by way of greeting, using the Norman language. 'The MacKinnon told me of this grievous tragedy. I will pray for the souls of these men.' Rhys inclined his head, but knew the priest had another reason for speaking. As he'd anticipated, the priest continued, 'But I beg you not to inflict your vengeance against our people. They are not your enemies.'

An invisible tension knotted across the space, and Rhys answered, 'We will only attack those who raise arms against us.' He glanced around at the people gathering for the funeral. 'Those who keep the peace have nothing to fear.'

His words would not convince the MacKinnons, he knew. Several mothers held fast to their children, as if they feared he would cut them down where they stood. He nodded to the priest by way of farewell and strode across the space.

But he had seen what the clan chief had spoken of. These people were thin and suffering. Their clothing looked as if the garments had been worn year in and year out. There was no prosperity, no sense of security here.

That was the reason why Rhys's grandfather, Fergus MacKinnon, had named Edward the heir, instead of a trueborn Scot. Without any children of his own, he had selected Margaret's grown son from her first marriage as the heir. And by bringing an alliance between Normans and Scots, Fergus hoped to end the vast poverty here.

His father had not lifted a finger, Rhys knew. Edward had no loyalty here, and he cared nothing for Scotland. To his father, this was a vast wasteland of primitive people whose customs were very different. And so, it fell upon Rhys's shoulders to change that.

A part of him wanted to walk away from this marriage and these people. He owed them no loyalty at all, not after what Sían had done.

But then, Rhys caught sight of a young boy standing near the kirk, perhaps thirteen years of age. The lad's hair was dark, like his own brother Warrick's, and his face was gaunt with hunger. Though he was taller than Lianna, the boy's arms were too thin. Most likely he would die this winter, if there was not enough food.

A weariness settled over Rhys, for *this* was the reason why he could not walk away. He had inherited Eiloch, and that meant taking responsibility for these people and their poverty. Regardless of his personal feelings, he would never turn his back on starving children. Providing for them was the right thing to do. He possessed the means to change their lives, forging new alliances that would serve his king in times of war.

As a boy, he had suffered his own personal nightmares of abuse. He'd tried to shield his brother from their stepmother Analise, but their father had never believed the truth about her. They had been alone, unable to defend themselves. No one had offered to help, and when Rhys stared at this boy, he saw the shadow of himself.

There was no turning back now. Not from these people, and not from this alliance.

Slowly, he walked with his men towards their

camp. They had deliberately left their belongings there, with the intent of returning tonight to take shelter within Alastair's house. He decided to remain isolated throughout the afternoon and early evening. Let them bury their dead without a Norman threat hanging over them.

And when he returned, he would wear their clothing as a sign of peace.

Her father released Lianna from her chamber to attend the funeral Mass for her brother and their kinsmen. By then, she had regained command of her emotions, steeling herself as they lowered the linen shrouds into the ground. She hid her shaking hands by gripping them tightly, and when the rain fell upon their graves, it felt like the tears she could not bring herself to shed.

After the bodies were buried, her father led her back to the house. Quietly, he said, 'You will return to your chamber and await Rhys de Laurent. I will send him to you, so that you may speak with him.'

She wanted nothing of the sort. But if she told her father she had no intention of opening the door, he would drag her below stairs and force her to meet the man publicly. She doubted if this Norman would listen to reason. His fierce bearing revealed a ruthless man who would act only upon his own accord.

Lianna held her silence as Alastair escorted her back. In the space of two days, her father appeared to have aged ten years. His demeanour was heavy with grief, and she slowed her steps. With a gentle squeeze to his hand, she murmured, 'We will miss Sían.'

He gripped it in return and closed his eyes, as if

to gather strength from her. 'You must take the place he could not.'

She didn't understand what he meant by that, for she could never lead the clan. But perhaps he intended for her to ensure that their people were protected, no matter what happened. And this she could promise.

'I will try.'

He took her back to her room and regarded her. 'I will send your meal to you here. And later tonight, Rhys will come and talk with you. Unless you would rather dine with everyone else?'

She shook her head. Her father knew how much she hated being among crowds of people. It was why she took her noon meal by the dolmen each day.

'I need you to make this alliance,' her father said softly. 'I believe that you have the strength to wed this man. And he will listen to you.'

He was wrong in that. Men never listened to her, and neither would a Norman warrior. But she went to sit beside her window, and her father closed the door behind him. As she'd predicted, he locked it, leaving her a captive once more.

Which was likely a good decision, given that she wanted nothing more than to escape. Lianna walked over to her bed and straightened the coverlet, pulling it so that both sides were even.

Her mind turned over the problem, wondering if there was something she could do—anything to avoid this marriage. But she could not see a pathway to freedom, no matter what wild ideas sprang to mind.

Her stomach lurched when abruptly there came a knock at her door. It was too soon. They had not eaten the evening meal, and she didn't imagine that her father could have brought the Norman to her this soon.

She ignored the knocking, her heart racing within her chest. And then a voice called out in Gaelic, 'Lianna, I need to talk with you.'

It was the Highlander, Gavin MacAllister. She had nearly forgotten about him in the midst of the funeral. But now she wondered if he could be useful to her.

'My father has locked me inside this room,' she said. 'Else, I would open it.'

To her surprise, she heard the turning of a key. 'Alastair gave me permission to speak with you. May I come in?'

She opened the door and saw that he was wearing the same saffron *léine* and trews that he'd worn before. His dark hair was cut short against the back of his neck, and the bristle upon his cheeks made her want to touch it.

'Why did my father send you to me?' she asked, inviting him inside.

'Because there is something I need to speak to you about. I was not entirely honest with you when we met.' He glanced over at the two stools on the far side of the room. 'Could we sit?'

'First, give me the key,' she demanded. She had no intention of allowing the Norman warrior to invade this room while she was talking with Gavin. She inserted it into the lock and turned it. 'If we are to speak, I do not want the Normans interrupting us.'

His mouth tightened. 'That is what I wanted to discuss with you.'

She led him to sit at the far end of the room, wondering if he had come to take her from Eiloch. He had said before that he had wanted to wed her. And though she hardly knew him, she could not deny that he made her blood race.

When he had kissed her, she had come alive in his arms, feeling desirable. No man had ever affected her the way he did, and a sudden, rash thought came to her. He could help her escape this unwanted marriage. Perhaps he could escort her to safety where she could avoid the Norman forces.

Her mind stilled with an unmistakable fact—if she wed Gavin MacAllister, they could no longer force her to marry Rhys de Laurent.

Her brain dismissed the idea, for she could not fetch a priest and speak vows with so little time. It would never work. But her mind was caught up with a storm of thoughts swirling within her.

'Do you still wish to wed me?' she blurted out, rising from her seat. She could not look at Gavin while she spoke, for his very presence unnerved her. 'Is that why you are here?'

He paused a moment. 'In a manner of speaking. There is more I need to tell you.'

Her body went numb with anxiety, and it felt as if her breath caught in her lungs. She squeezed her hands into fists and forced herself to face him. 'And what if I said yes?'

He hesitated again. 'You may not want to wed me, after we have spoken.'

She would wed the devil himself if it meant avoiding the Norman. And there was one way of doing so, a way that would end any chance of marriage with Rhys de Laurent.

Her face burned with humiliation, and she could hardly bring herself to voice her idea. Instead, she blurted out, 'Do you…want me?'

For a long, painful moment, he didn't answer. She closed her eyes, wishing she had never spoken at all. He would make excuses and leave. Her heart sank, and she berated herself for even asking. Of course he wouldn't want a woman like her. She was plain-faced with bright red hair and a body that was bony instead of soft.

But he rose from the stool and came to stand behind her. His hard body pressed against hers, and he drew her waist to him, so that she felt the warmth of his breath against her throat. 'From the moment I kissed you, I have thought of nothing else.'

Her breath released in a ragged gasp, and his mouth pressed against her nape. Gooseflesh rose over her skin, and she now knew that she could do what must be done.

'Then claim me,' she pleaded softly. *Seduce me so that I no longer have to wed Rhys de Laurent.* She needed to bind this man to her, to ensure that there was no chance of being forced to marry the Norman.

Gavin's body went rigid, and his demeanour transformed. Slowly, he turned her in his embrace, tilting her chin up to face him. 'Lianna, there is something you must know.'

She didn't want to hear reasons or excuses. This was her chance to escape a marriage she'd never wanted, and she was willing to sacrifice her innocence for that. And so she stood on tiptoe and pressed her mouth against his in a hungry kiss.

* * *

Rhys de Laurent knew he was a bastard. He had come to her room to tell her the truth, to reveal his true name to Lianna, and to discuss whether they should end the arrangement. He'd been willing to consider giving her to Warrick instead, especially after the death of her brother.

But from the moment she kissed him, offering her sweetness, all logic disappeared. She opened to him, and when he slid his tongue into her mouth, she gasped and moaned, pressing her hips to his.

His body was already rigid with desire, and her softness only ignited those forbidden needs. She believed he was a Highlander, a man who would take her away from Eiloch and give her the freedom she wanted. He knew that, just as he knew she would despise him if she knew who he really was. Was this seduction meant to bind him to her? Was she trying to escape their marriage?

Her hands slid through his hair, and she murmured against his lips, 'I can hardly breathe when you touch me.'

Rhys responded by bringing his palm to the curve of her breast. She wore a woollen gown, and he could feel the cockled nipple beneath it. He teased it with his thumb, and she shuddered.

He had been with women before, but none who reacted so strongly. The look of pleading desire on her face nearly brought him to his knees. He wanted to spend all night pleasuring her. But if he dared to voice the truth, all of it would end. This beautiful woman would look upon him with hatred, demanding that he leave. Although the voice of reason tugged at his conscience, he couldn't quite bring himself to speak. This woman would become his wife, and if he accepted her offering, there would be no turning back. All he had to do was remain silent.

Was it so wrong to desire a woman who begged for his touch? Especially when it meant consummating an arranged union? He decided that he would give her what she wanted, as long as she was willing. If she faltered or asked him to stop, he would do so without question. And soon enough, he would have his answers.

She reached for the laces of her gown. 'Will you help me with these?' Her brown eyes were hazy with need. 'My hands are shaking.'

He rested his hands upon the laces and pulled one out, then the other. 'Slow down, Lianna.'

She closed her eyes as he continued to unlace her. He lowered the gown to her shoulders and pressed his mouth to her skin. 'Are you certain this is what you want?'

'Yes.' Her voice was breathless, but the anticipation in her tone held fear as well. He hesitated, resting his hands against her shoulders, giving her time to pull back.

But instead, she pulled the gown lower, baring her shift. The fine linen was slightly sheer, and he could see the faint rosy tint of her nipples. Her auburn hair tumbled over her shoulders, and the force of his desire roared through him.

God help him, this was wrong. He knew he should not take this any further, for she would despise him once she learned the truth. But a dark hunger flared within him with the need to touch this beautiful woman.

Rhys was starving for a taste of her, and a vain part of him hoped that he could bring her such pleasure she would change her mind about wedding him. He cupped her cheek and slowly trailed his hand down her throat. She closed her eyes, her lips softening. Slowly, he lowered his hand, brushing his knuckles against her taut nipple.

A shuddering gasp erupted from her lips, and her hands dug into his shoulders. He stroked the erect tip, and she leaned her head back, her expression rapt with yearning.

Never could he give this woman to his brother Warrick—or to any other man. Not when she reacted so strongly to his touch.

Rhys lifted her in his arms and brought her to sit upon the bed. She started to remove the shift, but he caught her hands. He needed to give her one last chance to guard her virginity. For if they continued down this path, the marriage was inevitable.

'This wasn't the reason why I came to you, Lianna,' he said. 'If I join with you, you must become my wedded wife afterwards. Or if you want me to stop touching you, I will.'

She framed his face with her hands, her face flushed. 'Don't stop.'

Lianna knew this was wrong. She knew it down to her very soul, but she had come this far, and she could not wait any longer. Her father would come to her chamber with Rhys de Laurent, and if she were caught in Gavin's embrace, that would be the end of her betrothal to the Norman. Rhys would never accept a woman who could be expecting another man's child.

For that reason, she knew there was no return from this path of sin. She had made her choice, and she would abide by the consequences later.

'So be it,' Gavin growled. He removed his shirt, pulling it over his head.

She was spellbound by his hard muscles, fascinated by the reddened scar that ran across one rib. More than anything, she wanted to touch him, to know what it was to feel this man's flesh upon hers.

He knelt before the bed and touched her bare feet, tracing her soles. Instead of being ticklish, his touch was sensual, awakening her. As his hands passed over her ankles and up to her calves, he caught the hem of her shift and lifted it higher. She wanted to help him, but the intense stare in his dark blue eyes warned her not to move. His hands slid over her inner thighs, and she was aware of the sharp contrast between his heated palms and her cool skin.

Between her legs, she felt a yearning, to be filled by this man. He would take her body, and afterwards, she would no longer have to wed the Norman. This Highlander would free her from that prison. Her mind tried to warn her that her father would not allow it, but she silenced the words of reason. Her time was running out, and she had to see this through.

The Highlander moved his hand to her intimate flesh, and she was shocked to find that she had grown wet. His finger traced the seam of her opening, and she could not help but moan with the pleasure of his touch. She had always imagined that lovemaking was a necessary means for breeding children, where she would lie still, so that her husband could complete the act.

It had never involved such shocking feelings of need and urgency. She fought to regain control of herself, but her body warred against her mind.

Gavin guided her to lie back on the bed with her legs still open. Then he leaned in and covered her nipple with his heated mouth, over the linen. She nearly bolted off the bed when his finger slid inside her.

Sweet God Almighty.

'I—I can't think when you do that.' Reckless feelings tore through her, and she tried again to master her response. But her body craved his, aching with such fierce needs, she could hardly breathe.

'Good,' he answered, swirling his tongue over the damp fabric. 'I don't want you to think of anything else but me.'

Her body strained, yearning for something she could not understand. He circled her sensitive nodule while stroking her wet entrance. Then he switched his attention to her opposite breast, and she felt her body erupt with tremors.

'Don't fight it,' he said quietly. 'Your body will ken what it needs.' He slid her shift higher so it was bunched at her waist, and then he inserted a second finger. The pressure of his invasion, coupled with the suction of his mouth, was her undoing. A burgeoning spiral of desire made her arch against him, until she felt a surge of hot pleasure breaking over her with the force of a wave. She cried out, fisting the sheets as she rode out the release. His fingers were coated with her essence, and soon she heard him remove his trews. A moment later, she felt the blunt pressure of his erection at her entrance. He was so large, she feared he might hurt her. But he didn't force her at all. Instead, he remained poised there, his hands moving over her sensitive breasts.

'Do you still want this, Lianna?' he murmured.

'Yes.' There was no turning back now, not when the Norman could come to her door at any moment.

'Then take off your shift.'

It was still bunched at her waist, but she obeyed until she lay naked upon the bed. Now that the moment was upon her, she tensed, closing her eyes. Surely, he would thrust inside her, and it would be painful. But as he traced her nipples, she felt her body stirring once more. He slid in a slight fraction, and then stopped again. She didn't know what to think, but he withdrew and penetrated again. The motion startled her, for there was a yielding of her body, a craving to be filled. He continued his motion, and soon enough, she felt the hot shimmering sensation return.

'Gavin, please,' she begged.

The use of his name seemed to bring about a transformation in him. There was a sudden intensity, as if he hadn't liked to hear it. But he answered her cry, sheathing himself in her body. It did hurt a little, and the sudden breach throbbed, bringing about a different sensation. He didn't move, and she wondered if it was over. She was so conscious of his body joined with hers, of his breathing and the weight of him. He started to pull back, and she grasped his shoulders, silently pleading for him not to end it. She was certain that he had changed his mind, and she felt herself to blame for it.

But he thrust inside her, filling her completely.

His dark blue eyes burned into hers as he made love to her, mastering her body. She met his thrusts, lifting her hips, and was rewarded with another surge of pleasure. Gavin pulled her to the edge of the bed, palming her bottom and invading her wetness with his steel erection. Over and over, he penetrated in a steady rhythm that made her exhale in time with his thrusts. She was coming apart, her body shaking until once again he pressed her over the edge, making her body soar with another release.

She lay beneath him, feeling the slight change in tempo as he continued pumping until he reached his own crest of pleasure. His body filled hers once more, and then he finished, his hard body pressed against her own.

Lianna's heart was pounding, and she drew her legs around his waist, keeping him close. The Highlander kissed her sweetly, and she closed her eyes, trying not to let her mind dwell upon her father's fury. Right now, she felt deliciously bruised and swollen, her body fully satisfied by her impulsive move.

He drew the coverlet over them, holding her close. For a moment, she allowed herself to feel safe and protected. But she knew her father would come soon enough with the Norman. And she didn't know quite what to say to him.

Or worse, would the Highlander have to fight Rhys de Laurent for her? She didn't like that thought at all.

Gavin drew his hand over the outline of her ribs, his body still joined with hers. A low growl resounded from her stomach, and she blushed. 'I am sorry. It has been a long time since I've eaten.' She hadn't taken a meal at all, not since burying her brother. And then, too, her nerves gathered up into a tight knot at the thought of her father bringing her evening meal.

'Shall I bring you food?' he suggested.

'No.' He could not dare to leave her, not now. 'It isn't safe for you there.' She was afraid of what would happen when her father returned. The burden of guilt weighed heavily upon her, more so because she had found Gavin's touch so pleasurable.

He withdrew from her, still holding her to him. His thumb idly stroked her nipple, and a sudden tremor of pleasure echoed in her womb. 'Lianna, we need to talk about this.'

'I ken that.' But she was frightened to face what would come. 'I am afraid of what my father will say. I—I never imagined I would do something like this to avoid marriage to Rhys de Laurent. But he still wants me to marry the man who killed my brother.' She turned to face him, feeling the raw emotions rise up once more. 'I cannot marry him. I will do anything to escape this prison. Even wed a stranger.'

Her Highlander traced the outline of her face. There was a sudden hard cast to his expression, as if he recognised that she had used him in this way. She hoped he would understand why she had made this choice.

But at last, he stared into her eyes and admitted, 'Lianna, *I* am Rhys de Laurent.'

Chapter Four

Hatred rose up on her face with such ferocity, Rhys had no doubt that if she'd had a blade, she would have buried it in his heart.

'You black-hearted bastard,' she accused, shoving him away. 'How could you do this? You *lied* to me.'

He was not about to let her cast the blame upon his shoulders. 'I came here to tell you the truth. But you would not let me speak.'

'Because I thought your name was Gavin MacAllister!' She jerked the sheet away and wrapped it around her body. 'You deceived me, making me believe you were one of us. But you were only my enemy, from the moment I laid eyes upon you.'

He remained seated upon her bed. 'Your father suggested that I dress as a Highlander so I could learn what sort of woman you are. If you knew who I was, you would not have listened to anything I said. He wanted me to meet you before our marriage, in the hopes that we could start out differently, not as enemies.'

'You will be my enemy until you take your last

breath,' she swore. Her face was scarlet with rage and humiliation, but he would not leave her until they had settled this.

'I learned that you were a beautiful woman who cares deeply for her people. And when your brother tried to slaughter us, I told your father we should not wed.'

'And I agree!' she shot back. 'If you think for one moment that I will wed the man who killed Sían, I—'

'He killed my friend.' Rhys made no effort to curb the chill in his voice. 'Because of your brother, his wife is now a widow with a child on the way and no one to care for them. He shot Ailric from the shadows with his bow, like a coward.'

'And in return, you cut him down.' She stood from the bed, backing away.

Rhys rose to face her, striding forward without bothering to put on clothes. She took another step backwards, but then stopped and raised her chin to defy him. For a moment, there was a silent battle between them.

'I would never let any man harm my friends,' Rhys said coolly. 'Sían had no cause to attack us. I will not apologise for defeating him in the fight.'

She raised tear-filled eyes to his. 'Do you honestly believe I can forgive you for what you did?'

His face turned grave. 'The moment you gave your innocence to me, you bound us in marriage. I warned you what it meant. I gave you every opportunity to say no.'

Her fury stretched out within her, intensifying her guilt. For he was right. If she had never opened her arms to him, they might have avoided a union.

'My father sent you to me, didn't he? And you disguised yourself so I would not ken who you really were.'

Rhys's face hardened. 'I came to reveal the truth to you tonight. I wore the same clothing so you would know what I said was true.' His dark blue eyes narrowed. 'I told Alastair I would not wed you until I confessed my identity. You deserved that much.' He had known she would despise him and was fully prepared to face her hatred. But when she had kissed him, offering herself to him, the force of his desire had driven out all else.

Even now, bound up within the bedsheets, he found her beautiful. Her brown eyes gleamed with unshed tears, and her hair spilled over her bare shoulders like a fiery mantle. No longer did it matter that they were on opposite sides of this alliance. He would never let any other man touch her.

When Lianna had taken him into her body, it had felt as if it were meant to be, that they belonged together. He had understood what Ailric had meant about waking up beside a woman and feeling that sense of contentment.

He wanted that still, and he was determined to have her, in spite of her hatred.

'How do you know Gaelic?' she demanded.

'My grandmother spoke it with me, ever since I was a child,' he admitted. 'She visited us from time to time, and she insisted that I learn your language.' Because Margaret had known that he would one day take his place as chief of this clan. He could never assume that leadership without fluency in their language.

'And what of you?' he asked in the Norman tongue. 'Can you speak my language?'

He detected a flicker of recognition in her eyes, but she would not admit it if she did. She continued to speak Gaelic and insisted, 'I will never marry you. I would rather drown myself in the sea.'

'You have no choice now,' he said. 'You may be carrying my heir.'

Horror washed over her, and she shook her head. 'I'm not.'

'We won't know that for many weeks,' he said calmly. And given her fiery temperament, it would not be the last time she shared his bed. She might hate him now, but even she could not deny that he had satisfied her. Lianna had seduced him the first time, but he would claim her again.

She crossed her arms in front of her chest, still holding the sheet. 'I want you to leave my chamber. And do not return, unless you want my dagger buried in your heart.'

He picked up his trews and donned them, noting the flush upon her cheeks. Deliberately, he stood before her, tightening his muscles as he slid his *léine* over his head. Lianna bit her lip and then turned away.

He would not bother her again this night, for it was too soon. Only time would soothe the ragged edges of her hatred. 'I will send food to you. Then you will prepare your belongings. We will journey to Montbrooke where the formal betrothal will be signed and our marriage witnessed.'

Her eyes flared with anger, and she said, 'I will go nowhere with you.'

He changed tactics, knowing what meant the most

to her. 'I rode with my men throughout Eiloch earlier today. I have seen the poverty of your clan. They lack supplies to survive this winter.' She stiffened, and he drove his point in deeper. 'My family holds enough wealth to provide for every MacKinnon man, woman, and child. It would not be difficult for me to provide for them.'

He noticed the uneasiness in her demeanour, for she understood exactly what he was saying. 'But if you refuse to wed me, I have no interest in helping your clan. The land is already mine, by right.'

'You would starve children for your own gain?' she asked with incredulity.

'No, *you* would,' he answered. 'If you refuse to wed me, you condemn them to death.' He had no qualms about using whatever weapons were at hand. And Lianna MacKinnon cared a great deal about these people.

'If you have any heart at all, you would provide for those in need,' she shot back.

He let his gaze slide over her, remembering her sweet curves and the feeling of her body against his. 'You will ride with me on the morrow towards Montbrooke. And you will stay with me every night in my tent.'

'My father won't allow that,' she said.

'Your father is not travelling with us. He is sending a signed missive granting his permission for the wedding. It has been signed by every man of the clan as witness. Two of his men will accompany us.'

She paled and drew away from him. 'I will never wed you.'

'Look at the faces of the MacKinnon children

when you say that. Know the choice you are making.' He reached towards her waist, drawing her close. 'I don't even know their names. But I suspect you would care a great deal when we withdraw our support.'

'Why would you want to wed a woman who despises you?' she demanded. 'You could choose any other woman in this clan.'

'The arrangement was made years ago,' he said. He rested his hand upon her nape, and he felt the rise of gooseflesh beneath his palm. Lianna clenched her hands into fists, shoving him back. But he held steady, forcing her to meet his gaze.

'It could be a good marriage, if you would allow it,' he told her. 'I was well satisfied this night, and so were you.' His words were meant as an invisible caress, sliding over her skin. And he saw her face flush before she lowered her gaze.

With that, he released her and went to the door. 'We leave at dawn.'

Lianna never touched the food Rhys sent to her, nor did she sleep at all that night. Her bed coverlet was neatly folded across the mattress with not a single crease upon it. She had swept her room until all the dust was gone, and she had paced the floors in her bare feet.

But she could not undo the mistakes she had made—and because of them, she was bound to the Norman enemy she hated. He had known this would happen when she had tried to seduce him, and he had known that his deception would bring her downfall.

Dear God, she wished with all her heart that she had felt nothing at all from his touch. If it had been little better than rape, it might allay her guilt. Instead, she despised herself for taking pleasure from him, for it never should have happened. Even the kiss Rhys had stolen upon his departure had reminded her traitorous body of how dangerous he was.

He held power over her, enough to cast a spell upon her senses and make her feel things she didn't want to feel.

His assertion, that her people's welfare depended on this marriage, evoked such a rage that she nearly trembled with the force of it. He had no right to threaten innocent lives, simply to force her into a union she didn't want. He had killed her brother. Why would he ever imagine she would agree to join her life with his?

A quiet knock sounded at the door. Lianna did not answer it, for she had no desire to see anyone. When the door creaked open, she lifted her gaze and saw her father standing there. Alastair's expression was grave, and there was no doubting the displeasure in his eyes.

'I hope you have your belongings packed,' he said quietly. 'You leave within the hour.'

She remained seated on her bed with her hands folded on her knees. There was nothing she could say to convince him otherwise. Instead, she asked, 'Why would you send him to me in the guise of a Highlander? You lied to me as much as he did.'

'Because you would not give him a chance,' her father answered. He entered the room slowly, his pallor sickly. 'And when I met with him, I saw a man of ruthless strength who will protect us.' He sank down upon a stool. 'We need a leader who can guard us from our enemies.'

'Sían would have protected us.'

But her father shook his head. 'Your brother was too proud to listen to those wiser than himself. He was too impulsive.'

'You speak of him as though you are glad he's dead.' She stared at him in disbelief.

'I grieve his loss, as much as I grieve the mistakes I made with him.' He sat down, his face lined with sadness. 'I never intended for him to be chief, and he knew this. But he mistakenly thought that killing Rhys de Laurent would make me proud of him.' Her father closed his eyes and gripped his fists. 'Much of our clan's struggle is due to Sían's mistakes.'

His eyes turned upon her with seriousness. 'And now it will fall to you to correct them.'

'By marrying our enemy.' She nearly spat the words.

'You already shared his bed,' her father pointed out. 'By making that choice, you sealed the bargain. He swore to wed you quickly, so that any child you may have conceived will be born in marriage.'

'I did not know who he was!' she cried out. 'I thought it was a means of avoiding the marriage.'

'Then Fate has cast your defiance back on you,' he answered. 'You surrendered your virtue, and the consequences are yours to bear. You will travel with him and his men to Montbrooke. I am sending two men with you, to ensure that the betrothal documents are signed and witnessed.'

'But you will not come with us.' Her anxiety heightened for she would be alone, at the mercy of the Normans.

He shook his head. 'I am needed here, to heal the

damage your brother has wrought. The people need to be assured that their lives are safe, that the soldiers will not seek vengeance upon them. If you go with de Laurent, your actions will also mean a great deal.'

But she didn't believe that at all. The people would undoubtedly be glad to see her gone. Her shoulders lowered, and she tried one last time. 'Is there nothing that would prevent this marriage? Perhaps we could allow his men to live among us in peace.'

'The land belongs to his father,' Alastair pointed out. 'If you do not please him, then he has the right to cast all of us out.'

She closed her eyes, feeling trapped within this nightmare. It felt as if she had sold her soul to the very devil himself. For a time, she grieved the loss of her freedom and the life she had known. But then she steeled herself and stood. 'I may have no choice but to wed him, as you have commanded. But I swear to God, I will never obey this man, nor will I let him hold power over me. I will defy him at every turn.'

A slight noise caught her attention, and she glanced up at the doorway. Rhys de Laurent stood there, dressed in full chainmail armour.

'You may try to defy me,' he said softly. 'But you will lose.'

Rhys didn't trust Lianna not to ride away from him, so he held her in front of him on his own mount. It slowed their pace, but he understood the necessity of guarding her. She had remained silent throughout the first day of riding, though from the slight shifting of her backside, he suspected she was sore.

And he, too, had experienced his own level of discomfort. The pressure of her bottom against his manhood reminded him of the night she had seduced him. He was aching for this woman, wanting so badly to claim her once again.

But she held her spine stiff, as if his very touch repulsed her.

'Have you travelled south before?' he asked, attempting conversation. She said nothing, though he knew she had heard him. He prompted her again, but she maintained the silence.

With a sigh, he added, 'Despite what you may think, I am not your enemy, Lianna.'

At that, she turned her face to glare at him. 'You became my enemy the moment you cast your blade into my brother's heart. I have nothing to say to you.'

He didn't bother defending himself, for he could do nothing to change the past. In time, she would put it behind her—but not yet.

She stared ahead at the horizon, her fury palpable. The sun was sinking lower, and Rhys wanted to make camp for the night. Perhaps in the privacy of their tent, he could reason with her.

He didn't expect her to desire his touch, and she had good reasons for not wanting to marry him. But there had to be a truce between them, so they could do what was best for her people and for his.

'We will stop for the night soon,' he told her. 'My men will hunt and find food, if you will start a fire. Tamhas will stay to guard you.'

Lianna straightened again. 'I am not intending to run away, if you think one of my kinsmen must watch over me. I have nowhere to go.'

'My trust in you must be earned.' He didn't doubt

that she would try to find a means of avoiding him, were it possible.

Rhys raised a hand to signal his men to stop. There was a stream here for the horses to drink and graze, and the copse of trees would provide shelter from the elements. He helped Lianna dismount and noticed how she tightened her lips at the pain of moving. Not once had she voiced a complaint over their gruelling pace. They had stopped only once during the day, and she had eaten her noon meal of bread and dried meat quickly before they had continued south again.

Now she appeared weary, and he noticed her lean against a tree, surreptitiously rubbing at her backside.

Rhys gave orders for his men to set up the tents and find food. It bothered him to see the horse that had belonged to Ailric. He didn't want to give such terrible news to the man's wife, but there was no choice. The man's death seemed unreal somehow, as if Rhys could blink and see his friend among the others.

While he gathered firewood, he noticed Lianna doing the same. She made piles of different sizes of twigs and branches, along with another nest of tinder. He brought her heavier logs and set them down. She said nothing, but stacked them neatly, arranging the different branches so that the fire would have adequate air.

He was about to ask her if she needed help, but she had already gathered flint from her belongings and struck a spark to the tender, blowing the flame to life. Within moments, she had a small fire going, and she fed it carefully, until the logs caught.

'You did well,' he said.

'I ken how to make a fire. Even a child can do

that.' She continued making adjustments with the fire until at last she stood warming her hands. Her long auburn hair had escaped its braids, and she gave up on it, finger-combing the locks.

'It was a compliment, Lianna, not a criticism.'

She raised her brown eyes to look at him, and in her expression, he saw raw grief and dismay. It appeared as if she were holding back so many emotions, she could hardly keep herself together. 'I don't want you to be nice to me.'

No, she wouldn't, would she? She wanted him to be her enemy, for then she could never forgive him for killing Sían. It irritated him that he was trying to make the best of this situation, and she only wanted to blame him for being alive.

'You could try a little harder,' he warned. 'But if you don't want me to be nice, so be it.' He strode away and joined his men who had just returned with fish and two hares. The two Highlanders who had accompanied Lianna—Tamhas and Donagh—busied themselves by setting up the tents.

Lianna approached the soldiers and took the food from the Normans without a word. With her own dagger, she began cleaning the meat and the fish. She worked steadily, and though Rhys tried to pretend he wasn't watching, he saw that she paid close attention to the details. She saved the hare skins and expertly spitted the meat, bringing it towards the fire. Rhys helped her support two larger branches with stones, on opposite sides of the fire, with the spit mounted between them.

'Your woman seems to know what she's doing,' one of his men remarked. It was meant as praise, but he saw Lianna's shoulders stiffen. She might not admit it, but Rhys was convinced that her father had taught her the Norman tongue.

'She does,' he answered.

When the meat had finished cooking, Lianna brought each of the men a generous serving, giving Donagh and Tamhas MacKinnon the best pieces, before she took the last portion for herself. She chose a seat far away from the others, but Rhys would not allow her to separate herself.

'Come and sit by me,' he commanded. 'We eat together.'

'You may eat with them,' she insisted. 'But I have no place among you.'

'You will be my wife and their lady one day,' he corrected. He reached down and took her wrist, pulling her to stand. 'Do as I command.'

The look of fury on her face was matched only by his own. She might want to exert her power over him, but he would never allow that. Only once in his life had a woman held dominion over him—when he was an adolescent boy, forced to obey the bidding of his stepmother. Never again would he let himself be ruled in such a way. A hard resentment curled within him at the memory.

'And if I don't obey you?' Lianna tried to pull her wrist free of him.

His answer was to pick her up, bringing her towards the men. She pummelled him with her fists, demanding in Gaelic, 'Put me down.'

Her strength was no match for his, but he lowered her to sit on his lap, trapping her fists so she could do nothing.

His men laughed at her, and Lianna turned crimson. Rhys knew that he had humiliated her, but he was not about to let her behave like this in front of his men. He lowered his mouth to her ear. In Gaelic, he murmured, 'Behave yourself or I will punish you. I will touch you all night long until you beg me to thrust inside you.'

She paled at his threat, and immediately stopped. His men were still laughing, and Rhys sent them a dark look. 'That's enough. You will respect Lianna as my future wife.'

They obeyed, and one raised a flagon of wine in a silent toast to her. 'The food is delicious,' one said, by way of apology.

But Lianna only looked at her hands, ignoring the compliment.

'She does not speak our language well,' Rhys lied. He raised a bit of meat to her mouth, silently warning her not to protest. There was a quiet fury in her eyes, but she did eat. He could almost read her thoughts, and if she could have set him afire with her eyes, she would have done so.

When the meal was finished, she went to each of the men and took the remains of their food, disposing of the bones. She adjusted the fire again, working tirelessly until their camp was immaculate.

Then she glanced back at him. 'I am going to wash. You need not follow.'

Rhys had no intention of letting her go out alone but reached for his sword belt and trailed her. He kept a short distance from her, and she knelt beside the stream, washing her hands and then her face. She remained on her knees for some time, her shoulders hunched over.

'Please go,' she whispered. 'I want a moment to myself.' Her voice sounded fragile, as if she were barely holding her emotions together. But he could never let a woman remain unprotected. Especially one in his care.

'It isn't safe for you to be alone. I will stand guard until you are ready to go to our tent.'

At that, she scrambled to her feet and turned to face him. Her face held horror at the idea. '*Our* tent? We are not sharing a sleeping space.'

'We will be married soon enough,' he said. 'And though I trust my men, I intend to keep you by my side, where it is safer.'

'I cannot share a tent with you,' she protested. 'It would not be right. They would…talk about us.'

'It matters not any more, Lianna. They know that nothing will end this marriage. You might as well already be my wife. Where you sleep will not change it.' He took a step closer, noting that the droplets of water on her face strongly resembled tears.

'You ask too much. Have I not lost everything already? My home, my freedom. There is nothing for me any more.'

He closed the distance and took her hands in his. 'I've said it once, and I will say it again. You are not my enemy, Lianna. And if you want to make this a marriage based upon friendship, it is possible. We can start again.'

'You will never be my friend,' she swore. 'Would to God I had never let you touch me.'

Her words were a fierce weapon that infuriated

him. He had done all he could to treat her kindly, and she had thrown it back in his face. Instead of responding to her, he folded his arms across his chest and stared hard.

She met his gaze with her own rebellion, and in the moonlight, her features were alluring. Her red hair was wet and dark, her lips silver in the darkness. For a moment, she froze in place, uncertain of herself. No doubt she was trying to anger him so much he would stay away from her. He recognised her tactic, but he would not stand down or let her go.

Behind this woman's hatred lay a vulnerable girl who had lost her only brother and now, her freedom. She was fighting a war she could not win, and both knew it.

Finally, she strode past him, returning to the camp. He followed, keeping a close watch over their surroundings. When she reached the circle of tents, her expression turned stony. He took her hand and said to the men, 'Philip and Gilbert, take the first watch. I will take the last one.' He did not trust her kinsmen to guard the camp and did not include them in those duties.

He leaned into Lianna. 'I will lead you to our tent now. Do not cause a scene, and I will leave you alone when we are inside.'

She raised her brown eyes to his, studying him as if she could not tell if he was being truthful. But he meant what he'd said.

Releasing her hand, he walked towards one of the tents and pulled the flap back. When he studied her, he saw the anxious look in her eyes, as if she were still afraid. But he wanted only her obedience just now. He had no intention of forcing her against her will, for he was not that sort of man at all.

He knew, too well, what it felt like to be unwilling, manipulated by someone in a position of power—and he would not do that to her.

Lianna glanced around at the other men before finally entering the tiny shelter. Rhys nodded to the others and then joined her. Once he was inside, he started to unbuckle his sword belt. She straightened the ground cover before she sat upon it and withdrew a comb from her belongings.

He was fascinated by the sight of her long red hair spilling over her shoulders. She combed it slowly, and the locks held a slight curl. The urge came over him to touch the spun silk of those strands, but he did not. He lost count of how many times she combed her hair, but at last, she unfastened her *brat* and gathered it around her like a blanket. She lay with her back to him, not speaking a word.

'I know it has been a difficult day for you,' he said softly. 'And despite what you may think of me, I will never force you to share my bed. You always have a choice.'

She turned to face him. 'You will never touch me again, de Laurent. Not even if we are forced to marry.' Her bitter words were laced with sadness, and he knew not what to say. Time was the only thing that could heal her wounds.

Instead, he leaned back beside her. 'It is a long journey to Montbrooke, but I think you will like it there. Though you will have to speak our language.'

'I do not know it,' she lied, but he did not contradict her. Her face gave away her emotions too much for her to be ignorant of the Norman tongue.

'You will learn,' he said. 'My sister will help you.' His tension softened at the thought of Joan. 'She is like you, in many ways.' His sister took care of the household, though she was unusually superstitious, given the tragedies she'd suffered years ago. Even so, Joan would enjoy taking Lianna under her wing.

He told her of the castle, of his father's forces, and a little about his younger brother Warrick. But his bride said nothing, pretending to sleep. Her shoulders did not rise and fall in a natural rhythm, so he knew she heard every word he spoke.

'I am glad you are a strong woman,' he said softly. 'You will have need of it to face what lies ahead.'

Lianna closed her eyes, but the burning ache would not leave her. She knew she had spoken rudely to Rhys and to his men this night, but her control felt as fragile as an eggshell. His kindness had been her undoing. There was a rawness inside her, as if the world she had known had been torn asunder. And no amount of sweeping would tidy up the mess of her life.

Rhys left her in the middle of the night for several hours to keep watch. And when he was gone, the loneliness closed over her. Tears would not solve her problems, nor would they make her feel better. In the darkness, she tried to make sense of this new life, hoping in vain to force it back into order.

Several hours later, Rhys returned. Lianna held herself motionless when he lay beside her. She kept her eyes closed, even when he drew her body against his for warmth.

A flare of desire pooled within her skin, and she bit her lip to ward it back. But Rhys held her in his arms, resting his face against her hair.

Why was he insisting upon this marriage? It did nothing for him. If he was heir to both Eiloch and a Norman castle, he could have any woman of his choosing. He did not need her as his wife. Why, then, would he stay?

She didn't understand why he was treating her this way, as if he wanted to wed her. It confused her that he was being kind. Not that he had been lenient towards her in any way, no, but he had not forced her to share his bed. At least, nothing save the silent request that she lie in his arms while they slept. It bothered her to admit that she enjoyed being in his embrace.

His warm body pressed against hers, and she could feel the heat of his breath upon her nape. Her skin tightened at the memory of his kiss upon her flesh. Only one night ago, he had tasted her nipples through the veiled fabric of her shift. She bit her lip in memory of the heavy pleasure.

Her body was such a traitor to her brother's memory.

Rhys's arms remained around her waist, and though his breathing was even, she was aware of his arousal pressed to her spine. She could almost imagine him sliding her shift to her waist, caressing her intimately before he sheathed himself.

God above, the very thought made her go liquid inside. She needed to move away from this man, to avoid his unholy temptation.

Lianna gritted her teeth and realised that she would not sleep much longer. She started to move away, but

Rhys kept his hand at her waist. She sat up and saw him staring at her. 'Where do you think you're going?'

'I intend to prepare a morning meal for the men.' The activity and purpose would help push away the errant thoughts swarming within her mind.

He let go of her waist, saying nothing. She knew better than to imagine he would go back to sleep, but he did not follow her outside the tent. Two of the men were seated upon logs near the fire, holding spears in their hands.

Lianna went to her belongings which had been laid beside one of the trees. She withdrew oats, salt, and other ingredients for bannocks from the heavy sack. Then, she took a wooden bowl and mixed it all together, along with honey for sweetness and a little rendered fat she had saved. The men watched her with interest, and she set up an iron pan over the fire to heat. Then she greased the pan with the fat and poured the batter on it to cook.

One of the men smiled at her. 'It smells good, my lady. Thank you for preparing the food.'

His compliment was spoken in the Norman tongue, and though she understood all of it, she wanted to feign ignorance a little longer. Instead, she replied in Gaelic, 'It is no trouble at all,' knowing he would not know her words. Then she smiled and nodded.

When the cakes were done, she gave him one, and then a second cake to the other soldier keeping watch. She cooked the remainder of the bannocks, making a few extra for their journey this day. It would take nearly a fortnight to reach Montbrooke, and she had measured the oats carefully when she'd packed, knowing that they would grow weary of meat and fish.

Rhys had joined the men, sitting upon a log while he drank a cup of mead. She gave him a warm bannock and turned back to gather her utensils to clean them. But Rhys stood and interrupted her, breaking off a piece of his bannock. He raised it to her lips. 'You have not eaten, Lianna.'

'I will eat later,' she started to say, but he insisted, forcing her to bite off a piece. The warm bannock tasted delicious and she enjoyed the hint of honey she had added. Perhaps if she could find berries along their journey, it might add another flavour the men would enjoy.

But then her mood faltered. Why should it matter if she cooked food that was pleasing to the Normans? They had killed her kinsmen.

Her heart faltered, for she could not deny her brother's guilt. He had commanded the raid, attacking without warning. What had Sían been thinking? He had led them to their deaths. A dark grief took hold of her mood, but she was distracted by Rhys.

'I will not have you putting yourself last,' he said, brushing his thumb against her lip to wipe a crumb away. 'You are their lady. And mine.' He dropped a kiss upon her mouth, startling her with the sudden affection. He walked over to her belongings and began to prepare her horse for the journey.

Her mouth felt as if he'd laid a brand across it, and she understood that he was waging a silent battle. But he would not win. Kiss or no kiss, there was nothing to bring them together. She gathered the soiled bowl and started to reach for the iron pan, when Rhys called out, 'Use this.'

He tossed her a heavy piece of wool to protect her

hands. She nodded her thanks and then lifted the hot iron away from the fire. With her bowl under one arm and the pan clutched in the other with a woollen rag, she made her way back towards the stream. This time, Rhys did not follow, but she saw him lead her horse from the trees, keeping watch over her.

Lianna busied herself with washing the dishes in the stream, trying to push away the tangled threads of emotion. Inwardly, she grieved for the loss of her brother and his men…and yet, she understood that they had provoked the Normans.

If Rhys had attacked her kinsmen and the Scots had killed him, she would feel no guilt over his death. It would only be what they deserved.

Confusion reigned over her heart, and she locked away the feelings. The mindless work of scouring the soiled dishes was what she needed now. The water washed away the dirt, and made everything clean and bright again. She would not think of the days that lay ahead, nor of the attention she would receive as Rhys's bride.

And most especially, she would not lower her defences against this man. For he was a warrior who knew exactly how to lay siege.

Chapter Five

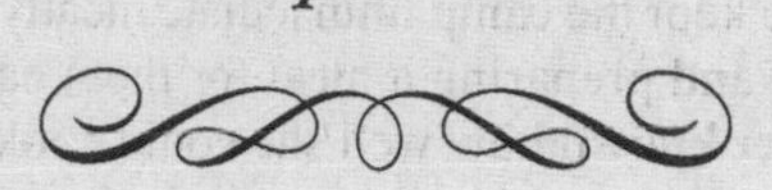

Rhys led their travelling party to the top of the hill overlooking the lands of Montbrooke. He felt Lianna stiffen against him, her fear evident as they approached his home. No doubt she would be uneasy about her place here.

Over the past fortnight, they had fallen into a pattern. She had slept in his tent every night, always far away from him. It had been a constant torment to share a private space with her and yet not claim her body. But Lianna had not forgiven him for Sían's death, and he knew better than to push the boundaries. It was a battle of control between them. Rhys would never yield against his own pride, nor would he admit any wrongdoing. He had defended his life, and her brother had died in the fight. He would not beg her forgiveness because he had lived and Sían had not.

In turn, Lianna behaved as if he were invisible. She barely spoke to him, and never would she let him touch her. But in the mornings, he would often awaken to find her curled up in his arms. Only then was her expression soft and content. Sometimes he imagined what it would be like to see her smile at him in the morning. Or better, to awaken her by kissing her, trailing a path down her bare skin. He would push aside the *léine* and her shift, cupping her breasts and stroking her sensitive nipples. But she would never admit her own desires.

Instead, he had given her space, watching over her as she kept the camp immaculate, neatly stacking firewood and preparing a meal for them each night. He'd never known how well she could cook, and her innate attention to detail brought its own rewards. One morning, she had asked him to stop for a moment. He had given the command, and she had picked blackberries for them to share. Later that night, she had mixed the berries with honey, a little flour, and God only knew what else. The cakes had been a rare treat that all the men had enjoyed.

Though she maintained the frigid demeanour towards him, she showed no trace of animosity towards his men. She looked after them, always ensuring that they had enough to eat. Her quiet presence made camp life comfortable, and because of it, the soldiers adored her. Lianna would indeed make a good lady of Montbrooke, for she put the people's needs first.

'You will meet my father this morn,' he told her, when he drew their horses to stop at the hillside. 'If you have need of anything, tell me, and it is yours.' Her face paled, and he reached out to squeeze her hand with reassurance. 'Don't be afraid.'

But she pulled her hand away. 'I am not afraid. Let us go, if we must.'

Rhys nudged their horse forward, and soon he saw her staring at the serfs working in the fields. Montbrooke was ten times the size of Eiloch, and she drank in the sight of everything as they approached the path leading to the drawbridge.

The castle had four rectangular towers and walls three feet thick. The surface of the walls was so smooth, no invaders could climb it. He knew that well enough, since he had tried to scale them as a boy.

As they passed by the castle inhabitants, Rhys raised his hand in greeting. Several of the people smiled and bowed their heads as he passed. Lianna held herself so stiffly, he could feel her nerves. It occurred to him that she was not dressed like a noblewoman. Before she was formally presented to Lord Montbrooke, he wanted her to wear a gown that revealed her rank as his bride.

'Follow me,' he murmured, taking the reins of her horse. He saw the gooseflesh rising on her arms, partially revealed by the green *léine*. She had combed her red hair many times this morn, but it was still slightly wind-blown from the journey. Rhys led them into the inner bailey, where a stable lad met them to take the horse. His own soldiers dismounted and followed a short distance behind.

Lianna risked a glance at them, and one offered her an encouraging smile. She had nothing to fear when it came to his personal guards—they would spread the word that she was a lady whom the people of Montbrooke would come to love.

Rhys saw his sister Joan standing at the top of the stairs. She smiled in greeting, folding her hands and waiting for them to approach. His sister was tall and composed in her bearing. Her brown hair was bound back from her face in a severe style, and she covered it with a veil. Her gown was a pure white, and she wore a cross around her throat and a bracelet made of beaten iron to keep the fairies away. Despite her odd manner of dress, she had a warm heart. He trusted her to take care of Lianna and to help her grow accustomed to their ways.

'I hope you had a good journey, Rhys.' Joan stepped forward to embrace him. Then she smiled at his bride. 'You must be Lianna MacKinnon.'

She stared at Joan as if in a panic, but did not speak at all. Rhys switched into Gaelic and said quietly. 'You can attempt a greeting, Lianna.'

'I cannot speak the language,' she insisted. Her face blanched, and she looked as if she wanted to flee from the spot.

Rhys covered for her, telling his sister, 'She is weary from our travels and would like to refresh herself before meeting our father. Can you find a suitable gown for her?'

'Of course.' Joan held out her hand to Lianna. 'She may also want to bathe beforehand. I can arrange it.'

At that, Lianna took his sister's hand and followed. Rhys was certain it was the offer of a hot bath that convinced her. She did wash her face and hands daily, and her skin always smelled of herbs and flowers. He liked that about her.

Once she had gone, he caught a slight motion behind him and saw his younger brother Warrick approaching. He gripped the young man in a fierce embrace, and said, 'I am glad to see you again.'

Warrick was lean, with dark hair and vivid blue eyes he'd inherited from their mother. Rhys's own eyes were blue as well, but not nearly as striking as

Warrick's. His brother was quiet and kept himself apart from the others. He busied himself on the training field, and it bothered Rhys that his brother did not share the same high status. Their father despised his younger son, and treated Warrick like the dirt beneath his feet, unworthy of anything. No matter how Rhys tried to talk with him, the roots of hatred ran deep.

He wanted to change that. Although he would no longer allow Warrick to wed Lianna, he could send his brother to lead the MacKinnon clan in his stead. The distance and time might ease the severed relationship, giving the man a chance for respect.

'Your bride does not seem eager to be married,' Warrick remarked. He glanced over at the two women, who disappeared inside the *donjon*.

'She has left her home and family to come here. Anyone would feel uncomfortable surrounded by strangers.' Rhys walked alongside his brother. 'But there's more.' He revealed what had happened with the failed raid, and the deaths of Ailric and Sían. 'She blames me for her brother's demise.'

'Were they close?' Warrick joined him as they walked the perimeter of the inner bailey.

Rhys wasn't certain how to answer that. Although Lianna behaved as if she and her brother had been friends, he didn't like the way her clan seemed to treat her like a servant. He shrugged. 'I don't know. But she won't forgive me for not dying in his place.'

A hint of a smile lifted the corner of his brother's mouth. They circled back to the stairs, and Warrick added, 'We've guests arriving in the next few days. Our father wanted to announce your betrothal with dozens of witnesses.'

'Perhaps you'll find a lady of your own among the guests,' Rhys suggested. But Warrick only shook his head, as if that were impossible.

The main door opened, and their father emerged at the top of the stairs. At that, his brother turned away to leave. 'I will see you later, Rhys.'

He didn't bother asking Warrick to stay, knowing that he was seeking his own escape. Instead, he bade him farewell before he walked up the stairs and greeted his father. 'Good morn to you, Father.'

Edward acknowledged him, saying, 'I see you fulfilled your duty and brought your bride home. But where is Alastair MacKinnon?'

'He had to stay behind,' Rhys explained. 'He sent his written permission for the betrothal, and it was signed and witnessed by the clansmen.'

His father appeared satisfied by that. 'And how do you find your Scottish bride?'

'She despises me and the very air I breathe.' Rhys saw no reason to hide the truth. He repeated the details of the attack for his father's sake and saw the tension lining Edward's face.

'You are fortunate that Alastair did not declare war, after you killed his son.'

Rhys folded his arms across his chest. 'The MacKinnon clan is starving, and they are poor fighters. Alastair knew we would slaughter every last one of them, if they dared to attempt revenge.'

He followed his father inside, noting the contrast between his family's home and the MacKinnon dwelling. Rich tapestries hung from the walls and silver and gold gleamed from goblets upon the tables. Savoury scents lingered in the air, reminding him of his hunger.

'I want to meet this bride of yours,' his father said. He led Rhys up to the dais and bade him sit at his place at the high table. Edward joined him and a maid poured him a goblet of wine, then another for Rhys.

'This marriage is an important one,' his father reminded him. 'It will give our king a place to shelter troops, if we go to war with the Scots.'

Already it felt as if his impending marriage would make him a traitor to the MacKinnons. Rhys took a sip of the red wine, choosing his words carefully. 'The clan will need our help to survive the winter. They have great need of food and supplies. It is why her father agreed to keep the betrothal—else most of their clan would die.'

'I won't ask if you want to wed Lianna MacKinnon. The answer is irrelevant. You will marry her, bed her, and then you can keep her in Scotland if you wish to remain here.'

Undoubtedly that arrangement would suit Lianna well enough. But Rhys didn't like the idea of being separated from her. 'I thought I would send Warrick there to govern on my behalf.'

Instantly, his father's face transformed into fury. 'I forbid it. He will not touch one acre of land. Not while I live.'

We shall see, Rhys thought. He knew better than to reason with Edward de Laurent. His father was rigid in his thinking, and once he made a decision, he stood by it—regardless of whether it was right. Their relationship was strained, for although Rhys was the eldest son and his father had raised him to be the heir to Montbrooke, Edward was reluctant to accept Rhys's ideas. Unless his opinions mirrored his father's, they were ignored.

But he would speak up on his brother's behalf. 'Warrick is a strong fighter, and he will protect our holdings in Scotland.'

'After what your brother did to Analise's daughter—'

'Never speak her name to me.' Rhys despised the woman with every breath in his body. His father's second wife had been little more than a witch with her calculating, sly ways. 'She was a liar, and you never saw her for what she was.'

He had been only fourteen when Analise had begun flirting with him. A grim fury settled over his darkened mood. Right now, he needed a means of expelling the anger, and he rose from his seat. 'I will eat later. I've lost my appetite.'

Edward's face was red with fury, but he was conscious of the bystanders. In a tight voice, he demanded, 'Sit down, Rhys.'

He didn't move. No longer was he a young boy, bound to obey the dictates of his father. He wielded his own power, and for a moment, he faced Edward in silent defiance.

But then Edward's wife approached the dais, her face filled with smiles. Rowena de Laurent intervened before they could argue further. She took both of Rhys's hands and stood on tiptoe to kiss his cheek. 'I am so very glad to see you, my dear. I think you've grown even more handsome over the years. But perhaps not quite so handsome as Edward.' She patted his cheek and sat down beside her husband. Within moments, she was pouring Edward another cup of wine. 'Do not quarrel already, when you've only just come home.'

The matron seemed to know just how to manage her husband's moods. With soft touches and a sweet voice, she soothed him. 'Let Rhys go off and greet his kinsmen. We can discuss the arrangements for the betrothal. Besides, we should eat when Lianna can join us.' With a discreet wink, she dismissed Rhys.

'I will join you then,' Rhys said. The very presence of Lady Montbrooke seemed to ease the frustration between them. He bowed to both of them and strode away from the dais, passing through the Great Hall. At this moment, he needed to cross swords with someone, to release the frustration building inside him.

He left the *donjon* and walked down the stairs, heading for the training field. Dozens of men were engaged in sparring, sharpening their weapons, while the older guards were instructing the younger men. He saw his brother Warrick standing apart from the others, inspecting one of the swords.

Rhys unsheathed his sword by way of greeting. Warrick raised an eyebrow. 'Has our father offended you already?'

'He spoke of Analise.' Rhys let out a breath. 'And I decided I would rather spar with you than listen to him speak of a woman whom I hope is burning in hell.'

Warrick's expression tightened, but he gave a nod. He picked up a shield and tossed it to Rhys in one swift motion before he seized his own. 'Guard yourself, Brother.'

It felt good to spar after being on horseback for so long. His brother was a strong fighter, despite being younger, and their swords clashed, time and again. Rhys let himself fall into the familiar pattern of swordplay, but he found himself thinking of Lianna, wondering if there would ever be peace between them.

Sweat beaded upon his forehead and his arm ached, but he welcomed the pain. He needed a means of driving out the past and keeping himself focused on the present.

He battled his brother until both of them were fighting for breath. Warrick grunted when he struck his brother's shield, and at last, Rhys called for a truce. 'I needed that,' he admitted.

Now that he had released his restless energy, he found that he was wanting to see his bride again. He wanted to see Lianna garbed in a silk *bliaud* and veil, wearing jewels and finery as befitted her new role. Perhaps then she might come to understand her new rank.

But he suspected that she would continue to defy him at every turn.

He was about to return to the keep when he saw a young woman standing nearby with a shy smile. Elia rested her hands upon her swollen pregnancy and lifted her hand in greeting.

'My lord, I bid you welcome. I have been wanting to ask you where my husband is. I hoped to see Ailric, and—'

The blade of grief sliced through him. There were no words of comfort he could give the woman. He could only say, 'I am sorry.'

For a moment, Elia stared at him in shock. Rhys shook his head and lowered it out of respect. When she grasped his meaning, her anguished cry tore through the stillness. She dropped to her knees, sobbing even as she cradled her arms around the swelling of her unborn child. 'He promised he would come back to me.'

'He died bravely in a raid,' Rhys said. With a heavy heart, he knelt down beside her and took her hand. 'I promised him that I would provide for you and for his child. You will not go hungry.'

'But he will never see his son's face,' Elia wept. 'I cannot bear it.'

Rhys comforted the woman as best he could, but words would not console her loss. She poured out her sobs, and the depths of the young widow's grief made him wonder how much Lianna was suffering after Sían's death. She had endured each day with no tears, but her pain was silent and deep.

Nothing he could do would bring back her brother. But he intended to be a good husband to her, giving her all the wealth she could dream of. And perhaps one day, she might smile again.

Lianna followed Joan into a small chamber away from the other guests. The woman had a practical air, which she liked, but the moment she stepped into the room, it felt as if her senses were assaulted. All manner of furnishings were cluttered into the tiny space, and there were at least three trunks scattered around the room. The bed was made, but one side was long, while the other was short. Her hands itched to straighten it.

Joan closed the door and eyed her. 'Do you understand my words?'

Lianna hesitated, not certain whether to say anything. Her nerves had gathered into a tight bundle, and she said nothing. She knew Rhys's sister was attempting to be her friend, but it felt wrong to become close to this woman.

She steeled herself and walked towards the window, not answering Joan's question. If she kept her distance from this woman, it would make it easier to separate herself from Rhys. She wanted him to set her aside and leave her behind in Scotland. Then everything could return to the way it had been before.

Outside, she heard the clang of swords and saw him sparring with another man, perhaps his brother. He moved with a predator's speed, lethal with each strike. Sían would not have had a chance. Her brother had been a skilled archer, but his hand-to-hand skills were weak.

A fresh wave of sorrow and guilt washed over her. Lianna rested her forehead against the stone, feeling lost and bewildered.

Joan came to stand beside her. 'I don't know what to say to you, except that I hope you will be happy here. I will try to help you.' She rested her hand upon Lianna's shoulder, and the gesture of comfort made a lump rise in her throat.

She knew she should turn and smile at the woman, but her emotions were so fragile right now, she had to keep a tight rein over them. Instead, she kept her gaze fixed upon the men.

There was no escape from this marriage. She would be bound to Rhys de Laurent, no matter what she might want. He would provide for her people, and she had to surrender her freedom in exchange. The air choked up in her lungs, and she struggled to calm the rising panic.

Joan stepped back and murmured, 'I will go and find something for you to wear. And I'll have a servant bring you water for bathing.'

Lianna waited until she heard footsteps retreating and the door closing. Only then did she step away from the window. Her heart was beating fast, and she fought to breathe normally. Panic and fear broke over her, until she dropped down to the floor by the bed, burying her face in her knees.

Dear God, what could she do? She was trapped in this place among strangers, promised to a man who had killed her brother. For the past fortnight, she had shut out every emotion, feigning obedience. But now the frustration and sadness stormed through her, drowning her sense of reason. If she allowed these people to dress her in the Norman style and present her as if she were a pawn, she would have nothing left of herself.

She fought back the tears and moved towards the bed, adjusting the coverlet so it hung evenly. Would that she could straighten out the edges of her life so easily. Then she dragged one trunk to the opposite side of the room. It was heavy, but she managed to make more space. She moved the last trunk beside it, until all three were out of the way.

The act of clearing the room and straightening it *did* make her feel better. She could bury herself in this, pushing away her fear and desolation. Though she could not control her fate, nor could she bring back her brother, she could put this room in order.

And perhaps it would alleviate the loneliness and grief.

It infuriated her that she had seduced Rhys, falling prey to his lies. Since that day, she had been acutely aware of his presence and the warmth of his skin beside hers. Lianna wanted to lash out at herself for being attracted to him, especially after what he'd done to Sían. But she simply had no defence against the weapon of his kindness.

A few moments later, there came a quiet knock at the door. Joan had returned with several gowns.

'I brought you a few gowns,' the woman said gently. 'I think the white one would be lovely with your hair. Or perhaps the blue. I haven't worn it in many years.' There was a slight catch of emotion in her voice, but she said nothing else.

Another knock sounded at the door, and Joan opened it for the servants, who brought in a small tub of water. 'I thought you might want to wash after your journey,' the young woman said. 'Then I will bring you to meet my father. He has been asking about you.'

Lianna fought to keep her expression emotionless, and she clenched her fingers tight. She didn't want to do anything just now. And most of all, she could not bear the thought of being put on display.

She wanted to be alone, to gather her courage and to face what lay ahead. But Joan said, 'I have a scented soap you might enjoy.'

But Lianna only shook her head and went to the door, opening it for Rhys's sister.

The young woman appeared hurt by the gesture, and she sobered. 'You don't want my help, then?'

Lianna shook her head. It was cruel, she knew, but

if she was around Joan any longer, she would crumble into pieces. She could remain strong in the face of adversity and strangers, but she was afraid of forming a friendship.

Rhys's sister sighed and obeyed. 'If you need anything, I would be glad to help you.'

Lianna went to the door and held it open, feeling like a terrible person. Joan was trying to be friendly, and she was pushing her away.

But she could not help but think it was better for the woman not to like her. If all went to plan, Lianna would never return to England again.

Rhys found his bride on her knees, scrubbing along the edge of the room. Everything within the chamber had been put to rights, and his bride had clearly not spent any time preparing herself to meet his father. The tub of water had gone cold, and two silk gowns were laid out upon the bed.

Lianna had tied her hair up with a veil, and he grew distracted by the sight of her bottom as she moved along the edge of the floor.

'We do have servants, you know.' He closed the door behind him, giving them privacy.

He knew any orders he gave would be ignored, so he went over to Lianna and stood in front of the area she was scrubbing.

'What are you doing, Rhys?'

'I came to bring you to meet my father. But I see you are not ready yet.'

'I'll never be ready,' she muttered. But she did fold the wet cloth into precise, neat corners.

'Did any of the gowns fit?' He knew Joan had

tried to find several choices, taking many from her own wardrobe.

'I wouldn't know. I didn't try them on.'

And there came the stubborn glint in her eyes. His sister had warned him that Lianna had been crying, and he could see it in her reddened eyes.

'Are you too afraid to meet my family?' It was a barbed dare, one he hoped she would seize.

'I'm not afraid,' she shot back. And there was the glimmer of temper he needed to see. It was easier to bring back her anger than to let her hide herself away.

'Good. Then you should bathe and dress yourself.' He pulled up a chair and sat. 'I'll wait for you.'

Just as he'd predicted, she glared at him. 'You will *not* stay here, de Laurent.'

'I could wash your back,' he offered, beginning to enjoy himself. 'You might not be able to reach it. Or perhaps I could hand you the soap.'

She strode towards the door and flung it open. 'Out.'

He remained seated where he was. 'You're going to attract the attention of the servants if you keep the door open.'

Her face was flushed, but she closed it and went to stand before him. 'I will go nowhere until you leave this chamber.'

Rhys slid his hands around her waist, then stood. Lianna put her hands on his chest, meaning to shove him away, but he held her fast with one arm. He unfastened the brooch at her shoulder, releasing the *brat* she wore. The voluminous wool sank to the ground, leaving her clad in a simple *léine* with narrow sleeves.

'Leave me alone,' she gritted out. 'I don't need your help.'

'I disagree. You sent away my sister and you've refused everyone else. It seems that you do need my assistance.' Despite her struggles, he unlaced the *léine*, until it fell forward, baring her shoulders.

'Rhys, no,' she protested.

The sight of her creamy skin ignited his desire, but he resisted the urge to kiss the slope of her neck. 'You have two choices, Lianna. Either you will undress and get into the tub of water. Or I will undress you and put you there.'

She glared at him. 'I do not need your help.' There was a trace of fear in her voice, as if she believed he intended to hurt her—which was not at all true.

'I only want you to come below stairs to meet my family, dressed properly.' He waited a moment and then asked, 'What is your decision?'

'My decision is for you to leave. Go and dine with your family and pretend I am not here.'

'So you can clean other rooms in the castle?' He understood it was her way of occupying her time, but he could not have her behaving like a servant. Why did she insist on trying to hide herself away? Was she afraid of his family?

'What I do is my own concern, de Laurent.'

'No. Your choices reflect on both of us. And I cannot have you avoiding my father and stepmother.' He kept one arm around her waist and he slid his fingers beneath the loosened *léine*. When his palm touched bare skin, she flinched.

And suddenly, the atmosphere shifted between them. Lianna ceased her struggles, and her brown eyes met his. Her breathing seemed to deepen, and when he caressed her shoulder, she froze.

'Don't do this,' she murmured.

But there was a different tone to her voice, one he didn't recognise. And though he had his suspicions, he wanted to know for certain.

'I said before that we need not be enemies, Lianna.' He drew his mouth to the upper curve of her neck. Her hands moved to his shoulders, but she did not push him away.

Rhys drew her gown lower and it trapped her arms within the narrow sleeves. He kissed the rounded curve of her breasts, and she gave a sharp intake of breath. He freed her red hair from the veil, letting it spill down her back like a curtain of silk.

Her breathing was unsteady, and his own desire was raging for her. But he knew that if he demanded too much from her, she would only despise him. It was a delicate balance, and he knew he had pressed her to the edge.

He edged the fabric a little lower, exposing her nipple.

'Rhys,' she pleaded, but he moved his mouth towards it. When he slid his tongue across the erect tip, she could not stop the moan that broke free.

He kept her in his arms, but no longer was she fighting him. Instead, she leaned her head back, welcoming his touch. And he rewarded her by tasting the opposite nipple, laving it until the nub was sweetly hard.

God above, he wanted this woman. His body was an iron ridge of desire, craving the feel of her wet folds surrounding him. But Rhys forced himself to step back. 'Get into the water, Lianna.'

She was trembling, but turned her back and removed the *léine*. The sight of her bare back and rounded bottom nearly undid him. But she stepped into the water, covering herself as she did.

'I will send a maid to help you,' he gritted out. 'And I expect to see you at the meal tonight.'

With that, he strode away from her.

Lianna had never felt like such an outsider in all her life. With the help of the maid, she had bathed and dressed. She had chosen a sapphire blue gown, and the maid had woven ribbons into her braids. From the startled smiles on the faces of the guests, she knew her appearance was acceptable.

But the moment she saw Rhys, her breath caught again. She hadn't forgotten the shocking warmth of his mouth upon her bare skin or the way he tempted her. He had caught her unawares, and she didn't know what to think of this man. He had forced her to wear Norman clothing, and now, he came to take her hand. It was time for her to be formally presented to Edward de Laurent, Lord of Montbrooke, and his wife, Rowena.

From the moment she'd laid eyes upon the earl and his third wife, an icy chill had suffused her body. She wanted to flee at this very moment, but Rhys leaned in. 'All will be well, Lianna.'

His warm breath made a shudder pass over her body. She bit her lip, reminding herself that she could not forgive him for his lies or for killing Sían. They were enemies, and she had to use every weapon at her disposal. For now, she would shut him out, shielding herself from the desires of her body.

When he presented her to Lord and Lady Montbrooke, Lianna curtsied. The earl reminded her of a falcon, with shrewd eyes. He would not hesitate to shred his victims, and she forced herself to stand upright.

'My lord father, I present Lianna MacKinnon, my promised bride,' Rhys said.

The earl stared at her, his eyes a bold blue. His hair was dark with flecks of grey, and Lianna felt rather like a prize of war. 'She will do.'

In Gaelic, Lianna responded, 'I care not what you think of me. I am only here because my father commanded it.' With a warm smile, she made her words sound like an appropriate response. What did it matter what she said to this man? He would not understand.

Rhys squeezed her hand tightly in warning. 'She is glad to meet you, Father.'

Lianna straightened, keeping the smile fixed upon her face. A silent exchange moved between the earl and Rhys, and then the earl responded, 'As am I.'

To her horror, he then switched into Gaelic. 'And I am glad to see that my son will wed a woman with a backbone.'

Lianna felt her cheeks catch fire. Why had she dared to address the earl in such a defiant way? She had mistakenly believed the man could speak only the Norman tongue. She was such a fool.

Rhys led her to an honoured place at the dais, and Lianna rather wished he could have escorted her outside so she could hide in the shadows. 'I deserved that.'

'Where do you think I learned Gaelic?' he responded. 'My grandmother taught Edward, and then she taught me.'

She wanted to bury her face in her hands for letting her tongue get away from her. 'Well, what's done is done.'

'It is. And on the morrow, our guests will arrive. Harold de Beaufort is a friend of my father's, and he will bring his wife and two daughters.' Rhys offered her a choice piece of capon, which she accepted, though in truth, she did not feel like eating.

'You look beautiful in that gown,' he said in a low voice.

'I had no choice but to wear it.' Her cheeks flamed at his compliment, for it only evoked memories of him kissing her. She bit her lip to cast away the idle thoughts and toyed with the food before her. 'Why must I wear the clothing of your women instead of my own? You're only going to take me back to Scotland and leave me there.'

He said nothing, and she waited for him to argue, claiming that he had duties to fulfil. But Rhys's silence only raised Lianna's suspicions. 'Rhys, you *are* taking me home again, aren't you?'

He met her gaze. 'I have not decided yet. There are times when your presence will be needed here.'

Panic boiled inside her. 'You cannot take me from my home. You've already taken away my freedom, what I wear, what I eat—' She stood up from her place, ready to flee his presence.

'Sit down,' he commanded. 'This is not the time, nor the place to discuss it.'

Although she obeyed, she made no effort to hide

her fury. Instead, she mustered a thin smile and said, 'You say you do not wish to be enemies. But you've stolen the life I had, leaving me with nothing. Not even my brother. Why would I ever want to befriend you?'

He reached out to touch her hand, but she snatched it away. 'I may hold no power of my own in this marriage. But I swear by God above, that I will never surrender my heart, my body, or my feelings. *That* much, you will never have.' Inside, she was trembling with the force of her anger. She had obeyed her father to prevent war and to protect her people. But if this man believed she would marry him and leave her beloved Scotland, he was gravely mistaken.

Lianna pushed her plate aside, disinterested in food. One of the Norman soldiers who had travelled with them caught her gaze at a lower table. He offered a sympathetic smile of friendship, but it did nothing to lift her spirits.

'You are right, Lianna. I did take your freedom, giving nothing in return.' She turned back to face Rhys and saw sincerity in his dark blue eyes. He nodded towards the crowd of people. 'But you are not the only one with obligations to your people. When my father dies, I am the heir to Montbrooke. I cannot leave my wife alone in Scotland.'

She distracted herself with a sip of wine. The fermented drink made her dizzy, and she forced herself to take a bit of meat.

'But I do not have a heart of stone,' Rhys continued. 'There is something I can do to ease all the changes that have happened.' His expression turned pensive, and he ventured, 'Is it your wish to be wedded in Scotland?'

She could not imagine being married anywhere else. Here, she was surrounded by strangers who could not speak her language, and she had to follow their customs. At home, at least, she had the safe familiarity of a place she had known all her life. 'Yes. I would rather be married at Eiloch than anywhere else.'

'Then I shall arrange it,' he promised. 'But in return, I ask that you fulfil the obligations of our betrothal and try to behave as if this marriage will be a good union,' Rhys said quietly. 'Play the part I ask of you, and I swear, I will take you back to Scotland to be married among your own people.'

She stilled at that, not knowing whether to believe him. He might well be lying, as he had done before.

'During the betrothal, I want you to demand it of your father,' she countered. 'When he grants his permission, then I will know that you speak the truth.'

Rhys nodded. 'So be it.'

During the next few weeks, Rhys noticed that Lianna had veiled all her emotions. She did not appear angry any longer, which was an improvement, but the sadness in her eyes was impossible not to see. It seemed as if she were a captive with invisible chains, and he didn't know how to make this any easier for her. Whenever he tried to speak to her, she answered in single words or hardly at all. No longer was there any hope that her animosity would thaw.

But there was no choice for either of them. This wedding would happen, regardless.

He didn't doubt that his father would forbid his

request to hold the ceremony in Scotland. Edward de Laurent would want everyone to witness the union. But Rhys knew that there were ways to convince the man that it was *his* idea and thereby change his mind.

Dozens of guests had arrived to witness the betrothal, and Rhys had noticed that his younger brother was fascinated by the maiden, Rosamund de Beaufort. For the first time, Warrick appeared utterly bewitched, and Rhys found himself wanting to help his brother. Rosamund was a beautiful heiress, and if anyone deserved to find happiness, it was Warrick.

This morn, Rosamund was sitting upon the stairs overlooking the training grounds. Though she had brought sewing with her, she sneaked gazes at Warrick when she thought he wasn't looking.

Rhys approached his brother, who was gaping at the woman. Warrick wore chainmail armour, and he looked as if he'd come to spar. 'Are you wanting her to watch, Brother?'

Warrick turned around, his expression frowning as if he didn't understand. Rhys smiled, knowing what it was to desire the interest of a young woman. And there was a way he could help.

'It matters not if she is there,' his brother answered.

Warrick wasn't about to admit his interest, though anyone with eyes could see it. 'I've seen the way you stare at her,' Rhys countered, handing him a quarterstaff. 'Spar with me a moment. I'll make you look good.'

But his brother shook his head. 'Her father would be furious if he saw her here. It's dangerous with so many men about.'

'That is her risk to take. And she does want to

watch you.' Rhys grinned, enjoying this chance to embarrass his younger brother. 'I think we should show her more.'

The confused expression on Warrick's face amused Rhys. He was intending to fight his younger brother, giving him a chance to impress the young woman. But then he caught a glimpse of Lianna standing at the window from one of the towers. Her long wavy red hair was unmistakable, and he guessed that she had been combing it when she heard their voices. He expected her to turn away, but instead, she studied them.

In her posture, he saw a frightened woman who had closed herself off from everyone. And though she had shown no interest in him whatsoever, he decided to try another means of getting her attention.

Rhys stripped away his chainmail hauberk and tunic, until he stood bare-chested. To Warrick, he said, 'If she's going to look, shouldn't you give her something to look at?' He gazed up at his bride, who was indeed watching.

Would Lianna ever look upon him with anything but hatred? No longer was he certain. And the prospect of years of this cool behaviour was not a welcome thought.

He distracted himself by helping Warrick with his hauberk. 'I'll wager her gaze is upon you this very moment.'

But he wasn't talking about Rosamund de Beaufort. No, he was thinking of the auburn-haired beauty who was watching him from the tower.

'This is foolish,' his brother insisted. There was a slight discomfort reflected in his face as if he didn't want Rosamund to see him in this way.

'Not for quarterstaffs,' Rhys argued. 'You don't need heavy armour.'

His brother hesitated, but then stripped to his waist. And the moment he did, Rosamund eyed him openly before her lips curved in a secret smile.

His brother gaped at her as if he'd forgotten how to fight. And it was time to change that.

Rhys lunged at him, and his brother deflected the blow with the quarterstaff. He showed no mercy to Warrick, for truthfully he wanted Lianna to see his strength.

You may despise me, but I am a warrior. He struck hard, using speed and strength to show her the sort of man he was.

His brother dodged a blow and found a weakness, striking Rhys hard in the ribs. He grunted from the blow and retaliated by aiming the quarterstaff at his brother's knees.

Warrick jumped out of the way, but Rhys used the young man's lack of balance to knock him to the ground. He glanced up to see if Lianna approved, but Warrick rolled away and caught him across the ankles, tripping him. His brother eyed him with suspicion. 'I thought you were going to make me look good.'

He had intended exactly that until he caught sight of Lianna. Rhys cursed and got to his feet just as Warrick did. 'I lied. But even so, she's watching you.'

Just as he'd hoped, Warrick turned his head. Rhys struck another blow, but his brother anticipated the move and avoided it entirely. He was rewarded by another smile from Rosamund.

Her approval spurred his brother to strike hard,

over and over again, moving with speed and intensity. Rhys continued to deflect the blows but retreated to make Warrick look good. His brother lunged hard, trying to knock him over, but Rhys dodged the blow, laughing.

'Go and talk with her.' He clapped a hand on Warrick's back, half-pushing him towards the young woman. At least one of them had the interest of a woman.

Rhys remained where he was, watching. He glanced up to the window and saw that Lianna was still watching, though her expression had not changed.

He remained at a distance while his brother approached Rosamund, drawing near to her. For a moment, it did not seem that Warrick could form a single sentence. But then, the young woman reached over her shoulder to pull a ribbon free from her braid. She tied it to his arm, and Rhys overheard her say, 'Now you have my favour.'

He didn't want to interfere with his brother's courtship, but he remained at a distance, picking up the quarterstaffs to put them away. A part of him envied his brother, to hold the favour of a woman. Although Rhys had enjoyed flirtations with a maid or two over the years, it had never been more than a brief liaison. He had needed to exorcise the demons of Analise's memory, and the women had been willing. He'd learned that giving physical pleasure brought its own power, and the maids had known he was betrothed to Lianna. Yet the only time Lianna had ever smiled at him was when she had believed he was someone else.

After Rosamund had gone, Warrick picked up her

fallen sewing. Rhys knew exactly what had happened, but he couldn't resist the urge to tease his brother. 'Are you thinking of picking up a needle yourself, Warrick?'

'She dropped it,' his brother answered.

'Did she? Or did she leave it on purpose, to give you a reason to see her again?'

Sometimes his brother failed to see the obvious answer before him. Warrick was about to pursue the young woman, but Rhys caught his arm. 'Not yet, Brother. Wait another day.'

But Warrick reached for his tunic and pulled it over his head. 'I'll give it to one of the servants to return to her.'

Rhys resisted the urge to sigh. 'Why would you? She deliberately left it for you.' He shrugged. 'Claim a kiss from her as thanks.'

'Her father would never allow a match between her and a man like me.'

That much was the truth. It was unlikely that Warrick would be permitted to wed a beautiful heiress, especially when their own father despised him. But Rhys saw no reason to destroy his brother's dreams.

'You desire her. Just as she desires you.' A darkness slid over his mood as he thought of the night he had spent in Lianna's arms. Not once had she reached towards him since that time. And ever since the night he'd forced her to change her clothing, she had avoided any contact with him. 'At least one of us might have a good marriage,' he ventured. Though Rhys had wanted to hope that Lianna would forgive him in time, it had not happened. Instead, the longer she spent at his father's home, the more she seemed to retreat inside herself.

'Lianna MacKinnon is a beautiful woman.'

'With a heart of ice,' Rhys finished. 'She despises the air I breathe, and with good reason.'

After he had deceived her, killed her brother, and taken her virginity, she hardly spoke to him any more. 'Were it possible, I would take her to Scotland and leave her there. That would make her happy.'

His brother's eyes turned sympathetic, but Rhys only shrugged. 'One day, you will understand what it is to be powerless to command your own life. God help you then.'

Chapter Six

It was the night before the formal betrothal, and Lianna sat upon the dais beside Rhys, picking at her plate.

'Is the food not to your liking?' he asked quietly.

It could have been dirt served before her, for all that she tasted it. 'It is fine.'

He broke off a piece of bread and gave it to her. 'I asked my father for permission to wed you in Scotland. He agreed, on one condition.'

A sudden wave of longing passed over her at the thought of returning home. 'What is it?'

'He asks that you speak our wedding vows before a priest, here at Montbrooke, first. It can be done privately, but he insists upon witnessing our union himself.'

Likely because Lord Montbrooke did not believe the marriage would be legal, unless the vows were spoken in England. Which also meant that Rhys's father would likely also demand proof of consummation. She flushed at the thought. 'W-when does he want this to happen?'

'That is your choice,' Rhys answered. 'The betrothal will happen on the morrow, and we can be wedded at any time after that. If you wish it to happen that night, we can speak the vows. Or if you want to wait a few days, that can also be arranged.'

He spoke of it as if he were collecting rents from the serfs instead of joining their lives in marriage.

'We can wait a few days,' she agreed. 'But I would prefer that only a few are present for the wedding.' She loathed the idea of being the centre of attention.

'I will see to it.' Rhys ate the bread, turning his attention back to the festivities. 'My father's wife Rowena has tried to provide entertainment for us this evening. We will play a game of stoolball.'

'I have never heard of this,' she admitted.

'It is a game of skill, and I think you will find it amusing.' He reached out to touch her hand, and offered, 'You may enjoy the moment of fun.'

She couldn't remember the last time she had indulged in an activity, purely for fun. Perhaps not since she was a child. And even now, Lianna didn't know if she wanted to join the others. She had kept silent for most of her time here, though she had spoken to Lady Montbrooke in the Norman tongue once. It had been unavoidable, and Rowena had been so pleased by the effort, she had smiled warmly, believing Lianna was only shy about speaking.

The meal ended, and Lord Montbrooke called for everyone to gather outside for evening stories, contests, and games. Lianna held back while the other young ladies went to join Lady Montbrooke. But Rhys guided her to stand among them before he departed to join his father.

'Will you join the other ladies in a game of stoolball?' Lady Montbrooke enquired.

Lianna remained behind them, but Rosamund de Beaufort welcomed her to come closer. She had met the young woman several days ago and had liked her. Not only was she beautifully talented with her needle, but she also talked a great deal and had a warm smile.

Rosamund stood beside her sister Cecilia and brightened at the prospect of a game. 'If you wish.'

Lady Montbrooke gave each of them a small tansy cake wrapped in linen, explaining, 'I know we usually play this game at Easter, but it's one of Rhys's favourites. These are the prizes.' Then she led them to an open clearing where six wooden stools were placed. On the opposite end, there were several wooden balls and a stick with a paddle on one end.

'Go and choose a stool to stand upon,' she directed the women.

From the broad smiles on the faces of the men, Lianna had a sudden suspicion what this game involved. Why else would young maidens be chosen to stand alone upon stools? It drew attention to them, and she suspected that the men would compete for their favour.

She hung back, unwilling to join them. In a low voice, she said to Lady Montbrooke, 'I have no wish to play. Let the others enjoy themselves.'

But Lady Montbrooke took her by the hand and led her away from the other young women who eagerly chose their places. 'You needn't be afraid, my dear. It's only a game, and Rhys has expressly forbidden the other men from bothering you.' She squeezed her palm and added, 'Our guests are here to honour you and my stepson. Please do not bring shame upon our household by refusing.'

The woman's quiet chiding had its intended effect. Though she loathed the thought of others staring at her, Lianna reluctantly chose the stool nearest to the men.

Several of the young maidens were laughing, and she overheard Rosamund asking about the game.

One of the others admitted that the men could choose which prize they wanted. 'Either the tansy cake or a kiss,' the maiden said with a wide smile.

Oh, no. She had no desire for Rhys to kiss her in front of all these people, particularly now. But it was the price of his agreement to hold their marriage celebration in Scotland. She could not humiliate him or his father in front of so many guests.

The game began, and the men lined up for their turn. The first soldier was one she recognised, one of Rhys's guards who had travelled with them back from Scotland. He was attempting to throw a ball at the stool Lianna was standing upon.

What on earth?

She had no time to discover what was happening, for another man defended her by striking the ball away with the stick. He ran hard around the line of stools, and his ball struck the base of it. After he had scored a point for his team, he returned to stand before one of the maidens. She offered him the cake, but instead, he took her face between his hands and brought her down for a deep kiss.

So she had been right about the prize. The men cheered, and the winner escorted the maiden away from the stools. Another young woman took her place.

Had Rhys chosen this game to force her to kiss him? It seemed unlikely, for he had left her alone these past few weeks. But then she saw him approach and pick up a ball. His brother Warrick took his place with the bat, intending to defend her.

'Don't hit it, Brother,' Rhys warned.

It was clear that he intended to claim her. Lianna stood motionless, afraid of being the centre of attention while Rhys aimed the ball towards her stool. She gripped her hands together, praying he would miss.

Her face must have given away her emotions, for Rhys's expression turned angry. It almost seemed that he was trying to force her hand.

But the moment Rhys released the ball, Warrick struck it hard with his bat. It bounded across the grass and struck Rosamund's stool hard. He ran past all the stools, a tense smile upon his face. He had ignored his brother's wishes, but Lianna realised that he had his own prize in mind. He approached Rosamund, and Lianna's heart softened at the sight of them. Warrick was staring at the maiden as if she were the most beautiful woman he'd ever seen. And Rosamund looked as if she wanted his kiss.

Lianna's heart ached at the sight of them. For a moment, she wondered what it would be like, if a man stared at her in that way.

Only weeks ago, Rhys had looked at her as if he were a starving man. She had revelled in his touch and in his kiss. If Rhys had been a Highlander, everything might have been different. Her brother would never have attacked and would still be alive.

For a moment, she met Rhys's gaze, wishing she could turn back time and return to the life she had known. She would not feel so trapped in this marriage… and she might even enjoy being with him.

Lianna was startled out of her daydreams when a ball struck her stool. Rhys strode towards her, a fierce expression on his face. One of the men teased, 'You already had your turn, my lord.'

But he was undeterred and came to her. For a moment, Lianna wasn't certain what to do. She held out the tansy cake to him, but Rhys ignored it. Before she could protest, he picked her up in his arms and started to carry her off.

'But…the cake,' she stammered.

'I hate tansy cake. Throw it to the dogs.' He continued walking away from the crowd, though she was aware of everyone's eyes upon them.

When she dropped the cake in the grass, one of the dogs devoured it hungrily. And from the look in Rhys's eyes, he was about to do the same to her.

'Why are you doing this?' she whispered.

'Because for weeks now, I've left you alone. I have not demanded anything of you, save your obedience. And you hardly say a single word to me.'

He stopped walking when they reached the inner wall. Slowly, he lowered her to her feet, trapping her against the wall with both hands. 'You seduced *me* that night, Lianna. And I know you enjoyed it.'

Her skin flushed, and heat rose through her body at his words. For she could not deny he was speaking the truth.

He pressed her back, his hand around her waist while he leaned in close. 'I know you despise me. I know you pray every night that you won't have to wed me.'

She faltered at that, for it was not true. The realisation shocked her, and she didn't know what to say. The very thought of wanting this man unnerved her.

Against the heat of his body, his breath warmed her lips. 'And I know you don't want to feel anything at all when I touch you. But I know you do. And before we wed, I want you to realise how it can be between us, if you allow it.'

His mouth descended on hers, but it was not a punishing kiss. No, this was designed to tempt her, his mouth moulding to hers as his tongue slipped inside. She felt herself yielding to his nearness, pressing her hips back against his own.

Desire roared through her, and she was so confused that she gripped his shoulders for balance. Despite all that had happened, her body's needs could not be denied. Her breasts tightened beneath the silk of her gown, and she could feel the hard ridge of his erection pressed against her thighs.

Her breathing hitched, and he continued to kiss her, drawing his hands down her back, cupping her bottom. She wound her arms around his neck, kissing him back. Her own tongue entered his mouth, and he deepened the embrace, his mouth capturing hers until she could scarcely breathe.

Rhys broke away, and her heart was thundering in her chest. His mouth rested above hers, and he said quietly, 'When you gave yourself to me that night, it wasn't enough.' He lifted her slightly, and she felt the hard thrust of his erection against her. A shuddering ache brought a wetness between her legs. 'I've never forgotten the sweet taste of your breasts or the tightness of your body sheathing mine.'

She yearned for this man, and the soft thrust against her was enough to build back the shimmering echo of need. He kissed her hard, his tongue sliding within her mouth in an echo of the lovemaking they had once shared. And God help her, she wanted more.

The probing length of his shaft rubbed against her through the barrier of their clothing, and it tantalised her. Her body arched against him, and he never ceased the assault on her senses.

Rhys was not a warrior who would be denied, and he was relentless in the endless kiss. Lianna cried out as an unexpected release tore through her in shuddering waves of pleasure. It embarrassed her that she had fallen apart so easily, and she buried her face in his shoulder as the aftershocks claimed her.

'I want to take you back to the *donjon* and claim you,' Rhys murmured, nipping at her ear. 'Soon enough, we will be wed. And if you allow it, every night, you will feel this way.'

Surely he had cast a spell of madness over her. When he let her go, her knees buckled beneath her. She caught the edge of the wall, not understanding what he had done.

Rhys held out his hand. 'Walk with me, Lianna. We must join the others again.'

She joined him, but it felt as if he had broken the edges of her invisible shield, leaving her vulnerable.

And she simply didn't know what would happen now.

At dawn, Rhys rose and dressed alone. He departed his chamber and walked down the spiral stairs, when suddenly he stopped. Near the bottom of the staircase, there was another opening in the floor, leading down to the underground storage chambers.

Rhys gritted his teeth in memory. When he was an adolescent, he had spent three nights imprisoned in that storage chamber, thanks to Analise. Even now, the memory of her voice twisted through his gut.

You are very strong, you know. I would wager you're stronger than your father. Let me see.

She had put her hands on his upper arms, trying to feel his muscles. Her touch had bothered him deeply, for he had never invited it.

Your father will be away for weeks, she'd whispered. *Come to my chamber, and we will talk awhile.*

His skin crawled at the memory of the woman. He had refused her unholy offer, but she'd been undeterred. Each day she'd brushed past him, and her coy smile had unnerved him.

He'd avoided her, but it had taken four years until he could touch a woman without thinking of Analise. Even now, he loathed the thought of her.

He passed by the open cellar entrance and walked into the Great Hall. His father was breaking his fast, along with several of the guests. Warrick was not among them, and he noted the absence of Rosamund de Beaufort as well. He knew his brother had been meeting the young maiden in secret, and he rather envied them.

There was no sign of Lianna anywhere, so he went to his sister to ask where she was. Joan took him aside and said, 'She is preparing herself for the betrothal ceremony later.'

'Did she receive the gowns and jewels I sent her?'

They were some of the gifts he would offer to her, as her bride price.

His sister nodded. 'But Rhys, I worry about Lianna. I've never seen a woman so unhappy. She doesn't belong here. And this betrothal…it isn't fair to either of you.'

'There is no longer a choice.' After Lianna had offered herself to him, there was no going back. She could not wed anyone else.

He heard footsteps coming down the spiral stairs and was startled to see Lianna wearing the *léine* and colours of the MacKinnon clan. She wore her long red hair down across her shoulders, and her feet were bare.

Her cheeks were flushed, her eyes bright. Even wearing these clothes, she had a vivid beauty that startled him. She stopped before him and waited.

'Why did you not wear one of your new gowns?' he asked. 'Was there a problem?'

She shook her head. 'I am a Scot, and it is better if I come into this marriage remembering who I am. We are making this alliance for my people, and I want to wear the clothing of my homeland.'

He understood her reasons, though his father would likely be displeased. Edward expected Lianna to be dressed as a Norman lady, not a chief's daughter. But the truth was, Rhys admired her spirit. He might feel the same, had he been born a Scot.

Rhys offered her his arm and nodded for his sister to go ahead of them. Joan obeyed, and he led Lianna towards a corner of the room. 'What have you decided about the wedding?'

'I would still rather be wedded in Scotland. Not

here.' Upon her face he saw the uncertainty, mingled with homesickness.

'The sooner we speak our vows here, the sooner we can go.'

His bride did not seem pleased with the prospect. Rhys rested one arm against the wall, shadowing her. 'Do I make you nervous?' he murmured. 'Is that why you are avoiding the marriage?' He didn't think she could be afraid of consummating the union—they had done that already, and he knew she had found it pleasurable.

Lianna stiffened at his nearness and said, 'We should join the others for the morning meal.'

'You haven't answered my question.' He reached out to touch her waist, and she shied away. It was as if she had no wish to be touched by him. At that, he stepped back, giving her space. He knew she had enjoyed his touch after the game yesterday. It seemed that she was confused about her own feelings, still wanting to maintain distance.

Lianna glanced over her shoulder to see if anyone was watching. 'I would rather not marry at all,' she admitted. 'But I know my people will rely on your family's wealth to save them. Eiloch has very little of value.'

'It gives the king a place for soldiers, if war breaks out,' Rhys said. 'There is already unrest in Scotland.' Not only that, but his Norman soldiers would provide protection for her people.

'And I am meant to sacrifice myself to bring the enemy amid my own clan.' She closed her eyes. 'You ask me to become a traitor.'

'This marriage will save their lives,' he countered. 'The Normans will not harm them. I will see to that.'

But she was already shaking her head. 'It won't be so easy, Rhys. You're an outsider. They won't accept you or your men.'

He knew that, but they had no other choice. 'I will live among them for a time,' he said. 'They will come to know me.'

It was clear she did not believe it, given the look on her face. With a shrug, she dismissed the idea and said, 'We should join the others.'

'Wait.' He caught her hand and held it. 'In a few hours, the betrothal will be signed and witnessed.' She paused, and he used the opportunity to press her further. 'After today, I want to begin anew. This silence has gone on long enough. I want a true marriage, not a wall of ice between us.'

Her expression was incredulous. 'How can you believe that could happen? Nothing you could say or do will bring my brother back.'

She tried to move away, but he caught her hand and drew her back. 'I regret that your brother died during the raid. But we cannot go on this way, Lianna. I know you're unhappy.'

He had mistakenly believed that giving her time to grieve would bring about peace. Instead, it had only heightened the distance between them.

Her fingers tightened on his. 'You could have wounded Sían. He didn't have to die.'

'No. He started the fight, and I ended it.' Her brother had been determined to kill him, and Rhys would not apologise for defending himself. Even if he had left the man alive, he had no doubt that Sían would have continued to attack.

'You cannot simply expect me to put this in the past and behave like a loving wife.' Her expression tightened with dismay. 'If I had killed Warrick, how would you feel? Could you begin anew and forget?'

He said nothing to that but released her hand. A rigid tightness rose within him, and he stared at her, suddenly realising what a mistake it was to think that this woman would forgive him and become his wife in truth. Theirs was an arrangement, nothing more.

Lianna took a step back and whispered, 'It matters not if we are wed this night or a fortnight from now. I will not share your bed.'

With that, she turned and strode towards his father to join him at the morning meal.

Lianna felt shaky after she had signed the betrothal document. Her father's letter had been added, along with witnesses from her clan, and the dozens of other guests Lord Montbrooke had summoned. Rhys had not spoken a single word to her since she had sworn she would not share his bed. His anger was palpable, a layer of ice between them.

Now, she wondered if she had gone too far. Gone was the kind man who had kissed her after the game, the man who had sent her jewels and gowns and promised a true wedding in Scotland. In his place stood a fierce warrior who would no longer bend.

She could not help but feel that, by denying him, she had issued a challenge. But she had been truthful. She could not imagine forgiving him for what had happened to her brother. Gowns and jewels would not change Sían's death. And even beyond that, she hated living here at Montbrooke.

She had no power here, no choices. Every decision was made for her—when to eat, what to eat, what to wear, and where they wanted her to go. She felt as if she were drowning, weighed down by invisible chains. And now, it would never change.

As a distraction, she studied each of the guests, trying to remember their names. After a time, she realised that Rhys's brother was missing, along with Rosamund. Although she did not know them well, it did seem strange that they were gone.

Her mind drifted as the men discussed the details of her meagre dowry, Rhys's bride price, and the land ownership of Eiloch. After hours of standing, her feet hurt, and she wished she could escape. Outside, the sun was shining, and in here, it was gloomy with so many people around.

She missed her daily rides. She missed Scotland and her family. It was a physical ache in her heart, and she longed to return to Eiloch.

A hand squeezed hers, bringing her back to the present. Lianna had no idea what had just happened, but Rhys said, 'We will wed on the morrow.'

The firm pressure on her palm warned that he would not be deterred. He had taken the decision from her. So, he intended for her to speak the vows so soon? Resentment dug into her mood. She felt as if the men had shoved her into the corner, with no regard for her own desires. Was this his reaction to her insistence that she would not share his bed?

'Good,' Lord Montbrooke proclaimed. 'I will make the arrangements.'

Lianna straightened and decided to exert her own wishes. She had been complacent long enough. Using the Norman tongue, she said, 'If we are to be wedded on the morrow, then afterwards, we will return to Eiloch. I have been away from my people for far too long.'

But the men behaved as if she hadn't spoken at all. Instead, the guests were speaking among themselves about this wedding, and now it was sounding as if it would be a large celebration indeed. Her throat went dry, and she tried to pull her hand out of Rhys's iron grasp.

He leaned in and murmured, 'Not here, Lianna.'

In turn, she whispered in his ear, 'Do not force this, Rhys.'

But he was not listening at all. She wanted so badly to retreat, to escape this crowd of people and get away from everyone. Her throat was tight with unshed tears, and she looked up in desperation at Lady Montbrooke. In the woman's eyes, she caught a glimpse of understanding.

A moment later, Rowena came forward and said, 'Rhys, I am taking your bride away, now that we have finished the betrothal. She needs to rest.'

Lady Montbrooke took her hand and tucked it into her own arm. Never before had Lianna been so grateful for her intervention. She went with Rowena, following her up the spiral stairs while below, the men continued finishing up the details of the betrothal.

Rowena led her to her own chamber, and only when they were alone, did Lianna release the tears. Lady Montbrooke put her arms around her and stroked her hair. 'I thought you might need a good cry.'

The woman's kindness only made her sob harder. Lianna felt so lost, trapped in a place where she didn't belong. And in truth, it felt as if she belonged nowhere.

'Rhys is a good man,' Lady Montbrooke said, rubbing her back. 'He will not be cruel to you.'

'I thought I would have more time,' Lianna managed, trying to gather command of her emotions.

'You will have the rest of your lives together,' the woman said gently.

But that wasn't what she had meant. Lianna wanted more time *before* the wedding, until she was forced into becoming Rhys's wife. He would never grant her the freedom she craved, nor would he allow her to retreat and be alone each day.

'What if I don't want to spend the rest of my life with him?' Lianna blurted out. 'Every choice has been taken from me. I cannot bear it.' Her heart ached with frustration.

Lady Montbrooke laughed and drew her back, drying her tears. 'My dear, you must learn how to manage a man. Let him believe that he is in command. But *we* hold the power when no one else is around.'

She didn't understand what the woman meant by that. The matron took her hands and said, 'I understand your wish to stand up to Rhys and assert yourself. But you must be more subtle about it.'

She took a breath, gathering her composure. 'How?'

'You allure him. Enchant him with your beauty and your intelligence. Make him long to please you, and then ask him for what you want when no one else is around. Believe me, he will do anything you ask. And never, ever defy him in front of his men. Let him keep his pride.'

Lianna wasn't certain she could be that woman, seductive or alluring. *But you seduced him that night*, her conscience chided. *And he took you willingly.*

Her body tingled at the memory, and she closed her eyes. 'I think I've already ruined any sort of peace between us. I told him I would never share his bed.'

'You were tired and feeling upset,' Lady Montbrooke soothed. 'But you can change everything. Put on your best gown for the wedding, wear the jewels he gave you, and then tell him you have changed your mind. Give him his body's desire and in turn, he will grant your heart's desire.'

Lianna took a step backwards, the fears closing over her. 'I don't think I can do that.' Not after all that had happened between them.

'Then start with a kiss,' Rowena suggested. 'A kiss offered freely, one that promises hope for the marriage. I know Rhys well. He is a proud man and one who will make an excellent husband. But first, show him your softer side.'

Lianna wasn't so certain. Right now, the desire to leave Montbrooke was stronger than anything else. 'I want to go out riding,' she confessed. 'I need to escape this place for a time.'

'Then take Rhys with you,' Lady Montbrooke offered. 'Go out together and spend the day alone with him. Try what I have suggested and see if it does not bring about the effect you want.'

Lianna sat down on a stool with her knees drawn up. She didn't know if she could behave in the manner Lady Montbrooke was suggesting. It wasn't at all the sort of woman she was.

But then, she knew full well that few people liked

her. Even her brother had laughed at her ways, ignoring all that she did for him and for the clan. Her past behaviour had brought naught, except others whispering behind her back.

She didn't want to pretend to be someone she wasn't. And yet, she desperately needed to seize back the power that had been taken from her. Only then could she be in command of her own life.

With a heavy sigh, she rose from the stool. 'Will you send word to Rhys that I wish to go riding? And will you ask that horses be prepared for us?'

Lady Montbrooke smiled. 'Indeed, I will. And Lianna, regardless of what others have led you to believe, *I* think you will make an excellent wife for Rhys.'

She didn't know if that would be true or not. But regardless, it was time to try another means of freeing herself from this prison.

Chapter Seven

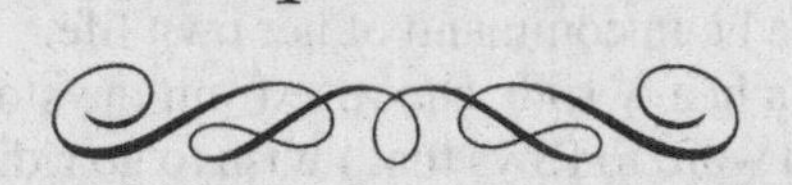

Rhys rode alongside Lianna as she drew her horse into a gallop. Her long red hair streamed behind her, and her cheeks were rosy from the wind. He didn't know why she had asked him to come with her on the ride, but it reminded him of the day at the dolmen when he had first met her. Sometimes he wished it were possible to go back to those days when she had offered a genuine smile.

The betrothal was finished, and he would wed her on the morrow. He saw no reason to delay it—not when she continued to push him away. It was clear now that she had no intention of trying to make their marriage a happy one.

And yet, he suspected she had a reason for inviting him on the ride. Her demeanour appeared nervous, and he decided to hear what she had to say. There might be a chance to soften the edges of her anger.

They reached a clearing on a hillside, and Lianna slowed her horse, stopping to look around at the landscape. The summer grasses spread out in a sea of green, while Montbrooke stood in the distance, a stone fortress well protected from enemies.

'Why did you want me to ride with you?' he asked. He suspected it had to do with his demand that they wed the next day. But her earlier declaration, that she would never share his bed, had demanded a response—and so he'd made his own move within the game.

'I spoke with your stepmother for a time,' Lianna said. 'And Rowena made me realise that you are right. I cannot behave as if this marriage does not exist, like I will wake up from a bad dream.'

She dismounted and walked a short distance, turning back to wait for him to follow. Rhys got off his horse and let it graze, walking a few strides forward. It felt as if she wanted to negotiate, to try to delay the marriage further.

'We are betrothed now,' he said. 'And we consummated our union before that. There is no waking up or turning back.'

'I ken that.' Her voice was quiet, and she chose a seat upon a wide limestone outcropping. 'But I do not like what has happened.' Her *brat* slipped down from her shoulders, and she pulled her hair to one side.

She looked back at him, and her eyes held misery. But even then, she was beautiful. Her lips were soft, and there was weariness in her gaze. 'I miss Scotland,' she told him. 'Please take me home.'

Her red hair brushed the edge of her cheek, and her brown eyes were pleading. He stood beside her and was startled when she reached up to take his hand. It was such a contrast from the anger she'd shown earlier, he didn't know what to think.

But her thumb grazed the centre of his palm in a startling move of affection. Not once had she reached out to him since the night she'd seduced him. His body hungered for hers, and he squeezed her hand in answer.

Was this her attempt at a peace offering? There was still a vast distance between them, but she had taken a single step.

Rhys lifted her hand to his mouth and kissed it. And this time, she did not pull away. Her deep brown eyes studied him for a moment, before she gazed downwards with shyness.

For a time, he remained silent, watching as the wind swept a path through the meadow. And then he offered, 'We will leave after the wedding vows.'

Her face brightened, and he saw the first true smile in a long time. 'Thank you, Rhys.'

Had they been lovers, she might have embraced him or offered a kiss. But it was far too soon for that, and he did not press her for more. Instead, he continued to hold her hand.

In the distance, he saw a rider approaching. 'Kneel low into the grass until we know who this is,' he warned Lianna.

She obeyed, and he kept his hand upon his sword to guard her. There were two people on the horse, and soon, he recognised his brother and Rosamund de Beaufort.

'I thought they might be together,' Lianna whispered. 'They were missing from our betrothal ceremony.'

'I noticed that, too.' He rested his arm behind her spine. 'In many ways, I envy them their freedom.'

Her face softened, but she did not appear offended

by his remark. 'Neither of us was given a choice, were we?'

'No.' He regarded her for a time, wondering what her life had been like in Scotland. 'Did you ever want to marry another man?'

She gave a wry smile. 'I was reminded from the time I could walk that I was promised to you. I did not dare look at anyone else. Nor did they look at me.'

'They looked,' he said. 'But I suppose your father would never let them have a chance.'

She let out a half-laugh. 'You don't ken my people, Rhys. They hardly saw me at all.'

'Then they were blind.'

He rested both arms on either side of her waist, and she tensed. But he did not steal the kiss he wanted. Instead, he remained a breath away, studying her face. He tried to understand what sort of upbringing she'd had, to believe that anyone could think her invisible.

She was like a trapped wild animal, fighting back against those who wanted to help her. And perhaps the only way they would return to peace between them was for him to release the bonds.

She closed her eyes, and said quietly, 'I will wed you on the morrow. But I ask that we have only a few guests. I do not want to be surrounded by a crowd.'

'That was my father's doing, not mine. But they will be expecting to witness our vows.' He did not know how to avoid it without offending the visitors. He knew that Lianna hated to be singled out. 'I will try to find a way,' was all he could offer. 'I can make no promises.'

She lowered her head in a nod.

And for now, it was enough.

On the morning of her wedding, Lianna was startled to hear shouting and men gathering weapons. She hurried to her window and saw Lord Montbrooke arguing with Harold de Beaufort. Their forces were joining together, and she saw two of the guards dragging a young boy towards the keep.

A maid entered her bedchamber, and said, 'Good morn to you, my lady.'

'What is happening below?' Lianna demanded. 'It looks as if they are preparing for war.'

'I cannot say.' It was unclear whether that meant she could not or would not say.

The maid picked up a green silk *bliaud* and began helping her to dress. Lianna hardly cared what she wore, but she did worry about the boy outside. Something terrible must have happened, and she wanted to know what had caused the men to gather weapons and assemble as if for battle.

When the maid had finished helping her, Lianna picked up her skirts and went below stairs. She hurried towards the Great Hall and immediately saw Rhys waiting for her. He approached and caught her hand. 'There is a problem, Lianna.'

'I saw the soldiers.' She was about to ask him what had happened when the two guards entered, dragging the adolescent boy with them. His face was white with fear. 'Who is that?'

'Go back to your chamber,' Rhys ordered. 'You should not be here right now.' The dark look in his eyes suggested that the boy was about to face a serious punishment.

'Not until you tell me what's happened.' And even then, she intended to find out what the adolescent had done. He couldn't be more than three and ten. Why would he be seized by soldiers?

Rhys kept her hand in his and led her back towards the stairs, out of the way. 'He is Ademar of Dolwyth. Apparently, he helped my brother Warrick escape with Lady Rosamund de Beaufort last night.' His face turned grim. 'They intend to question him. And once they know where Warrick and Rosamund are, they will hunt them down and punish them both.'

Lianna was horrified by the thought. 'Why would they run away? Could they not be married?'

Rhys shook his head. 'My father and younger brother have been enemies for years now. He would never allow such a match for Warrick.'

'Why?'

But Rhys only shook his head. 'Suffice it to say, he believed the lies told by his second wife, Analise.'

At the far end of the Hall, Lianna winced when she saw the guards seize Ademar and hold his arms behind his back while another man backhanded his face with his fist.

'Where are they?' the guard demanded.

'I—I—I d-don't kn-know,' the boy stammered.

The guard mocked Ademar's stutter. 'You'd better th-th-think harder, boy.' And with that, he struck the lad across the face, over and over, until blood ran from his nose.

Lianna dug her nails into Rhys's sleeve. 'Please stop them. He's just a boy.' And the more they questioned Ademar, the more evident it became that the lad had a speech difficulty. He could not voice any words without the stammer, and the more they questioned him, the more he was beaten. She could hardly believe the men would treat an adolescent boy in such a way as they questioned him. How could they mock his stutter and continue to strike him, when he could give no answers?

'I will do what I can,' Rhys promised. 'But you must stay here.'

She nodded and ducked back into the shadows of the spiral stairs. He strode through the Great Hall, ordering, 'Enough of this.'

Lianna craned her neck to see what was happening. Lord Montbrooke appeared displeased at his son's interference, but Rhys went to his father's side and spoke to him quietly. Then he addressed Lord de Beaufort in a low voice while the guards continued to hold Ademar. The boy had sagged to his knees, blood dripping down his face and nose.

Rhys moved forward and leaned down to speak with Ademar. The boy raised his head, and tears mingled with the blood. But he did answer the questions in a tremulous stutter.

Rhys motioned for another servant to take the boy away, and then he returned to his father's side. Within moments, the men were gathering arms and leaving the Hall.

Lianna stayed on the stairs for a moment, wondering what would become of the young lad. It didn't seem right that they had punished him for helping a man and a woman in love. She decided to tend the boy's bruises and talk with him awhile.

No sooner had she taken a single step forward before Rhys caught her hand. 'Come to the chapel within the hour.'

She faltered at the suddenness of his command and hardly knew how to respond. 'So soon?'

He nodded. 'My father wants to witness the vows before he goes in search of Warrick.' He squeezed her palm. 'You needn't worry. It's unlikely there will be more than three guests.'

She understood that this was another way of delaying his father's pursuit. And she found that she wanted to help Rhys. It was wrong for Edward de Laurent and Harold de Beaufort to search for the lovers with the intent of forcing them apart.

'Will we then travel to Scotland?' she asked him.

Rhys reached out and traced the edge of her face. 'I must follow my father and Lord de Beaufort while they search for my brother. But after that, yes.'

There was a hard cast to his tone, as if he didn't want to go. 'What do you plan to do?'

He expelled a breath and admitted, 'I plan to help my brother in any way I can. Once they find Warrick, they might try to kill him for daring to take Rosamund de Beaufort. I only hope I can stop them.'

A numb feeling settled in the pit of Lianna's stomach, for she knew exactly how he felt. She had been unable to prevent her own brother's death at the hands of Rhys. But with each day that passed, she was finding it more difficult to look upon him with hatred. Her mind and conscience warred with one another, and though she wanted to despise him, he had been nothing but kind to her.

Confusion clouded her mood, and she took a step

backwards. 'I will meet you in the chapel within the hour. But I want to tend Ademar's wounds first.' And with that, she retreated, needing the task at hand to steady her mind.

Lianna walked past the guests, asking one of the servants where the boy had gone. When she learned that he was outside near the training grounds, she ordered the servant to bring her clean water and linen.

As she left the keep with a pitcher of water and the linen, she saw Rhys joining the other men. He risked a glance back at her, and her cheeks warmed at the sight of his intense stare. It was as if he were reminding her that she would be his wife within the hour. And dear God, it made her body soften at the very thought.

She shut her eyes tightly, trying to push back the unbidden images. No. She would not allow it.

To avoid thinking about him, she hurried towards the training ground where the servant had told her she could find Ademar. She found the boy seated against one of the outer walls, his shoulders slumped forward. Lianna walked towards him and crouched down. At first, he didn't seem aware that she was there.

'I am Lianna MacKinnon,' she told the boy. 'I've come to tend your wounds.'

He didn't look up but kept his shoulders slumped forward. From the slight motion, she guessed he was crying.

'Will you let me see your face?' she asked softly, kneeling down beside him. He still refused to meet her gaze, and so she began to talk. 'I heard of how you helped Warrick and Rosamund. Few grown men would dare to do what you did.'

'I b-b-betrayed them,' he managed.

Lianna poured some water on to a linen cloth. 'I don't believe that. And neither will they.'

'H-he was my friend. And I told Lord Montbrooke where they were t-travelling.'

Lianna touched the wet cloth to his forehead, and at last he looked at her. His eye was swollen, and he had bruising along his jaw. His nose was still bleeding, though it was not broken. She washed away the blood and then dipped the cloth back in the pitcher, wringing it out again. 'Hold this to your eye.' He obeyed, and she said, 'They would have tracked them down eventually. It's not your fault.'

'I should have b-been stronger.'

She rested her hand on Ademar's shoulder. 'You cannot change what happened. And trust me when I say, they will not blame you.' He was only a young adolescent and could hardly be expected to endure such brutal questioning.

Her words seemed to have an effect on him. Though Ademar kept the wet cloth held to his eye, he straightened. 'One day, I w-will not be so w-weak.'

She smiled at him. 'No, you will be much stronger in time.' Nodding towards the kitchens, she suggested, 'Go and get something to eat. You'll feel better for it.'

His expression dimmed, as if he didn't think that were possible. Lianna added, 'Don't be afraid for Warrick. Rhys will help him.' She poured water on to her own hands, washing them, before she folded up the linen cloths to take them away.

She gave the pitcher and linen back to a servant and returned to the *donjon*. Then she ascended the spiral stairs to the chamber where she had stayed these past few weeks. It was an easy matter to pack her remaining belongings, tucking them into the trunks for the journey home. She studied the elaborate Norman gowns Rhys had given her. A part of her wanted to leave them behind, to pretend as if she held no part in his heritage. But then, there might come a time when she needed them. With reluctance, she packed them away, along with the jewels.

A knock sounded at the door, and when she called for the person to enter, she saw Joan. Rhys's sister was wearing white, as she always did, along with the simple iron jewellery. The young woman said, 'They are ready for you at the chapel. I will take you there.'

Lianna rose from her knees. For a moment, she wanted to ask for Joan's forgiveness. The woman had offered friendship, and Lianna had pushed her away. She regretted that decision and wanted to make amends.

But what could she say? How could she even begin? The words failed her, and Joan led her towards the small family chapel within the *donjon*. Lianna felt as if she had stepped into someone else's life. She wore clothing that did not belong to her, and she was living in another place where no one loved her.

When they reached the doorway, Lianna stopped her. 'Will you…stay to witness the vows?' She meant it as an invitation, a chance for them to start anew.

But Joan shook her head. 'I shouldn't. My presence would only bring bad luck to you.'

It was a strange thing to say, and Lianna reached out and took her hand. 'Don't say that. We would like to have you there.'

The young woman's expression turned sad, and

Lianna wondered the cause of it. She knew that Joan had never married, which struck her as strange. Edward de Laurent was not a man who would miss an opportunity to arrange a good marriage for his eldest daughter, binding her in matrimony to a nobleman.

Joan squeezed her hand and said, 'I wish you both happiness, and I *do* think you will come to love Rhys as I do. I would not want my presence to cast a shadow over your union. Believe me when I say it's better this way.'

And with that, she turned her back and left. Lianna felt her nerves gather into a tight ball, feeling more alone than ever.

Inside the dim chapel, the priest was waiting, along with an impatient Lord Montbrooke and four other men she didn't recognise. She stepped inside, and the earl remarked, 'At least you are more appropriately dressed this time.'

Lianna wanted to blurt out a scathing reply, but she stopped herself. Instead, she asked, 'What will become of Warrick when your men find him?'

Edward de Laurent shrugged. 'It is no concern of yours.'

'Since he is to become my brother through marriage within a few minutes, I think it *is* my concern. What has he done wrong, except to run away with the woman he loves?'

The earl's countenance turned black with rage. 'You know nothing of what Warrick has done. He deserves to be flogged for harming an innocent maiden.'

'From what I saw, she wanted to be with him,' Lianna answered. 'I hardly think love is a reason for a flogging. It should be the two of them getting married, as well as Rhys and myself.'

'He will never wed Rosamund de Beaufort. Or any other woman, save a common wench.' Edward crossed his arms and glared at her. 'It would be well if he did not survive the flogging.'

'How can you say that about your own son?' She wanted to understand his reasons for the violent hatred.

'Because he killed my youngest daughter. And that, I will never forgive.'

She was shocked into silence, and Rhys entered a moment later, followed by the priest. There was far more to this story than Lord Montbrooke knew, but from what Rhys had said, Edward believed his former wife's untruths.

There was no time to argue, for Rhys took her hand in his and the priest began the wedding ceremony. Lianna's hands grew cold, and she could hardly grasp what was happening. Suddenly, everyone was staring at her, and she knew not what to say. Rhys leaned in. 'I know this was not the wedding we should have had. But I will give you a proper celebration in Scotland when we arrive.'

She managed to nod, and the priest took that for her consent. He blessed the pair of them, and Lianna felt dizzy that it should be over so quickly. Rhys kissed her mouth swiftly, and it was done. He was now her husband.

There was no Mass, for Lord Montbrooke was already leaving the chapel in search of his younger son. Rhys held her hand, drawing her back until they were alone. He lowered his mouth to her ear. 'Pack your belongings and be ready to leave as swiftly as you can. We have to follow them north.'

She understood his haste. 'My belongings are ready now. If you want to send the wagon with my trunks back to Eiloch while we follow your brother, we can meet up with my men later.'

He relaxed at her suggestion and nodded. 'Good.' But even so, he did not release her hand. Lianna glanced at the doorway, wondering why he was holding her back.

'I should send you back to Scotland with your own guards,' he admitted. 'This isn't your battle to fight. But I don't want you to be alone. I would rather protect you myself.' His voice was warm, and it suddenly made her nervous.

She wanted to pull away from him, but Rhys rested both palms on the wall behind her. She was cornered in his arms and didn't know what to do.

Lady Montbrooke had counselled her to soften towards her husband. And yet, everything about Rhys de Laurent set her off balance. Her heart beat faster, and she could hardly catch her breath.

'I didn't give you a proper kiss of peace,' he said, tilting her chin up.

Lianna wanted to turn her face away, but she didn't dare to move. Her body grew aware of his presence, and she was spellbound by the hard planes of this man's face and his sensual mouth. Heat burned through her skin, and she tried not to let herself feel anything.

But then Rhys's mouth covered hers, and he pressed her back against the wall. She could hardly grasp a single thought when he kissed her, and she was caught up in the storm of his warm mouth upon her lips. He caught her waist and pressed himself against her so that she felt the hard ridge of his need. And she could not deny the restless response rising within her.

Confusion and guilt roiled through her, and she broke free, feeling helpless. 'Y-you should go and prepare the horses.'

He stared at her, and in his gaze she felt the unfulfilled promise. 'This isn't over, Lianna.'

And God help her, she knew it.

One week later

His brother was lucky to be alive.

After being flogged, Warrick's bleeding body had been left behind at Dolwyth. Rhys had taken him away, bringing Warrick back to his own camp before their father could find him. For four days, they had travelled north to Scotland, while Lianna did her best to tend his brother's wounds.

Their father had ordered the punishment—and perhaps Edward had wanted him to die. Icy resentment gathered up within him as he wondered how any man could treat his son this way. But he didn't know how he could solve the hatred between the two men. Warrick had done nothing wrong, despite the accusations against him. But Edward had been only too eager to believe Analise's lies.

The familiar anger kindled inside him, and he strode towards the tent he'd shared with Lianna. He had been so distracted by his brother's fate, he had not touched his new wife in the past sennight. The irony didn't escape him, but perhaps it was better that he left her alone for now.

'How is he?' he asked her.

The tent was immaculate, his brother lying prone while she had a basin of water and bandages laid out in neat rows beside her. Lianna pulled back the edges of Warrick's shirt, which they'd had to cut away with a blade since the blood had stuck the garment to his skin.

'He is still in pain, and he has not spoken to me. But he has eaten.' She removed an older poultice and began making a new one with garlic and yarrow. Despite her healing efforts, Warrick's back was deep red from the lash marks, and there was no doubt he would be scarred. It seemed impossible to imagine that their own father had ordered this done to him.

Lianna reached for a wooden bowl filled with warmed water and one of the rolled linen cloths. She began washing Warrick's wounds, and he shuddered the moment she placed the new poultice upon his back.

'Where is she?' he demanded, his voice barely above a whisper.

Rhys didn't have to ask who Warrick was talking about. He exchanged a glance with Lianna. 'Her father took her away. He intends to wed Rosamund to Alan de Courcy.'

His brother was silent while Lianna wrapped the bandage around his torso. There was a grim cast to his features, and at last he demanded, 'When?'

Rhys shook his head. 'I don't know.' Likely as soon as possible. He helped Lianna finish tying off the bandage and said, 'I'm sorry.'

His brother cursed beneath his breath. There was a bleakness in his blue eyes, and he admitted, 'You should have left me there to die.'

No. Never that.

But before Rhys could speak, Lianna reached out and squeezed Warrick's hand. 'There is always hope.'

His brother stared up at the darkened sky. 'Not for me.'

There was such torment in the young man's eyes, Rhys understood that there was little he could say. Words would not make his brother feel any comfort. It was best to leave him be, and perhaps in time, he might find another woman to love.

'I will make a tea to help you sleep,' Lianna offered. Her eyes held sympathy, before she went back to get the herbs.

Rhys was about to follow her, when Warrick murmured, 'Stay a moment.' His brother waited until Lianna was out of earshot and then added, 'Our father ordered my punishment because I wedded Rosamund in secret. But now her father is having the marriage annulled.'

Rhys let out a slow breath of air. 'You are fortunate to be alive.'

'I wish I weren't. Death would be better than knowing they will marry her off to another man.' His brother leaned back and closed his eyes.

There was nothing he could say to ease his brother's frustration, so he reached out and touched his shoulder gently. 'Try to sleep. Lianna will be back with the tea in a little while.'

He closed the flap of the tent behind him. It was cooler outside, and mists gathered along the edges of the hills. He spied a forest in the distance, where the tree trunks were almost black against the grey sky. In a few more days, they would arrive back at Eiloch.

He saw Lianna retrieve a small chest from her trunk of belongings. They had met up with her men along this road, only two days ago. She frowned after opening it, and he asked, 'What's wrong?'

She shook her head. 'I need more valerian, but I don't know if any grows nearby.'

It was still early afternoon, and Rhys offered, 'Take a guard with you, and you can look. If you think it will help him.'

'It will.' Her face fell, and she said, 'But even chamomile and valerian won't cure what's hurting inside him.'

Rhys walked with her towards the edge of the clearing. He rested his palm at the small of her back, and her long red hair brushed the edge of his hand. Lianna wore the colours of her clan, and the green and brown clothing contrasted against her hair.

She halted her steps and asked, 'Was there something else you wanted?' Her voice held a slight tremor of nerves.

'There was, yes.' He drew her closer and rested his forehead against hers. 'We've been wedded for over a sennight.'

Lianna drew her hands to his chest, as if to keep him away. Her expression grew nervous, as if she were frightened of him. 'Rhys, I don't think—'

'Have I ever forced you against your will?' he asked quietly. 'The only night we were together, it was your choice.' He slid his palm over her cheek, and she lowered her gaze. 'And I watched you come apart in my arms when I was inside you.'

Her mouth opened slightly, as if shocked by his words. But he continued the assault on her senses, wanting to tempt her further. 'I want to touch you again, to feel your body beneath mine, skin to skin. I want to feel your wetness surrounding me as I take you over the edge and you dig your nails into my back.'

Her eyes widened, but she did not pull away from him. He felt the tremor in her hands, and her breathing grew unsteady.

'All I've demanded thus far is for you to share my tent. To lie beside me at night.' But Rhys would not deny that he wanted more than that. After witnessing his brother's savage flogging and the heartache Warrick now endured, he wanted to feel the warmth of his wife's body against his. He wanted her touch and the comfort of her presence.

'I have never claimed you, though it is my right to do so.' He caught her nape and drew her close again. 'My patience wears thin. And when I have none left, I will tempt you with my mouth and hands until your body is begging to be filled with mine.'

She still appeared startled by his words, but this time she rested her hands upon his shoulders. Rhys had never felt such a hunger for this woman. He kissed her, devouring that beautiful mouth until her hands wound around his neck.

Her mind and spirit might defy him, but her actions spoke otherwise. She kissed him back, and when he pulled her closer, she grew pliant in his arms. The weeks of celibacy had only sharpened his needs, and he wanted far more.

He released her, and said, 'Go and get your herbs. But stay in view of the camp and take a guard with you.'

She stumbled back, her lips swollen. But she nodded and hurried back towards the men. Tonight, he decided. He would coax her into desiring him, until she surrendered in his arms.

Lianna's thoughts were troubled when she strode towards the glen. God help her, Rhys made her blood race. In truth, her feelings were torn into pieces. One moment, she despised him for killing her brother, and the next, she recalled that Sían had set out to murder Rhys. The raid had been unprovoked, and her husband had only defended himself.

A narrow lake stretched out across the space, but she could see no valerian plants. It might be better to search within the small wooded copse. She walked among the trees into the centre of the forest.

Her heart was so confused by what to do now. For she was starting to see that Rhys was not the monster she'd believed he was. There were traces of the handsome Highlander she'd believed him to be. And seeing how he had rescued Warrick and had taken such good care of his brother, she realised that remaining married to this man would be very different from her imaginings.

She walked towards the outer edge of the woods alone, not bothering to take a guard with her. For what purpose? There was no one here, and if she shouted for help, Rhys would be there in a moment with his men. Right now, she wanted the solitude to gather her thoughts. She had been wedded only a short time to Rhys, but in that time, she was starting to understand him. He was not a man who made rash decisions. He was a strong fighter, fiercely loyal to his family and friends.

But more than that, he knew how to tempt her, reminding her of the night he'd claimed her innocence. Even now, her lips were softened at the memory of his kiss. Eventually, she would have to lie with him. But the thought no longer tormented her…it aroused her.

She walked amid the alder saplings, following a stream that cut across the forest. While she searched for the valerian, she tried to decide what to do. Lianna closed her eyes, breathing in the scent of the forest. All around her, it was silent, and she took a moment to still her thoughts. From behind her, she heard a rustling noise, and the crack of a stick. It was likely her husband or another guard, come to watch over her. Lianna smiled to herself at the thought.

But then a hand clamped over her mouth, and she saw three Highlanders she didn't recognise. They must have hidden themselves in the forest before her arrival.

She kicked at them, desperately struggling to remove the hand from her mouth. She tried to scream, but the muffled sound would not come out.

Then they shoved a handkerchief in her mouth, binding it tight, and hauled her away.

Chapter Eight

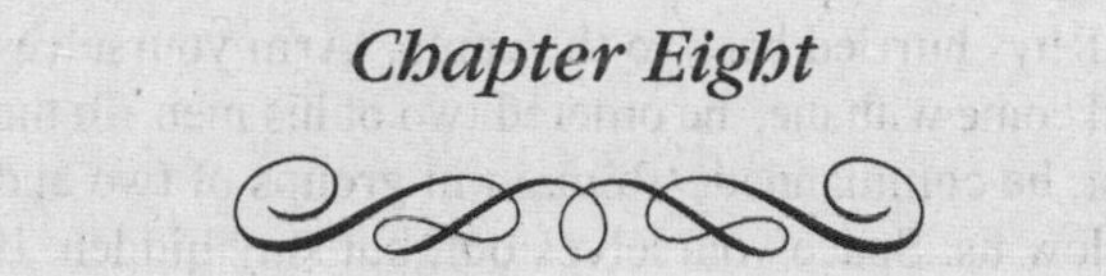

Rhys returned to Warrick but was startled to find his brother gone. His bedding was rumpled, and even his shoes were still there. It might be that he'd left to relieve himself, but he had not seen his brother walk since he'd been rescued.

His instincts tightened with unease, and he returned to his men. 'Have you seen Warrick?'

'No, my lord,' one of the guards answered.

It was then that Rhys did a count of the men and realised that all of them were present. Lianna had not taken a guard with her—and likely, that was why his brother was gone. She would have passed by the tent on her way towards the glen, and Warrick must have followed her.

Rhys traced his brother's footsteps towards the glen. A few paces out, he saw a fragment of Warrick's bandage. Then, at the edge of the forest, he saw another piece of linen tied to a sapling.

A coldness flooded his veins, for this was a game they had played as boys. They had hidden from their sister Joan, leaving clues to find each other. His brother was deliberately leading him in this direction. But why wouldn't he have simply accompanied Lianna, if that was his reason?

Because Warrick had suspected danger. It was the only possible explanation. His brother must have seen something. But what?

Rhys hurried back to the camp. 'Arm yourselves and come with me,' he ordered two of his men. To the rest, he commanded, 'Remain in groups of two and follow us. Space yourselves out, but stay hidden. If we encounter enemies, I want them to believe there are only three of us.'

He donned his helm and took the lead. He trusted his younger brother with his life, and if anything had happened to Lianna, Warrick would lead him back to her.

He only prayed he could find them in time.

Lianna could not see where they were going, for one of the Highlanders had slung her over his shoulder. Her hands were bound with ropes, and her mouth was dry from the handkerchief in her mouth. It had been tied around her head so tightly it was impossible to make any noise at all. Were it possible, she would have screamed as loudly as she could. But when she tried, nothing came out, except a muffled moan.

From her upside-down position, she could not see the features of the man who had taken her, save his dun-coloured trews and shirt. When she tried to shove free of him, he laughed and patted her bottom.

'There's a sweet lass. You shouldna be alone in the forest,' he said. 'Especially when Normans are about.'

His hand moved to her backside again, and she fought to escape him when he squeezed it.

Her mind was seizing up with fear. Despite her attempts to kick at her attacker, his grip only tightened. He was broad-shouldered and tall, perhaps a little older than herself. Lianna had no idea why he had stolen her, but she prayed that Rhys could somehow find her.

She tried to see past the other two men to learn where she was. The glen and the forest were gone, and it seemed that they had carried her deep into the hills. From this elevation, she could see for miles, but there was no sign of Rhys or their men.

Worst of all, she spied a cave concealed by the underbrush. The thought was terrifying, for Rhys might never find her there.

'Are ye going to share her?' one of the men asked with a leer.

'Only when I've finished,' the first answered. He entered the cave, and inside, the coals of a dying fire illuminated the space. It smelled stale, and she wondered what the men were doing so far from their homes.

When they set her down, she took in every detail to keep her mind from the rising panic. These men had little wealth, for their hands were blistered and worn. Each had a dagger at his waist, and the only other weapon she saw was a thick wooden staff. The man who'd carried her had black hair and a black beard, as well as a white scar across his nose and cheek. Her other two captors were smaller, one fair-haired and the other brown-haired. Their beards were sparse, as if they were younger men.

'She's the MacKinnon's daughter,' the black-bearded man predicted. 'With that hair of fire.' He twisted it around his wrist, trapping her in place. 'I knew we'd find her if we tracked the Normans.' With a grin to his friends, he said, 'Her father will pay to get her back. He owes us.'

'The Norman might pay more,' the fair-haired man taunted. 'I heard he meant to wed her.'

The bearded man had a hard cast to his face, as if he despised the Normans. 'I've a better use in mind for a fair lass. She should have a taste of a real man.'

At that, Lianna tried to break into a run. She didn't care where she went, so long as it was away from these men.

But the bearded man caught her waist and struck her hard. Pain roared through her cheek, and Lianna dropped to her knees. The world seemed to slow down, and she grew aware that her cheeks were wet. Was she crying?

She tried again to scream through the binding around her mouth, but no sound came forth. Her fears multiplied, and she understood now why Rhys had demanded that she take an escort. But she had been too proud to take a guard with her, believing that no one was nearby. Her foolishness might now cost her life.

'Hold her down,' the bearded man ordered. 'And let us see what lies beneath this gown.'

One of the men grabbed her bound hands and raised them above her head, pinning her to the ground. The first seized her bodice and tore it to her waist, revealing her breasts. Lianna struggled against them, her heart pounding with fear.

Dear God, they were going to rape her, and there

was nothing she could do to stop them. Bile rose within her stomach, and she locked her ankles together, trying to fight them.

Never had she imagined this could happen to her. The thought of Rhys was a prayer, though she doubted if he could track her this far.

A rough hand fondled her breast, and she tried to twist away from the unwanted touch. She kicked at the bearded man, fighting to get away from them, and the men laughed at her efforts.

The world seemed to slow down, magnifying her fears. She was trembling, and it felt as if she were underwater, with a roaring echo within her ears.

Dimly, she grew aware that the hands holding her down had softened their grip. She didn't know why, but she twisted again, trying to free herself. A slight noise broke through the stillness, and without warning, the black-bearded man released his grip. His eyes grew sightless, open in shock.

Through her tears, Lianna stared at the sight of a blade that had impaled the man's spine through his stomach. The other two men scrambled to get away, but within seconds, both were dead—cut down by a broadsword.

A sword that belonged to her husband.

Lianna sobbed with relief as Rhys covered her bodice and reached back to untie the gag. Then he unbound her hands and lifted her into his arms. Her body was shaking, and she closed her eyes tightly, so grateful he had found her.

Rhys gave his sword to his men and said, 'Let me speak with my wife in private for a moment. Let no one inside.'

For a moment, she simply clung to him, needing the strength of his arms around her. 'Y-you came for me. How d-did you find me?'

'Warrick saw you leave alone, and he followed you.' He kept her in his embrace, stroking her hair while she trembled. 'I am glad he left a trail for me.'

She didn't know how his brother had managed it in his wounded state, but she whispered, 'I am so grateful.' The tears broke forth, and she could hardly speak. 'Rhys, I am sorry. I never meant for this to h-happen.'

'I know.'

She could not let go of him, and he didn't seem eager to push her away. With his mouth at her temple, he asked, 'Did they hurt you?'

'They would have, if you hadn't come. But no, not yet.' Her husband had killed the men with a ruthless expertise, an undeniable warrior. He had been trained to slaughter his enemies, and this day, she was grateful for his skill.

No one could fight against a man like Rhys de Laurent and win.

The shell of grief cracked apart as she realised her brother's mistake. Sían had lost his life, trying to strike down a master of fighting. She wept, releasing the pent-up emotions from the past few weeks. The tears were cleansing, and Rhys kept her in his arms until she managed to gather command of herself.

'Take me back to our camp,' she pleaded.

He framed her face with his hands, his blue eyes fixed upon hers. 'I'm here, Lianna. I won't let anyone hurt you.'

She met his gaze through the haze of tears. Then he

lifted her into his arms and carried her out. She hardly cared, for she doubted if her knees would support her. She breathed in the scent of Rhys, knowing that he'd meant what he'd said. He would keep her safe.

It felt as if the world had shifted out of position. No longer did she see him as a vicious enemy who had murdered her brother. Her heart ached as she was forced to confront the truth. That wasn't the sort of man he was. Rhys kept a cool head about him, and though he was a strong warrior, he did not rush into battle.

In front of her, she saw his men paired up, evenly spaced. If he had not struck down the three clansmen, he had a dozen men to back him up. The knowledge deepened her respect for his strategy, and she understood that he had planned out every possible outcome. After a time, she said softly, 'I can walk now, Rhys.' He had been carrying her down the hillside, hardly seeming to care about her weight.

When he said nothing, she asked, 'Am I not too heavy?' She was starting to feel embarrassed, but he continued walking as if it took no effort at all.

He slowed down and looked at her closely. 'No, you're not too heavy. But Lianna, I won't be letting you go.'

And when she looked into his eyes, she saw an air of possession that brooked no argument.

Rhys watched her carefully through the rest of the evening and into the night. Lianna prepared a meal for the men, clearing away their dishes and showing her gratitude through her actions.

But when they were alone in the privacy of their

tent, her demeanour grew even more quiet. She lay down beside him, and he pulled her close for warmth. Never would he forget the horrifying sight of Lianna being held at the mercy of those men. And he wondered if she had withheld anything from him. She seemed restless tonight, as if she wanted to talk but couldn't find the courage.

'Are you all right?' he asked her. 'You've hardly spoken a word.'

She didn't answer, but rolled to face him. Her knee brushed against his, and she moved in closer, resting her cheek against his bare chest. It was the first time she had reached towards him in weeks, and he went motionless. It seemed as if she needed to be in his arms, and he pulled her nearer, stroking her long red hair. For a time, he did not press her; he only offered comfort and security.

The longer he remained still, the more the stiffness slid away from her body. Like ice melting, droplet by droplet, he felt her resistance beginning to soften.

'I hated feeling so powerless,' she admitted. 'They spoke of ransoming me, but in truth, if you hadn't come, they would have hurt me.'

A hard edge of fury sharpened inside him at the thought of anyone harming his wife. He wished he could turn back the hours so she had never been taken at all.

'Did you know them?' It seemed strange that only three men would be so far away from their clansmen.

'I think they recognised me. There were some MacDonnells who travelled through Eiloch last spring. My father made certain I was kept away from them.' Her face grew pained. 'Now I understand why.' She took a deep breath and added, 'They were tracking me, once they saw your men. They believed you or my father would pay a ransom for me.' She slid her arms around him, her hands upon his back. The unexpected touch was a welcome warmth he hadn't expected.

Rhys kept her in his embrace for several moments, waiting to see if she would say more. When she didn't, he asked, 'Did I frighten you when I killed them?' When he had seen the bearded man holding her down with her bodice torn open, he'd struck the killing blow without voicing a single question. Only afterwards did he realise that he'd likely terrified his wife into silence.

Her breathing was even, but her hand stroked a light pattern over his skin. 'No. I was glad you killed him.'

She moved her face to rest against his heart, her lips brushing against the rapid beating. Heat roared over him, scalding him with unbridled desire. His body hardened, and when she pressed her hips against his, he bit back a groan.

'I was never more glad to see you in all my life,' she murmured. 'I prayed you would find me.' She took an unsteady breath and added, 'Though I ken that I didn't deserve it. I have not been much of a wife to you.'

He understood how difficult it must have been for her to admit it, but he would not blame her for it. 'I was not the man you wanted. And neither of us was given a choice in this marriage.'

'No.' She seemed to be struggling for the right words to say. He breathed in the scent of her hair and she answered it by embracing him tightly. 'But we could…start again.'

Her hands moved up his chest to his throat, where she wound her arms around his neck. She lifted her leg over his, and the action made her shift rise nearly to her waist. Rhys was still wearing his braies, but his erection strained at the wool.

God above, Lianna was driving him into madness.

And when she lifted her mouth to his, she murmured, 'Hold me, Rhys. Help me to face my fears and forget about them.'

He needed no other invitation. He kissed her gently, reassuring her with his mouth. She leaned in closer, and he drew his hands down to her hips, sliding the shift up until she helped him remove it. He discarded the remainder of his own clothing until they were naked in the darkness.

Her soft curves pressed against his body, tempting him to touch her. Lianna lay upon her side, and the touch of her cool skin upon his evoked a surge of need.

'Do you remember the night you first came to me?' she whispered.

'It has been burned into my mind for weeks.' He drew his hand down her hair, over her bare back, tracing the curve of her bottom.

'Pretend that you are still that Highlander,' she whispered. 'And that none of the rest happened.'

He understood that she needed him to push back the harsh memories, replacing them with better ones. 'I am still your Highlander,' he said, switching into Gaelic. Though his words were not as strong, he murmured endearments to her. Telling her how brave she had been, how beautiful she was now.

Lianna put her arms around him again, and it pressed her bare breasts against his torso. 'Touch me the way you did on that first night we were together.'

His blood coursed through his veins with a wildness barely controlled. When she lifted her mouth to his, he fought to maintain command. She kissed him with the innocence of a maiden, but her body held its own invitation. He slid his tongue into her mouth, and she shuddered, delicately touching it with her own. The erotic kiss wove a spell between them, and he felt her skin growing warmer, prickling as she responded to him. He caressed her hip, moving his palm over the lean, long legs. Then he drew his mouth down her throat, feeling her arch against him as he caught a sensitive place.

On that first night, *she* had seduced *him*, but now he intended to tempt this woman beyond reason. He craved her body and wanted her to know exactly what she had been missing these past nights.

He learned the edges and curves of her, then captured her nipple with his mouth. She let out a gasp, but he soothed her, swirling his tongue over the hardened tip.

'It feels good when you do that,' she said softly. He rewarded her honesty by suckling her nipple, and she moaned in response.

He moved his attention to her other breast and at the same moment reached between her legs. She was wet, and when he pressed his thumb against her centre, she dug her fingernails into his shoulder.

'Rhys,' she gasped.

He locked his gaze with hers. 'I am your husband now. You are mine, Lianna.' He emphasised his words by circling the hardened nub of her flesh with his thumb. She was trembling at his touch, but she did not deny him.

Then he brought her hand to his hardened shaft. 'And I am yours.'

She seemed slightly afraid, but she curled her hand around him, sliding it upward. Then she squeezed him gently and the erotic sensation forced a sharp intake of breath. Her thumb grazed the thick head, and he caught her wrist.

'Did I hurt you?'

'No.' But he was shaken by how her single touch had nearly driven him to spill his release. This woman held a power over him that he had never anticipated—and he could not allow it. 'But I want to touch you more.'

He guided her hand away, still shaken by her simple caress. He distracted himself by suckling against her nipple, sliding a single finger inside her depths. She was wet, and he found that arousing her was sharpening his own pleasure. He found that she was far more sensitive when he stroked the hooded flesh, and she could not stop herself from leaning into him.

'And what of this?' he asked against her breast. 'Do you want more? Or should I stop?'

When he stilled his hand, she cried out, moving her fingers towards his. 'No, don't stop. Please.'

She grew reckless, panting as he kept up the rhythmic caresses. He kept two fingers deeply inside her while he continued to circle. She was moving her hips against him, arching and trembling. Her breasts were erect, her body slick with perspiration as she strained against him.

He slowed his strokes, but kept the pressure steady. Lianna cried out, holding his mouth to her breast, when suddenly she quaked within his arms, trembling as she came apart. It was like a wave that pulsed through her, and as she rode out the release, he gave in to his own needs. He positioned himself at her wet entrance, and when she lifted her knees, he sheathed himself deep inside in one fluid motion. She arched her hips, and he felt the wild trembling of another release crashing over her, squeezing him as he thrust.

'Rhys, I need you,' she blurted out. 'Please.'

He lost himself in her, no longer able to keep himself under control. All the weeks of yearning for this woman had wound him into a tight ball, and now he had no choice but to thrust inside her. Though he tried to be careful, there was something about Lianna that challenged him. Her brown eyes stared into his, demanding that he surrender.

'I don't want to ever think about those men again. I want only you.'

Her words were an invisible caress, making him rock hard within her body. And when he penetrated her, over and over, she raised her hips, seizing him and pulling him deeper.

No longer was she the careful, calm wife. Instead, she gave in to her wild urges, digging her fingernails into his back. He drove harder, and she bit back a scream as he ground against her. It was a savage lovemaking, but he could not stop himself any more than he could have stopped a thunderstorm.

He felt her body spasm against his, and she let out a keening noise as her body milked his shaft. She drove him into madness, wrapping her legs around his waist as he pumped, and when she kissed him, he lost control.

His body erupted within hers, and he clung to her, riding the tide as the wave knocked him asunder. Her body accepted his seed, bowing beneath him as he thrust a few more times. And when he collapsed atop her, his heart was pounding as if he'd run a thousand miles.

And for a night in Lianna MacKinnon's arms, he would do just that.

Lianna was sore for the next two days, and she felt her cheeks burning, though she tried to pretend as if nothing were different. Yet, the men knew that everything had changed between herself and Rhys.

She told herself that it did not matter. She was his wife now and was expected to bear him children. How else could she do so unless she shared his bed?

But her conscience chided her that she was enjoying him far too much. He had even stopped to set up camp early last night, and his men sent her teasing smiles when she served them meals. Her own kinsmen were cooler in their demeanour, making her feel as if she had surrendered too easily.

They were drawing closer to Eiloch now, and the thought made her nervous. Would her people come to accept Rhys? Would they understand that she'd had no choice but to wed him? And what would her father think of it?

She rode alongside Rhys, her gaze fixed upon the

crofters' homes and the condition of the fortress. Her mind made detailed notes about the broken fences and the homes in need of repair. She memorised the faces of the thin children and the elderly. And when she passed by the house of Iona, she smiled to see the swollen pregnancy at her friend's waist. Despite all the changes in her own life, there was still the familiarity of home. And now that she had married Rhys, they would bring prosperity back.

Her husband kept his voice low and remarked in the Norman tongue, 'They do not seem pleased to see us.'

'That will change, thanks to the supplies you've brought.' She had been overjoyed to learn that he had not forgotten his bargain when their travelling party intercepted the rest of the men. Her own belongings were there, along with four other wagons Rhys had ordered, by way of a bridal present.

He slowed the gait of his horse and caught her hand, stroking her fingers. 'You did not ask for a true bride price, Lianna. Only food for your people.'

'I need nothing for myself.' Her cheeks warmed when she saw the undisguised hatred upon the faces of her people. They eyed her as if she were holding hands with a monster.

'Even so, there is another gift I will give you tonight,' he murmured. 'Perhaps you will wear it for me.'

She didn't ken what she should say, except to nod. 'If you wish.'

'And you may plan the wedding you wanted,' he said. 'Whatever feast you wish, whatever you desire for the celebration, you shall have.'

A softness slid over her face at the thought. She wanted to begin anew with her people, offering them a reason to celebrate. Despite her brother's death, they would survive this winter and perhaps learn to accept Rhys and his men.

Warrick hung back with the rest of the soldiers, and she decided to find a place for the Normans to stay together. The young man had remained stoic throughout the journey, but she owed him a favour for rescuing her.

She realised that Rhys was waiting for an answer regarding the wedding, and she said, 'I will begin the preparations on the morrow.' He seemed to relax at that.

Their marriage had improved somewhat, but she still felt awkward during the daylight hours. It always seemed as if others stared at them, and only when she was alone in her husband's arms, did the boundaries disappear. Sometimes it felt as if she were living two lives—one as his wife, and the other as a chief's daughter and a Scot.

When they reached her father's house, Rhys dismounted and helped her from her own horse. She was eager to see Alastair once again, to embrace him and share the news.

But after a kinsman led her to his room, she was dismayed to see her father lying in bed, his pallor grey and cool.

'Father,' she called out, hurrying to his side. She picked up his hand and was relieved to find that he was still alive. But he was not at all well.

Alastair managed a wan smile. 'So, you've returned. I wish I could have been at your betrothal, Lianna.'

'It was witnessed by several dozen men,' Rhys said. 'All went well, and we spoke our wedding vows a fortnight ago.'

She noted the slight flare of disappointment in his eyes. 'I had no choice, Father. Lord Montbrooke would not allow us to leave until we were wedded. But Rhys promised me that we would have another wedding here with our clan and with you.' She squeezed his hand. 'You must promise me that you'll get better. I want you to be there.'

'Nothing would please me more, my wee lass,' he said quietly. 'I have missed you.'

She warmed to his words. 'Don't worry, Father. I will set everything to rights at Eiloch.'

'I ken that you will.' He reached up to her cheek and said quietly, 'You look different than before. If I am not mistaken, this marriage has changed you.'

She couldn't stop the blush upon her cheeks. It had indeed changed her, but perhaps it was because she now believed that Rhys had never intended to kill her brother. It had been Sían's choice to fight a battle he could not win.

'I am well,' was all she could say.

'Good.' Alastair leaned back against his pillow. 'Go and do as you will, while I rest my eyes. I will see you at the evening meal.'

She leaned down to kiss his cheek before stepping back with Rhys and leaving her father alone. Inside the large gathering space, she saw that the rushes had not been changed. Upon the floor were scattered bones and refuse. It was almost as if the people had abandoned Eiloch, leaving it to decay. A flare of annoyance caught her, but she would not allow this neglect to continue.

'You look ready to declare war, my wife,' Rhys said against her ear.

'And so I am. They have not carried out their duties when I was away.' She would speak with Orna and find out why tasks had been left undone.

'I will speak with Alastair about it and find out why,' he offered. 'One of my men can oversee the clansmen, if necessary.'

She bristled at the idea of a Norman soldier telling her people what to do. It would not go well at all. 'Let it be, for now. I will visit with each of the crofters and learn what has happened while I was away.' Her mind was spinning off with all the duties left to her.

'And then you'll report back to me all that you have learned.'

When he put it in those words, it sounded as if she were spying on his behalf. Lianna hesitated and answered, 'I will tell you what repairs need to be made and what the needs of my people are.' She had no intention of creating problems where there were none.

Rhys seemed to sense her reticence and slid his palm against the small of her back. Leaning in, he murmured, 'And during the noontide meal, you'll ride to the dolmen, won't you?'

A ghost of a smile tugged at her mouth. 'I do not ken if that's possible until I have finished my duties. But perhaps later.'

'You might find a Highlander waiting for you,' he said against her mouth.

A flare of heat rose between her legs, and her cheeks flushed. 'I—I need to go, Rhys.'

He seemed to understand his effect on her. 'Find out what has happened, and I will hear from the others. My men can help with distributing the food at a later time.'

She nodded. 'Will you have our men organise the grain stores into forty portions?' she asked. 'We need to begin dividing the supplies.'

'In a few days, perhaps. For now, I want to inspect your defences and make changes where they are needed.'

Once again, she felt a sudden uneasiness. *She* knew these people better than Rhys. And though she had anticipated that Rhys would take the leadership role, she did not want it to feel like a conquest.

'Do not make too many changes, too soon,' she cautioned. 'They may not listen to your orders.'

His expression darkened. In a cool voice, he said, 'They will listen and obey every command I give. Or they will find themselves without a home. I will not tolerate rebellion here.'

She stiffened at that, not knowing how to respond. If he began issuing orders, her people might rise up in anger. 'They are already afraid. We must tread carefully so they accept you and your men.'

He sent her an incredulous look. 'Fear is no reason to abandon necessary tasks. They must work together and not neglect their responsibilities.'

She knew that, but she worried about how the people would respond to Rhys. He was not the chief of this clan. Now that Sían was gone and her father was ill, the tasks should fall upon her shoulders, for she fully understood what was needed. She wanted his permission to make decisions on behalf of the clan.

'Will you let me help you?' she asked quietly. Some of his tension dissipated when she kept her tone soft.

He hesitated as if he didn't want to surrender dominion to her. But she waited, giving him time to think it over while he led her towards a corner of the room. A few of the MacKinnons stared at them, but Rhys ignored their hostility.

'Go and find out what has happened while we were away,' he relented. 'But keep a guard with you at all times.' His hands moved around her waist, and she felt self-conscious with her kinsmen watching them.

Rhys kissed her in front of them, making it clear that she was his wife in truth. Although she had come to enjoy his affection, at this moment it felt like a mark of ownership. She could feel the silent fury of the MacKinnon clansmen, though she tried to ignore it.

When she left the gathering space, she saw Warrick outside among the other Norman soldiers. She could see from the circles beneath his eyes that he was not sleeping well. 'Will you walk with me?' she asked. He obeyed, though she suspected he was still in pain. She decided to send a healer to him later to see if his wounds had improved.

Warrick shadowed her footsteps, but she waited for him to walk alongside her. They passed Rhys, who was gathering the rest of the soldiers around the wagons to begin sorting through the supplies. He raised a hand in greeting to Warrick and smiled at Lianna.

She couldn't quite return it, for she was aware of how her kinsmen were judging her. As they walked towards her maid's house, she told Warrick, 'I am grateful to you for saving me from those men a few days ago. I cannot thank you enough.'

He gave a nod but said nothing else. Then she probed a little more. 'Does your back still hurt?' It must have tormented him to follow her when he was still recovering from the wounds.

He continued walking beside her, his face expressionless. 'I endure it.'

She felt badly for his pain, wishing she could ease it. 'I hope that one day soon your suffering will end.'

A wry smile crossed his mouth. 'My suffering will never decrease, Lianna. I lost my ' He paused and rephrased his words. 'I lost Rosamund, and now her father will force her to marry Alan de Courcy.'

She slowed her steps. 'You loved her.' He didn't answer, but she could see it in his face. Then she tried again. 'Is there anything we can do to help you?'

'Not unless you can stop the marriage.' He admitted, 'I know Rhys wants me to remain here. But I need a sword in my hands. I need to fight, to blur my mind from the memories of her.'

He wanted no life without Rosamund, Lianna realised. She reached out to take his hand in hers. 'I hope that time will ease your pain.'

When they reached the home of her maid Orna, Warrick stood back but kept his hand upon his sword hilt. Lianna's maid smiled, embracing her as they spoke. 'It's good to see you again, my wee girl. We've missed you.'

And though she knew her elderly maid spoke her own truth, Lianna wasn't so certain about the others. 'The clan members are angry with me, aren't they?' she ventured. 'I see it in their eyes.'

'They will come to their senses, soon enough,' her maid assured her. 'It's been hard with Alastair so ill. Eachann tried to take on the chief's duties, but he divided the clan. Some understand the reasons for your marriage, but there are many who believe you should be driven out with your husband.'

Lianna's spine stiffened at that. 'And after I've brought them food and grain to survive the winter?'

Orna patted her hand. 'In time, they'll come to see the truth. 'Tis hunger that makes them so angry.'

Lianna supposed that was true enough. She spent time with the older woman, talking of the clan and hearing the gossip. Then she said, 'I was married already in England, but Rhys has promised that we could celebrate the wedding again here. Would you help me with the arrangements?'

Her maid's face faltered for a moment, then she composed herself. 'Of course.' She thought about it and suggested, 'I've an old gown of your mother's set aside. You could wear it, if you like.'

A slight ache caught at her heart at the mention of her mother. She wished so badly that Davina were still alive, so she could be with her on this day. She had only a few memories of the woman, of the way she had combed her hair exactly seventy-seven times, and the way she had braided Lianna's hair into a long plait, with not a single hair out of place.

Her parents had been happy together, and her father had never remarried. He had claimed that no one could replace Davina.

A part of her wondered if her own marriage could ever be like that. Perhaps her mother's gown would lend luck to them during this second ceremony.

'I would like to wear the gown,' she answered Orna. She wanted the MacKinnon clan to see her husband in a different way, not as a conqueror, but as one of them.

And the wedding might lift the spirits of everyone, with feasting and celebration.

Chapter Nine

Rhys was not pleased by what he'd seen at Eiloch. Although he had busied himself with dividing up the grain and supplies, he hadn't yet distributed any of it. The open animosity from the people was unwarranted, and even more than that, he hadn't liked the way several of the men had spoken about Lianna.

They didn't know that he spoke Gaelic fluently, a fact that he'd deliberately concealed. For now, they believed he knew only a few words, and many spoke openly of their disdain for the soldiers. But soon, he would have to address their disrespect.

'What do you want us to do with the wagons?' one of the soldiers asked.

'Guard them for now, until your lady tells you where she wants the grain.' He passed by one of the larger men, Eachann MacKinnon. Rhys had taken an instant dislike to the man, especially given the way he behaved as though he were superior to the others.

'Norman bastard.' Eachann spoke in Gaelic and smiled at him, behaving as if he were giving Rhys a complimentary greeting. 'Ye had best be on your guard around the MacKinnons. Else we'll slit yer gullet while ye are sleeping.'

The insult made his fists clench. He paused and stared back at Eachann, keeping his eyes upon the man. He let no trace of emotion show but let the man continue digging his own grave.

Eachann bowed his head and continued, 'Ye might have wed Lianna MacKinnon, but none of us wanted her. She's not right in her head.'

At that, Rhys's hand shot out and seized the man by his throat. He made no effort to hide the icy rage in his voice as he answered in the same language. 'Do you think I don't understand every word that comes out of your mouth?'

The man paled at that, and Rhys tightened his grip. 'You can think whatever insults you wish about my men and me. But as for my wife…' He pushed the man backwards until he was forced up against a thatched house. 'If you expect your family to receive any of the food she brought for this clan, you had best get on your knees and beg for her mercy. Or you'll get nothing at all.'

He released the man, and Eachann gasped for air. He appeared stunned at Rhys's speech, and could not bring himself to say anything else.

'Tell the others,' Rhys said. 'Treat her well, and they will survive the winter. Or if you do not, then expect nothing from me. I care not if you live or die.'

He strode away from the man, irritated by the man's insults towards Lianna. She had done nothing to deserve them, and he intended to put a stop to their contempt. Did they have any idea that she was responsible for their well-being? His irritation intensified with each step, and Rhys passed by several crofters' homes before he found her pounding a wooden peg into a broken gate. Seeing his wife behave like a common servant was the final blow.

Rhys didn't say a word, but simply took her hand and pulled her away from the gate.

'I wasn't finished yet,' she argued.

'I was.' He needed to speak with her alone, to make her understand that no one had the right to treat her with insolence. 'We are riding out to the dolmen.'

'Wait a moment,' she said. 'I will summon the horses and get food for us.' She gave the orders to one of the young boys, and he felt his patience slipping away until the lad finally returned with horses and a bundle of food.

'We only need one horse,' Rhys said, lifting Lianna up and swinging behind her. He rode towards his men, where he found his brother Warrick. 'I leave you in command for the next hour or so.'

His brother gave a nod of acknowledgement, and then Rhys wheeled the horse around, riding hard towards the coastline. He knew his anger was out of proportion, but he needed to understand why Lianna tolerated this behaviour from her own people.

The wind tore through her red hair, nearly blinding him, but he pushed it aside and held her close. When they reached the stone altar, he dismounted and helped her down. She set the bundle of food upon the dolmen, and he reached for her, kissing her hard.

Something about this woman ignited his desire, and the more he claimed her, the more he wanted her. Her lips met his, and she kissed him back.

'I don't like the way they speak of you at Eiloch,'

he gritted out. 'They do not give you the respect you deserve.'

She wound her arms around his neck. 'It matters not what they think of me. It is my duty to keep them safe and to see that their needs are met.'

'They are behaving like spoiled children,' he argued, lifting her to sit upon the dolmen. She wore a gown laced up the front, with a *brat* around her shoulders. His attention was caught by the swell of her breasts, and he reached out to unlace her bodice.

When she was exposed to him, she grew embarrassed. 'Rhys, what are you doing?'

From a fold in his cloak, he withdrew the gift he'd been saving for her. It was a ruby, the size of a quail's egg, hanging upon a golden chain. He lifted it over her head, and the ruby nestled between her breasts.

'This is my bride gift to you,' he said.

Her eyes widened, and she reached down to hold it. 'It's beautiful. But Rhys, truly, I do not need jewels.'

'It pleases me to see you wear it.' He drew the ruby over her swollen nipple, then across her opposite breast. She closed her eyes, and he saw her grip the edges of the stone in response.

He covered her nipple with his mouth, and the hard tip tempted him into taking her right now.

'Rhys, someone could see us,' she ventured, her cheeks flushing. With her red hair falling across her shoulders, and her bare breasts exposed, he had never seen anyone more lovely.

'That's what makes it dangerous,' he murmured. 'We'll have to steal this moment before anyone finds us.' He slid his palms up the backs of her thighs, and she parted her legs. When he reached between them, he found that she was already wet. 'This excites you, doesn't it? The fear of someone finding us together.'

Her brown eyes locked with his, and she reached down to help him unfasten the trews he'd worn. Her hands slid over his erect length, and she moved to sit at the edge of the dolmen. Rhys guided her legs around his waist, and sank within her.

She gasped as he filled her, and he used the ruby to tease one of her nipples. 'Those people don't know all that you do for them,' he said, revelling in her moist warmth surrounding him. 'And until they show you the respect you deserve, they will get nothing from me. No food. No supplies.' He penetrated her, cupping her hips as she lay across the stone table.

She lifted her hips to take him deeper, but he made love to her slowly, tantalising her as he entered and withdrew.

'I don't want anyone to suffer,' she answered, her voice breathless. 'They need the food. Especially the ch-children.' She shuddered as her own arousal rolled over her. He could feel the inner quaking of her muscles, and he wanted more.

'If they accept you as their lady and treat you with the respect I demand, they will have all they need.' He drew her to sit up on the dolmen, and he thrust hard, taking her swiftly. 'But if I hear of insolence or disrespect, I swear to you, they will get nothing.'

She gasped at the invasion of his shaft. He remained embedded there, holding her thighs as she was balanced upon the stone. Her face held shock, as if she had never imagined he would do such a thing.

'Just imagine it,' he murmured against her mouth.

'Someone could come upon us at any time. They would see me thrusting inside you.'

He imitated his own words, sliding in deep, and watching as she softened to him, accepting his intrusion. Her hands gripped his shoulders, and he supported her back as he laid her down, taking her upon the table.

'We have to hurry before they find us. And I won't stop claiming you, until you cry out with pleasure.'

His words provoked her, and her face grew pained as she strained towards the release point she craved. She moved her hips against him, pressing him close.

'Rhys,' she moaned, as he slowed his pace. 'I cannot bear it.' She was like heated silk around his length, and he loved watching her unravel.

Lianna cried out, her nails digging into his skin as he increased the pace. He was careful not to abrade her skin against the stone table, but he showed no mercy, wanting to drive her wild with need. He leaned down and took her nipple into his mouth, suckling hard as he continued to penetrate her body, over and over.

Her reaction was carnal, and she went liquid against him, shattering as he pounded, again and again. 'Rhys!'

'Yes,' he growled. 'Beg me for more. You know that I am the only man who has ever made you feel this way. The only man who will ever touch you.'

Her body bowed beneath him, seizing up as her release rolled over her. Her breath came in keening cries in rhythm to his lovemaking.

Only then did he give in to his own urges. Her

body tightened around him, shuddering hard as he entered her.

'I need you,' she cried out in Gaelic.

And her words warmed him, sending him past his own edge of release. He held her closely, his body erupting against hers. They were both mostly clothed, except for her skirts tossed around her waist.

He could feel the pounding of her heart as he laced up her bodice again, hiding the jewel from view. 'When do you want to be wedded for the second time?'

She tightened her legs around his waist, her brown eyes hazy with passion. 'In a few days.'

He cared not how much time she needed for the preparations. Already she belonged to him, and he would not be parted from this woman.

Even so, he did not delude himself into believing that the clan would accept him. He had made an enemy in Eachann MacKinnon, and soon enough, he would have to face the man.

Lianna rode away from the dolmen, her body feeling swollen and deliciously used. The weight of the ruby rested between her breasts like a hidden caress. Her mind was overwhelmed by confusion. She did not understand her marriage with Rhys, for he would not reveal what he thought of her. He would not allow her to make decisions for the clan, in spite of her father's illness. And she didn't trust him to know what her people needed.

When she reached the outskirts of Eiloch, she dismounted and walked alongside her horse. She began traversing the perimeter of the fortress, noting that

Eachann's house had fallen into disrepair, and sections of thatch had rotted.

Orna's cottage was neat, but she knew that the old woman had only a little food remaining. She would ensure that Orna received her fair portion first, for her maid had always been faithful in service.

When Lianna reached the far end of the wall, she saw several fallen stones. She let her horse graze and knelt down, stacking the stones and repairing it as best she could.

Nearby, she heard some of the men talking, but none of them stopped to help her. She had nearly finished the last stone, when their conversation ceased.

Rhys strode forward, and she recognised the growing anger in his demeanour. In Gaelic, he spoke to the men, 'Would you care to explain why my wife is on her hands and knees repairing a wall, while the rest of you stand around and do nothing?'

Hamish had the grace to look sheepish, but he gave no answer. Another said, 'Lianna does as she wishes, and we do not interfere.'

Her husband's face turned thunderous. 'I want the three of you to get mortar and repair the wall so that the stones will not fall again. Lianna, come with me.'

She stood up and went to his side. In a low voice, she said, 'Rhys, it's nothing. I merely put the stones back.'

'And what else did you see while you were walking through Eiloch?' His tone held a sharp edge, and she faltered before telling him of the rotting thatch and she pointed to another section of the wall that needed to be repaired.

'Give the orders,' he demanded.

'Rhys, these are free people. I cannot order them to work.' If Eachann chose not to repair his own thatch, it was his roof. And as for the wall, it took hardly any time at all to replace the stones.

'Then I will give the orders.' He eyed the men who had not yet left to fetch mortar. In truth, Lianna doubted if they would do anything at all. They were about to go hunting for their evening meal, and feeding their families was more important.

In a loud voice, Rhys demanded, 'I will not stand aside and allow you to treat Lianna as your slave. If a section of our wall has fallen, I expect the men of Eiloch to help rebuild it. And if one of you needs help repairing your roof or walls, then it shall be given.'

There was an uneasy stare among the men, and Lianna felt their unspoken frustration. They saw him as a Norman invader, an outsider who did not belong among them.

She needed to speak with Alastair, for he might know what to do. She said to her husband, 'I must go and tend to my father now.'

He nodded permission for her to go, and Lianna returned to her home. Her heart remained troubled, for although she knew Rhys's intentions were fair and good, he should not build dissent by issuing orders to these men.

She walked into her house and was relieved to see that the rushes had been changed. Her father was seated at the dais, reading a scroll of parchment. His wrinkled face held concern, and she went to sit beside him. 'Is everything all right?'

Alastair set the scroll aside. 'King William's forces are gathering. They have asked me to send men.'

An ache settled in her stomach, for she understood that he was caught in the middle. By allowing Norman soldiers to dwell among them, it was as if he were harbouring the enemy.

'But that is not for you to worry about, my lass. Dine with me, and tell me what troubles you.' He raised his hand, nodding for one of his men to bring wine and bread.

'I feel trapped,' she admitted. 'The people will not follow Rhys's orders. And sometimes I think they wish Sían were still here.'

Her father paled, and reached for her hand. 'Do you miss your brother?'

She nodded. 'He was supposed to be chief after you, and the people resent Rhys for taking his place.'

'That isn't what I asked,' Alastair said. His wrinkled hand squeezed hers. 'Think of how Sían behaved towards you. What would your life have been like, had he been chief?'

She stared at him, not understanding. Alastair sighed and shook his head. 'Sían was my son, and before God, I did love him. But he could never have become chief. He was unfit to rule anyone.'

'He gave many commands, and the people obeyed him,' Lianna started to argue.

'His friends pretended to obey him. But they never saw the man he was.' He steepled his hands together. 'Sían took coins from you, and he stole from the people, gambling with the MacDonnells.'

'But why?' A sinking feeling permeated her stomach. 'He had everything he needed.'

'Stealing was a game to him. I caught him in the

act many times, but he denied it. Lies and truth meant nothing to him.'

She didn't know what to believe. 'You never punished him.'

'A fault of mine,' Alastair admitted. 'But if I had done so, he would have lashed out at our family and at the clan. When he grew enraged, his mind was not right, Lianna.' He closed his eyes. 'I do not doubt he would have brought war among us.'

'There may still be war.' She nodded towards the parchment. 'We have to defend our clan.'

He smiled at that. 'Your marriage will do that. King William cannot demand our men, now that we have followed the terms of the contract. I will send word to him that we have a blend of Normans and Scots living among us. It will keep Eiloch neutral, even if war comes.'

'I hope so,' she said quietly. She took a sip of wine and picked at the bread. Already she could smell the mouth-watering scent of roasted venison for the noontide meal.

'And what of your marriage?' Alastair enquired. 'Does Rhys de Laurent make you happy?'

She could not stop the flush that suffused her cheeks, remembering how he had loved her against the stone dolmen. 'I am growing accustomed to the marriage.'

Her father's demeanour warmed. 'I see the way he looks at you, Lianna. I think it will be a sound marriage, and I am well pleased by it. I look forward to celebrating your wedding here, among our people.'

She tried to push back her uncertainties. 'Do you

think the MacKinnons will accept him? He is already giving orders, and many do not want to obey.'

'But you ken what must be done. They will follow you.'

She laughed at that. 'They ignore me, Father, and always have. They taunt my ways.'

He shook his head in denial. 'Some do. But most ken all the hard work you do when you think no one is looking.' He tore off a piece of bread. 'Had you been a boy, you would have made a very good chief, Lianna. But you will be a leader in your own way. Influence Rhys, and all will be well.'

She wanted to believe that could be true. But when she saw her husband enter the house, his presence dominating the room, she questioned whether he would listen to her at all.

It took only two days for Rhys to realise how astounding his wife's memory was. She knew the names of every person in the clan and could recite details about each one that revealed the needs of each family. While some viewed her ways as strange, he believed her brother had undermined her, making others believe that her attention to detail was odd. There were several of Sían's friends who mocked Lianna behind her back. He would not allow it. If they refused to grant her the respect she deserved, he would uphold his promise to give them no supplies.

'Are you certain you want to wear that?' his brother Warrick asked, eyeing the Highland attire Rhys had chosen.

'They need to know that I will be one of them,' he

answered. It was the best way to show unity, and he believed it would please Lianna.

Tonight, she had invited the clan to witness their wedding vows for the second time. She had ordered a large feast and had asked several friends to play songs for dancing later tonight. Already, the scent of roasting meat was tantalising.

Rhys adjusted the garment and walked outside to the gathering space. Warrick followed, and they approached the small stone kirk at the far end of Eiloch. The evening sun was descending in the sky, and garlands of flowers were hanging upon the doorway of the kirk. A few children stood nearby, watching with curiosity, but there were only two guests. Lianna's maid was one, and her father was the other.

A sudden uneasiness passed over him, and he eyed his brother, wondering where the rest of the clan was. Warrick only shook his head.

'My lord.' Lianna's maid Orna curtsied. Her face held worry, and she said, 'I ken that you and Lianna wished to be wedded before the clan, but perhaps you should wait.'

Wait for what? Rhys wondered idly. By their absence, the MacKinnons had made their point clear enough. But it irritated him that they would hurt his wife's feelings in this way. She had worked tirelessly over the past few days, trying to make a feast that everyone would enjoy.

Alastair leaned heavily upon a walking stick. 'This is Eachann MacKinnon's doing,' the chief admitted. 'I suppose he thinks that if no one witnesses your wedding, it cannot be recognised.'

'We are already married,' Rhys pointed out. 'This was meant to be a celebration to share with them.'

'They do not want to celebrate the presence of the Normans,' Alastair said quietly. 'Orna is right. It may be best to wait.'

'This was Lianna's wish,' he said. And it infuriated him to see her treated like this. After all she had done to ensure their comforts, they would turn their backs on her now? Did they think he would allow them to humiliate her in this way?

It was wrong.

Although Eachann MacKinnon might be responsible for the actions of the clan, Rhys would not let the man hold such power. It was time to confront the man and end this silent war.

'Summon the clan,' he told Alastair. 'I wish to speak with them.'

'I am not certain that is wise,' the chief said. 'Especially given their emotions right now.'

'Eachann MacKinnon thinks to take your place as chief. And that role is not his.' He spoke quietly, knowing what must be done. To Orna, he said, 'Go to your mistress, and tell Lianna, that our wedding must be delayed.'

But the older woman's face fell. 'It's too late for that, my lord.'

Rhys glanced up and saw Lianna. She was already walking towards them with a worried expression. Her red hair gleamed in the afternoon sunlight, crowned with purple heather. She wore it down around her shoulders, and it contrasted against the blue and green gown she wore. Around her throat, she wore a torque of beaten silver, but when she saw the absence of guests, there was only dismay upon her face.

Rhys turned to Warrick. 'Go and summon the rest of the clan. I want them all here to listen to what I have to say.'

'No,' Alastair argued. 'Let me send my men to fetch them. As you say, *I* am the chief here.'

He deferred to the man's wishes and awaited Lianna. When she reached his side, she asked, 'What has happened? Where are our kinsmen?'

He didn't know what to say. It would hurt her feelings to hear the truth, but there were no other explanations. 'No one wanted to come.'

Though he expected anger or frustration, he was surprised to see her emotions turn into sad acceptance. 'I suppose I should have expected this.'

'Why?' He made no attempt to hide his own anger. 'Because they always treat you like dirt?' She bristled at his remark, and he wished he hadn't said it. Softening his voice, he said, 'I am angry with them, not you.'

'I cannot change the way they think of me,' she argued.

'I can.' He took her hand in his, waiting for Alastair to return. It was past the time to address these people and change their behaviour towards his wife.

Her fingers were cold in his, and she murmured, 'I don't ken if we should speak our vows tonight. Not like this.'

He started to insist that they could go through with this wedding, but he understood that she did not want to be the centre of attention when people were forced to come.

One by one, the families emerged from their homes.

Many appeared apprehensive, but they did not dare disobey their chief. Alastair awaited them near the kirk, and they approached until all were gathered. Rhys spied Eachann MacKinnon standing nearby, annoyance upon his face.

'My daughter invited you to witness her wedding vows,' Alastair began. 'But you chose not to attend. Your choice has caused a division within our clan, and Rhys de Laurent has asked to speak to you.' He paused, and Rhys stepped forward to meet their gazes.

Most made no effort to hide their distaste. He knew they resented him and his men, but he intended to put a stop to their disrespect towards Lianna.

He moved to Alastair's place and fixed his gaze upon the men and women. Deliberately, he spoke in Gaelic. 'Many of you remember when my grandfather arranged my marriage to a MacKinnon maiden. He was your chief at that time, and he wedded a Norman lady, my grandmother Margaret.'

Eachann spat upon the ground at that, and Rhys nodded towards his men, who surrounded the Scot in a silent threat.

'He made this bargain as protection for you, because he knew that war would come. And it is my intention to keep that agreement. But I will not tolerate disrespect towards my wife.'

He stared at each one of them. 'This land belongs to me now, and there are some of you who have joined Eachann MacKinnon in wanting to disobey orders.' Rhys gestured to his men to escort Eachann forward. He met the man's insolent glare with his own hard warning. 'Either you will obey me as your leader, along with Alastair, or you will leave Eiloch. The choice is yours.'

'I will not take orders from a Norman bastard,' Eachann sneered.

He had no time to react when the Scot charged forward, swinging his fists. Rhys pushed Lianna out of the way and sidestepped the blows. They circled one another, and a deadly calm passed over him.

He'd always known it would come to this. Eachann would not accept him as the leader, and he had to make an example of the man.

The Scot swung again, but Rhys avoided the blow easily, watching the man closely to learn his fighting style. The MacKinnon fought with no precision, only raw fury. Rhys allowed him to throw punches, again and again, and each time, his fists met only empty air. The Scot roared out his frustration, but Rhys moved with lightning speed. He counter-attacked, punching the man in his stomach, until the Scot gasped for air. He used the opportunity to kick the man's legs out from under him, and Rhys pressed him to the ground, twisting the man's arm so that he could no longer fight.

'And now? Will you take orders from a Norman?' he demanded. When there was no answer, Rhys struck him across the nose, and blood ran down his face.

The Scot closed his eyes. A woman cried out in fear and rushed forward, dropping to her knees. 'Please do not kill my husband. I swear, we'll both be obeying yer orders, my lord.'

At that, Eachann glared at his wife. He was about to speak, but she clamped her hand over his mouth. 'Do not be a sheep-headed fool. Ye've lost, and that's an end to it. I willna have ye drive us from our home because of yer stupid pride.'

Rhys kept the man pinned down, even as he studied the others. 'There will be changes here, and I demand your obedience. Or I will have you removed from Eiloch to survive on your own. If you dare to return from exile, you will be killed.'

He released the MacKinnon, and Eachann was wise enough to remain on the ground. 'If you stay, you obey me and you obey Lianna. You will treat her as one of your leaders.' His fury rose higher, and he added, 'Have you not seen the attention she pays to your families? Do you not understand that *she* was the reason you had anything at all during these past few years?'

It was time to address the death of Sían, and he said quietly, 'Sían MacKinnon led a group of men to attack us, in the middle of the night. He shot an arrow into the heart of one of my friends, a man whose wife was expecting a child.' He glanced down at Eachann's wife, who flinched and rested a hand over her middle.

'There was no cause for the attack, and I defended my men. As I will defend you, should any harm come upon this clan.' He looked back at Lianna. 'I regret the death of Sían MacKinnon, but he brought it upon himself. It is my hope that we can now bring peace among us.'

No one spoke, and their silence held its own weight. He met the stares of each man, woman, and child, but only fear remained on their faces.

Lianna came to stand beside him and took his hand in hers. To her people, she said softly, 'I had hoped that you would join in witnessing a second wedding.

But I see now, that this is impossible.' Her brown eyes gleamed with tears. 'Even so, I invite you to share in our feast. Let us put the past behind us and begin anew.'

He could see the fragile command she held over her emotions, and nodded for the men to obey her. Eachann finally got up from the ground, wiping at his bleeding nose. His wife led him away, and neither looked back.

Rhys knew not if the peace would last, but he had made his point. Eachann MacKinnon could either obey them or leave. He would not stand for any further dissent within the clan.

Lianna moved to speak with two of the men, and within a few moments, they began bringing out the food. It had her intended effect of shifting the mood of the people. No one would turn down the feast, and soon enough, the MacKinnons took food and sat nearby to enjoy it. Children raced around in delight, after receiving portions of roasted mutton and pheasant.

But Rhys was well aware of his wife's misery. Her dreams of a wedding at Eiloch had been shattered, and he could do nothing to change it.

Though he wanted her at his side, he noticed her distancing herself from the rest of the clan. She busied herself with passing out food and drinks, easing her way back to her father's house. And when everyone had finished feasting and was standing around in conversation, Rhys realised that his wife had not eaten at all.

He crossed the space to her side. 'Will you not join us?'

She shook her head, and he noticed that her face was pale. 'I am weary. I would rather rest just now.'

He placed his hand upon the small of her back. 'You should eat, Lianna.' It bothered him that she had not enjoyed her own feast.

But she shook her head in refusal. 'I cannot. The thought of food turns my stomach.' She apologised and admitted, 'Let me go and rest, Rhys. It has been a long day.'

He escorted her back to the house, and a sudden thought occurred to him. If his wife was feeling weary and unable to eat, there could be another reason. 'Are you with child, Lianna?'

She jolted at that. 'N-no. At least, I don't think so.' But from the sudden startled look on her face, it seemed that she had not considered it. He was struck by the fear in her eyes, and it echoed within him. If she were carrying his unborn child, he had to keep her safe at all costs.

'Rest, then, and I will join you later.' He kissed her, but she seemed caught up in her own thoughts and did not return the affection.

She gave an absent nod and started to walk away, when he ventured, 'It will be different from now on, Lianna. I will stand for nothing less.'

But the sadness in her eyes said she didn't believe him.

Three days later

Lianna strode through the circle of crofters' homes, feeling the burden of melancholy weighing upon her. Why had she ever thought she could wed a Norman and be accepted by the people? Despite Rhys's demands that the clansmen respect her orders, they behaved as if she were invisible.

Her husband came to her each night and made love to her, but she was careful to keep her heart distanced from him. With each day at his side, she fought her emotions, despite how much she enjoyed his embraces.

Soon enough he would return to Montbrooke, and she knew not if he meant to leave her here. Her father's illness had improved, but he was not at his full strength yet. Worst of all, she feared that Eachann MacKinnon was only biding his time for vengeance. Her kinsman would not forgive such a public humiliation, and she did not trust him.

She unloaded a bag of grain from her horse and went to visit her friend Iona. She would give birth soon, and Lianna wanted to help in any way possible.

She knocked on the door, and when Iona called for her to enter, she found her friend pacing.

'I've brought you more grain,' Lianna said.

Iona's face was pale, and she gritted her teeth, placing her hands upon her back. She took a slow breath and stood in one place. 'Put it over there.' She nodded towards the far end of the cottage.

'Are you well? Is it the babe?' she asked.

Iona nodded. 'But 'twill be hours yet.' She opened the door and said, 'Walk with me awhile. I've a need for fresh air before I'm confined to bed.'

'Where is Malcolm?' she asked, not knowing where her friend's husband was.

'I sent him out hunting early this morn. He doesna ken that I'm in labour, and it's best to keep it that way. He'll be too worried.' Iona stopped walking for a moment and took slow, deep breaths. Her fingers clenched into fists, and she stood motionless.

'Shall I stay with you?' Lianna offered. 'I've more grain to deliver, but I could have one of Rhys's men take care of it, instead.'

Her friend's mouth hardened. 'Lianna, no one wants your pity.'

She faltered at that, feeling a sudden flush of uncertainty. 'It's not pity. Everyone needs the food, and I won't have anyone starve this winter.'

'None of us wants to be beholden to the Normans,' Iona said, gasping as another pain rolled over her. 'No one believes that we'll be protected. Your husband will return to his lands in England, and we'll have no means of defending ourselves.'

Lianna couldn't tell whether Iona's anger was genuine or whether it was labour pain that bothered her. 'His brother Warrick might stay,' she offered. The young man had spent his days training with the other Norman soldiers, keeping to himself.

But Iona only rolled her eyes. 'Can you not see that we don't want outsiders, Lianna?'

'They aren't outsiders. Rhys wants to help us.' Her husband had done all that he could to distribute food and supplies—but he had withheld some of the stores from certain folk.

'Our enemy, you mean.' The young woman shook her head as if she did not believe the Normans could ever be anything else.

'He's not my enemy,' Lianna started to protest, and Iona started pacing again. She strode beyond the house, towards the centre of the fortress. More than once, she stopped to take a breath and her hands rested upon her spine. From the pain etched in Iona's face, Lianna wondered if she should summon the midwife. It did seem as if the labour pains were increasing.

Her friend made a face. 'Rhys de Laurent gives us orders and expects us to obey. He doesn't belong here. Alastair is our chief, not him.'

'The land belongs to Rhys,' Lianna pointed out. 'He deserves to live here as much as anyone else.'

Iona stopped walking again, panting slowly. 'Tell yourself that if you want. But everyone sees that you're whoring yourself to him. You care naught for Eiloch, and you've forgotten Sían. You have an enemy in your bed, and you want him there.'

Her cheeks turned scarlet at Iona's accusations. How could her friend say such things? 'I am not whoring myself. He is my husband,' she countered. 'And you're wrong. I do what I must for the survival of this clan.'

Her friend's eyes lifted to something behind her, and she shook her head. In a low voice, she murmured, 'You betray us every night, Lianna.'

Her anger rose hotter. She had done everything she could for the clan, and none of it was ever good enough. Though she knew part of Iona's accusations were born of anguished pain, she could not stand aside and let her say this.

'I have *never* betrayed you. I am a MacKinnon and that will not change, no matter who my husband is.'

Iona met her gaze, and her expression revealed disbelief. When she only shrugged, it made Lianna's fury boil over. 'Rhys is a Norman whom I wed because I had no choice. I was promised to him before

I was born. No matter what I might have wanted, I was forced to marry and bed him.'

Her friend had gone silent. Then she turned back, returning to her home. Lianna was about to follow, when a shadow crossed over her. She looked over her shoulder and saw Rhys standing there. From the dark expression on his face, he'd heard every word. And so had the dozen or so clansmen standing nearby.

'Is it such a trial, then?' he asked, his voice cutting like a sword. 'Do you pretend to enjoy my touch, when all the while you wish I would leave you alone?'

She could not answer. The fury in his eyes burned through her, and she felt sick to her stomach. Everyone was staring, and she could not gather the right words.

In the end, Rhys didn't wait for her to answer, but strode away. Silently, Lianna berated herself for what she'd said. She *did* enjoy his touch—far too much. But it confused her to be torn between her kinsmen and her husband. She didn't deserve happiness with Rhys, not after all that had happened.

Misery filled up inside her, along with the wish that she had never said anything at all.

Chapter Ten

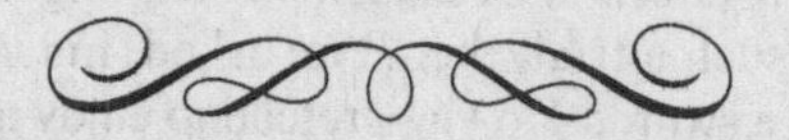

During the next fortnight, Rhys was careful not to touch Lianna. He left her alone in their bed, waiting to see if she would deny his accusation. If she offered even the slightest affection, he would return it. But she kept to her own side of the bed, turning her back each night.

It was torment lying beside her with the scent of her skin and the warmth of her body so close. But he would not reach for her any more. His pride refused to allow it.

This had been an arrangement, and he knew she'd been forced to wed him. But there had never been any force within their bed. Her claim that there had been no choice rankled him. He knew what it was to have power taken from him, to be touched without his consent—and he would *never* do that to her. Lianna had been the seductress on that first night, and he had enjoyed every moment of pleasuring her. He loved watching her come apart, her body convulsing around him as he gave her the release she craved.

Why, then, had she claimed that she had been forced to share his marriage bed?

He could have forgiven her for the idle words, had she reached for him, even once. But night after night, she kept to herself. And he would not touch her unless she asked him to.

He kept himself busy each day, training the Highlanders. The men were interested in Norman fighting methods, and he had learned about their own style of clandestine attack. It was a tentative peace, one that grew with each day.

Eachann had joined the men, though it was mainly due to his wife's interference. Janet was an outspoken woman, fiercely protective of her family, and she would not allow her husband to rebel any longer.

Rhys didn't trust the man, but at the same time, he understood that he had to give Eachann a second chance. There was still resentment within the Highlander, though it seemed that he respected Rhys's fighting expertise. This day, he was sparring with the man, and Eachann nearly won the match.

'Good,' Rhys complimented him. 'Your balance is improving. Keep working on your speed.'

The man gave a slight smile. There was a hesitancy in his demeanour, as if he wanted to say something. Rhys waited, and then prompted, 'Was there something you needed?'

The Highlander glanced over to a small group of MacKinnons where his wife was standing. 'I never thought I would say this, but I was wrong about you and your men. It's...better at Eiloch now.' He exhaled a breath, which was visible in the cool autumn air. 'My wife is expecting our first child, and now I ken that we will have enough to see us through the winter. We are grateful for the supplies.'

'That was Lianna's doing,' Rhys responded. 'She saw the need and demanded the grain as her bride price. She took nothing for herself.'

'Her brother Sían used to mock her,' Eachann admitted. 'If we agreed with him, he rewarded us with silver. It amused him to put her down.' His expression turned grim. 'I am sorry I ever did.'

'And where did he get this…silver?'

The Highlander shrugged. 'I don't ken, but Sían did wager a lot. Some MacDonnells travelled through our lands last spring. He bragged that he won coins from them, but we never saw them.' Eachann thought a moment, and added, 'The clansmen were angry with us, and I overheard one talking of vengeance.'

Rhys wondered if they were the same men who had attacked Lianna earlier. If they ever dared to travel through Eiloch again, he'd not hesitate to run his sword through them. He eyed Eachann again. 'There will always be dangers from other clans, but we will be ready for them.'

Eachann nodded. 'So we will.' He accompanied Rhys back to the house and added, 'What of your Norman estate at Montbrooke? Will you have to go back?'

'In time, yes. My brother will remain here, along with Lianna. Alastair will continue to be chief.'

Eachann's expression dimmed. 'He isn't well, is he?'

Rhys shook his head. 'But he will remain chief for as long as he can. I will see to it that his orders are carried out.'

His words seemed to satisfy the Highlander.

'Alastair has been a strong leader. And when he is gone, I suppose you will take his place.'

Rhys hesitated, for he had other responsibilities. Truthfully, he had intended for Warrick to take on that role. 'There is time before that decision must be made. But Lianna will help the clan with their needs.'

'Does she ken that you're leaving her behind, when you go to Montbrooke?'

Rhys shrugged. It hardly seemed as if it mattered any more. Lianna pretended to be asleep when he came to bed, and he wasn't about to touch her if she did not want him. The frigid ice had returned, and he was weary of it.

'My wife would murder me in my sleep if I went away and did not take her with me,' Eachann admitted. 'Janet is demanding in her ways.' He spoke then, of the child they wanted, and in the man's eyes there was a light of excitement. 'She wants a son, ye ken, but I wouldna mind having a daughter. A wee lass with her mother's eyes.'

Rhys thought of Lianna, but it was too soon to know if she was with child—especially since he had stopped touching her at night. Nor had he pressed her for answers. He would never force her to share his bed.

He parted ways with Eachann and went into the house. As always, it was neat and tidy, with nothing out of place. Lianna had an ironclad command over the household, and everything was always where it should be.

And suddenly, he had the desire to rearrange it all, to break through the façade of control and see if there was an emotional flesh and blood woman beneath it all. If he tore through her carefully arranged life, what then? Would he shatter the ice? Or would she only retreat deeper into her restricted world?

He found her in their chamber, scrubbing the floors. Though she tensed at the sound of his entrance, she gave no greeting, nor did she cease her efforts. Instead, she continued her work, carefully ensuring that there was no dirt upon the wood. The sight of her on her knees with her backside raised brought a flare of interest, but he tamped it down.

It was as if he were married to a stranger now, and she hardly spoke to him. Were there any emotions in her at all? He decided to broach the subject of his estate in England to see how she would respond.

'I am leaving for Montbrooke in the morning.'

At that, her hand stilled upon the rag and she turned to face him. 'So soon?'

He nodded. 'It has been weeks since I left. I need to speak with my father and attend to my responsibilities.'

She sat back on her knees. 'I do not know if we can leave so soon. It will take time to pack our belongings and ensure that while we're away—'

'I said *"I"*, not we.' Rhys moved towards the small trunk containing his clothing. 'You will remain here with Warrick.' He knew that she hated England, and he saw no reason to bring her back.

Lianna paled and got to her feet, folding the cloth into neat squares. 'But my place is with you.'

'Is it?' He moved closer, and she took a step away. 'I thought you were forced into this marriage. It was never your choice.'

'It wasn't,' she whispered. 'But as you said, we need not be enemies.'

He didn't know what to think of her words. Her actions had made it evident that she wanted to keep her distance from him. Why would she want to return to England?

'Do you want to journey to Montbrooke?' he asked quietly.

'What I want to do and what I must do are two different things.' She lifted her brown eyes to his, and his mood darkened. The implication was not lost on him, for she had not offered any affection at all. It was likely that she regretted the marriage, particularly since they had never celebrated a proper Scottish wedding.

'Is that what I am to you?' he asked, not bothering to hide the edge to his voice. 'A duty you must endure?'

She winced, as if his words had been a physical blow. 'Rhys, I will accompany you. It is expected of me, whether I want to return to England or not.'

'I do not need you to shadow me. I know you did not like my father's house.' Without letting her speak, he said, 'You can remain here while I go back.'

'But—'

'I don't need or want you at Montbrooke.' Likely she felt it was necessary to argue, but Rhys knew she preferred to stay behind in Scotland. And why not? Her family and home were here. There was no reason for them to see each other, if she did not want to go back to England. The bargain had been made, and they had consummated the marriage.

'We need only see one another a few times a year,

to conceive a child,' he said. 'After that, we could live apart.'

Her lips pressed together as if the thought frightened her. She raised her brown eyes to his, and for a moment she appeared so vulnerable, he regretted the words. But he needed to know if she truly wanted him gone.

Her silence hung between them, and it gave him the answer he'd expected. So be it.

'Is that what you want?' she asked at last, her voice flat and devoid of emotion. He searched for some sign that she cared—anything that revealed her feelings. But there was nothing at all.

'I suspect that you find my touch distasteful now,' he answered. 'I won't burden you with it.'

'That's not true,' she blurted out. The three words gave him a glimmer of hope. He took a step closer, wanting to see if she meant it. With no warning at all, he caught her waist and slid his hand over her breast. Gently, he stroked her nipple, and she jolted, trying to push him away. The instinctive reaction belied her words. But he would not stay where he was not wanted.

'See that my belongings are packed,' he said dully. 'I leave at dawn.'

Without another word, he left her behind.

Lianna felt as if she'd taken a blow to her stomach. Rhys's sudden touch had caught her off guard, and her breasts were overly sensitive just now. She had flinched at his caress, for it bordered on pleasure–pain. The reaction had shocked her, but she knew how it must seem to him.

A part of her wanted to hurry after him, to plead with him to stay. But she was caught up in shock right now, and her mind could not grasp what had happened. Was he truly leaving her?

He must still blame her for what she'd said. Ever since she had claimed to Iona that the marriage was not her choice, nor the wedding bed, she had felt the sense of wrongness. The words had been born of her own embarrassment, for how could she admit to her kinsmen that she cared for Rhys?

He had slipped into the edges of her life like a missing piece. He had never mocked her for her rigid habits but accepted her as she was. He'd even begun removing his shoes whenever he entered their bedchamber.

Her heart ached at the thought of losing him. When had this happened? When had he become such a part of her life that she needed him at her side?

Lianna sank down upon a stool, feeling faint. She had tried to distance herself, trying to return to the woman she had been in her former life. But it was impossible to imagine living without Rhys. These past few weeks had tormented her with heartache, for he had left her alone, virtually ignoring her. She felt the physical distance between them and did not know how to heal it. Patient waiting had done nothing, and she was now convinced that he despised her.

She allowed herself to cry, letting out the tight rein she'd kept upon her feelings. It had taken every ounce of control not to break down in tears before him.

For she believed she was pregnant with his child.

She had not had her menses in over a month, and her breasts were terribly sensitive. But the thought of childbirth terrified her. Already, she felt as if her body would no longer obey her wishes. The slightest scent turned her stomach, and it was difficult to eat without feeling sick.

For the past fortnight, she had tried to deny the signs, but even her maid Orna suspected it. Instead of feeling joy, fear clouded her mind. Her own mother had died giving birth to a stillborn boy. Lianna had never forgotten the anguish of burying them together.

No, the thought of giving birth alone was unthinkable.

What if something happened to the child or to her? She needed Rhys's steady presence to reassure her. The thought of spending the winter alone was impossible to bear.

A knock sounded at her door, and when she opened it, she saw Warrick standing there. He stepped inside her chamber without waiting for permission and demanded, 'Why is my brother leaving on the morrow? He wants me to stay and help govern Eiloch.'

His words broke apart the fragile command over her feelings, and Lianna no longer cared if he saw her weep. The buried emotions swept over her like a wave until she could do nothing else but cry. She lowered her shoulders and sobbed for the loss of Rhys.

'I am sorry, Lianna.' Warrick softened his tone and came to kneel down beside her. 'I thought you sent him away.'

'He is leaving me,' she sobbed. 'And I don't ken how I can get him back.' She was well aware of how awful she looked, but her emotions were ragged.

Warrick let out a sigh. 'Rhys is a proud man. He won't yield in a fight. But he will come back to you, Lianna.'

She didn't truly believe that any more. 'He t-told me to stay here. That he had no need of me at Montbrooke.' She wiped at her tears, not knowing what to do. But she doubted if pleading with him would make any difference at all.

'What do you want? Do you want to follow him?'

She nodded. 'My place is at his side, whether that is in Scotland or England. Especially now.' Her hand moved unconsciously to her waist, and Warrick understood the words she had not spoken.

'Does he know?'

She shook her head. 'And if I tell him I am with child, he will tell me to stay here.' It was the last thing she wanted, for she knew not if Rhys would ever return. He had said himself that he would only need to come back to her to conceive a child. And now that it might be true… She closed her eyes, trying to hold back her feelings.

'It would be safer,' he agreed. 'But it's early, yet. There is no reason why you cannot travel.'

Lianna tried to regain command of her feelings and asked, 'What should I do, Warrick? He is angry with me for…things I said.' She wished she could take back the words, but it was too late.

Warrick thought a moment and then stood. 'If you want to be with Rhys, then you should follow him. Even if you do apologise, it may not make a difference. He was always too proud to yield.' His expression dimmed, and he added, 'But I will escort you. I have to travel south anyhow.'

She sent him a questioning look, wondering why he would leave after his own father had ordered him flogged.

'I was invited to witness Rosamund's wedding to Alan de Courcy. Our father sent the missive.'

A sense of indignant anger rose within her. 'Why would he ever believe you would attend that wedding? After all you endured?'

'He wants to gloat,' Warrick admitted. He went to stand by the open window and was silent for a long moment. At last, he spoke again. 'I need to see Rosamund one last time.'

Lianna softened and went to stand beside him. Below, she could see Rhys giving orders, packing supplies. He had given Warrick a place to stay, but it was not enough. She could see in the man's eyes that he yearned for Rosamund, even now.

'You want to save her, don't you?'

He kept his gaze fixed upon the horizon. 'She told me that she could not be with me any more. I thought she would fight for us. But in the end, she cowered to her father's orders.'

'And what if she had no choice? Will you try to stop the marriage?'

He shook his head. 'Only she can do that. But I want her to know that I am there. And if she chooses to marry de Courcy, I will never speak her name again.'

Lianna reached out to touch his shoulder, and she swallowed hard. 'Are you certain you want to go?'

He gave a hard nod. 'I must.'

'Then I will pray that she changes her mind.' She felt a pang of sympathy for Warrick, wishing she could do something to help. But perhaps his presence would be enough to convince Rosamund.

'Go and stop her from marrying de Courcy,' she urged. 'Tell her that you love her.'

Her heart warmed at the thought of Warrick returning to Rosamund. He would fight for her, and she felt certain he would win. There was no doubt in her mind that Rosamund loved him. Surely they would find a way to be together.

And then she understood that *this* was what she needed to do—fight for the man she wanted. For she had already given Rhys her heart, and a part of him grew within her womb. Despite all that had happened, she loved him. If that meant becoming the Norman lady he wanted, she would do it.

'I will begin packing my belongings,' she said. 'You should do the same, and we will join Rhys.'

But he surprised her by shaking his head. 'No. We should not travel with my brother.'

'Why?'

'Because he will find reasons for us to stay. He wants me to be the acting chief in your father's stead.' Warrick's face grew solemn. 'But this is not my home. I don't belong here, Lianna.'

She knew it was true, though her kinsmen had come to accept him. 'My father is well enough to govern Eiloch. But I still don't understand why we cannot simply convince Rhys that we are going to Montbrooke, despite his wishes.'

'Wait two days and let my brother have time to regret his words,' Warrick advised. 'Let him arrive at Montbrooke first, and when I escort you there two days later, it will be too late to send you back.'

She wasn't so certain about his plan, especially

after the way his own father had treated him. 'What about you?'

'I will continue on to Rosamund's wedding once I have delivered you to my brother.'

His advice made sense, for he was right—after denying her permission to accompany him, Rhys would only send her home again. It was better to simply arrive when there was no choice but to let her stay.

She would pack her Norman gowns and jewels, transforming herself into the lady her husband wanted. If it meant speaking their language and obeying their customs, she would do everything in her power to change.

Her hands rested upon the soft swelling at her stomach. She had a strong reason to fight for her marriage… and she refused to let her husband turn away.

Montbrooke Castle, two weeks later

'You should have left Warrick at Dolwyth,' Edward de Laurent said. 'After everything he's done, you think to make him chief of Eiloch?' He shook his head in disbelief.

'And what did he do that was so wrong?' Rhys countered. 'He ran away with Rosamund de Beaufort and married her in secret.'

'It was no marriage at all,' his father countered. 'Her father already had it annulled. But God's bones, why would Warrick believe he could wed an heiress? He's lucky I let him live.'

The hatred in his father's voice spurred an even greater fury in his own mood. He had stood by for years while Edward had treated his youngest son like dirt. And though he had tried to stand up for Warrick, his father had never listened.

'Analise was a liar. She killed her own child and blamed Warrick for it.'

'You are wrong,' Edward insisted. 'I saw him holding my dead infant daughter with my own eyes. He did not deny it.'

'Because Analise threatened him.' He gritted his teeth. 'All these years, you've believed her lies. But I swear, by God above, you never knew her. She used you, and after what she did to us…' He stopped speaking, for what was the use?

'She had nothing but praise for you,' Edward said. And though he supposed his father thought it was a compliment, Rhys was glad Analise was dead. The secret touches, the sly flirtations—all of it had turned his stomach. And when he had refused to touch her, she had punished him with her own cruelty.

'Her heart was rotten to the core, and I hated her.' Even now, he could not remember the woman's face without a shudder. 'Be glad of the wife you have now. Rowena is worth far more than you know.' He stood and excused himself from the meal, not wanting to spend another moment in his father's presence.

He left the Great Hall, striding through the castle until he reached the outside. As he was descending the stairs, his sister Joan hurried towards him. She wore white, as she always did, and she had an anxious smile, as if she were eager to speak. He couldn't think what it was she wanted, but greeted her, 'Good morning, my sister.'

'There is a visitor who has come to see you,' she explained. 'A lady.'

Rhys had no idea what Joan was talking about. There had been no sign of visitors, and none of the guards had alerted him to the presence of anyone. 'Are they arriving now?'

She shook her head. 'She arrived earlier this morning.'

There was no reason for a lady to visit him, save one. 'Is it Rosamund de Beaufort?' Perhaps the young woman had come to learn Warrick's fate.

But Joan denied it. 'She is not the visitor. It is someone else.'

'I have no time for games, Joan.' He had been away for so long, he wanted to learn more about the dissent between King Henry and King William of Scotland. He needed to fully understand the threat against both properties, and he wanted to speak to his father's soldiers.

'She awaits you in the solar,' his sister continued.

'As I said before, I have no time. She can speak with my father if she does not wish to wait.'

Joan stepped in front of him and pressed something into his hand. 'She thought you might say that. And she bade me to give you this if you refused.'

Rhys opened his palm and saw the ruby necklace he had given to Lianna. 'Where did you get this, Joan?'

She smiled and walked past him. Over her shoulder, she answered, 'Perhaps you should ask your wife.'

Rhys clenched the necklace and returned up the stairs towards the solar. Lianna was here? How had she managed to slip inside the gates without attracting notice? Had she dared to travel alone again? Worry clenched within his gut, and he hastened his pace.

He didn't bother knocking on the door, but opened it. For a moment, he stared at the woman standing before him. Lianna was dressed in the manner of a Norman lady, with an emerald *bliaud* and her red hair bound up beneath a veil. The sight of her caught him off guard, and he stared at her without knowing what to say.

'My lord husband,' she murmured, curtsying before him.

Nothing could have surprised him more than to find her here. But it explained why the guards had willingly let her enter. 'Why have you come?' he demanded. 'Is your father—?'

'Alastair is well, and he is looking after Eiloch, just as he has always done.' Her demeanour was serene, as if she had not just travelled hundreds of miles.

'What about my brother?'

At that, she hesitated. His suspicions darkened, and he narrowed a stare at her. 'Lianna…'

'Warrick escorted me here. And now he has gone to Rosamund's wedding.'

She spoke with calmness, as if nothing were out of the ordinary. But Rhys knew there had to be a strong reason for her to travel all this way. It was completely unlike Lianna, and he wanted to know why.

'I told you not to come.'

A sudden flicker of emotion shadowed her face before she answered, 'I ken that you did. But as I told you before, my place is here.'

'I see no reason why you should think that. The MacKinnons need you more.' He didn't truly trust Eachann, and without Lianna or Warrick there, he could not say what would happen.

'My father is more than capable of governing the clan. It is his right.'

But it was Lianna who had truly ruled over the people. Her father had been the chief in name, but it was his daughter who deserved that title.

Rhys studied her and noted the shadows beneath her eyes. She must have followed him closely, for he had arrived at Montbrooke only two days ago. 'If you stay, then I would caution you to keep to yourself. I have my own duties to attend.' He hesitated a moment, waiting to see if she would take a step towards him. But she didn't move from her place.

Go to her, his heart urged. *Embrace her.*

But his mind hardened, for Lianna was here only out of duty. Perhaps her father had shamed her into accompanying him.

He clenched the ruby necklace a moment before holding it out to her. 'This belongs to you.'

She reached for the necklace, her fingers brushing against his as she accepted it. When she hung it around her throat, the jewel nestled between her breasts.

A surge of interest flared within him, and he longed to tear down the walls between them, holding her skin to skin. But then, she had disobeyed his orders, travelling all this way. There was no reason for her to stay at Montbrooke, and it would be better if she returned home.

She reached for his hand and squeezed it. 'I've missed you, Rhys.'

Her unexpected words startled him, and he didn't quite know what to say. Then she stood on tiptoe and touched the outline of his jaw, sliding her fingers over his cheek. He went rigid at her touch, and she tried to pull his head lower. He felt the warmth of her breath against his mouth, and she kissed him lightly. The gesture was unexpected, but he didn't kiss her back. Right now, his suspicions were heightened, and he needed answers.

She stepped back and said, 'I ken you must return to your own duties now. But I only wanted to see you first.'

He knew he ought to kiss her hard, to hold her and let her know that he had missed her, too. But something about this visit felt unusual to him. She was hiding something, as if she had done something wrong and was trying to atone for it.

She was holding back secrets, he was certain. And he needed to know what they were.

Chapter Eleven

Lianna muttered a curse after he left. Stubborn Norman. Didn't he realise just how far she had travelled to be with him? She had tried to follow his stepmother's advice, tempting him with a kiss—but he hadn't even kissed her back.

She left the solar and found her way to his chamber. It was neat and tidy, with his trunk pushed to the far wall, almost as if she had prepared the chamber herself. The tidiness irritated her, for she had come with the hopes of straightening their shared chamber. And she could not even do that.

A wave of dizziness washed over her, and she forced herself to sit down on the trunk. She had learned that the best means of controlling the morning sickness was to eat frequently. Bread and cheese made it easier to forget the nausea, but many times she found it difficult to remain standing for long periods of time.

Lianna leaned back against the wall, wondering what to do now. She needed time with her husband, time enough to seduce him and show him that she did care. Not once had she ever been forced to share his bed, and she wanted him to understand that her idle words had been false.

But Rhys was being stubborn and proud, and if she sent for him, he would only leave again.

No, she had to be patient and continue to be the sort of lady he wanted, making herself useful at Montbrooke. Joan might show her what she needed to know, or perhaps his stepmother, Rowena.

And in time, she could tell him about the baby.

The familiar fear gripped her, though she told herself that women gave birth safely all the time. It was easier to block out the worries, for there was nothing she could do until the child was born.

She left his chamber and saw his sister Joan in the hallway. The young woman offered a tentative smile, and Lianna shrugged. 'Thank you for bringing Rhys to me. He is still angry, and I don't ken how I can change that.'

'Rhys wants to be in command,' Joan admitted. 'He doesn't want to be told what to do.'

She was well aware of that. But she intended to do everything in her power to win back his favour. She confessed her plan to Joan, who considered it.

'I will do what I can,' his sister offered. 'But my brother can be stubborn.'

Lianna understood that, but if it involved seduction, she thought it might be possible to convince him to relent. Especially if she pleased him. She was determined to be the sort of wife he wanted, to prove that she had not meant those words. If he saw her as a proper Norman woman, it might end his bitterness.

She simply could not imagine living like this for the rest of their days.

When she turned back to Joan, she said, 'I ken that I was…not kind to you the first time I stayed at Montbrooke. It was hard for me to be away from my home.'

'You did not want to marry my brother, I know,' Joan answered. 'But Rhys is a good man. Even if he can be pig-headed at times.' Her face warmed with a gentle smile.

'I will do everything I can to be the wife he wants,' Lianna said. 'If you will teach me your ways.'

The young woman's expression grew thoughtful. 'I can show you our customs if you like, but you should be yourself, Lianna. Don't worry about trying to be someone you are not.'

Though she understood Joan's assurance, Lianna saw no other choice. She had grown accustomed to Rhys, and she did not want to live without him. She needed him, especially now. And if that meant wearing different clothes or behaving like a Norman lady to please him, she would do it. When they were at Eiloch, he had worn the clothing of her kinsmen and had tried to fit in among them. Could she not do the same while she was here?

'I want to try,' she insisted. 'But I will need your help.'

Joan gave a nod. 'If you wish it.' She led her down the spiral stairs. 'Truly, to behave like a Norman lady means to listen more than anything else.'

Lianna nodded. 'So be it. But in the meantime, will you show me Montbrooke? I fear that I paid it little heed when I was here last.' This time, she intended to see what the needs of the estate were, and she could share them with Rhys.

'Certainly. And later, you may join us for the noontide meal. My father will want to speak with you.'

The thought had little appeal, but it was part of claiming her place here, Lianna supposed. She walked down the stairs, mimicking Joan's behaviour as she took slow, graceful steps. Near the bottom of the stairs, she saw a servant lift up a small door in the floor that led to another set of stairs belowground.

'Is that for storage?' she asked Joan.

The woman nodded. 'It is mostly for wine, but sometimes it's used for hiding weapons or food supplies in the case of a siege.'

The servant returned with a small barrel, closing the door behind him. Then Joan took her outside, showing her each of the outbuildings. Lianna saw that the kitchens were well stocked, and she was pleased by the food preparations. As they passed the guard tower, she held up her hand. 'Grant me a moment, Joan.' She approached some of the soldiers who had accompanied her on the first journey. Their faces brightened at the sight of her.

'Lady Lianna,' the commander greeted her. 'We are pleased at your return.'

She smiled at him and asked, 'Do your men have all that they need? Is there anything I can do for you?'

The commander seemed pleased by her question. 'Thank you for asking, my lady. But no, we have everything we need, though the men always enjoy a good meal, my lady.' He smiled warmly, and Lianna promised to send them honeyed cakes and sugared almonds.

Before she departed, she asked him, 'How is Rhys?'

The soldier's face turned grim. 'Although he has only been here for two days, he behaves as if he is preparing for war. But he will not tell us of the threat. He trains the men for hours, and we respect him, for he is the best fighter among us.'

She wondered if it was in preparation for war between Scotland and England but could not be certain. 'Has he…said anything about Eiloch?'

The commander shook his head. 'But he is on edge. All of us can see it.' With a wry expression, he added, 'Your presence may do him good.'

Lianna hoped he was right. After thanking the commander, she returned to the keep and found Joan waiting upon the stairs. The young woman appeared uncertain and warned her, 'It is unusual for a Norman lady to speak with soldiers.'

Lianna understood her concerns, but they were unfounded. 'These men guarded me upon my first journey here. They are good soldiers,' she explained.

'That may be true. But my father and Rhys would not be pleased at your interference.'

Lianna could hardly call it interference when it was merely sending additional food to the men. She decided to be discreet about it. 'I understand.' She kept her voice quiet and demure, though she had no intention of ignoring anyone in need at Montbrooke.

They crossed through the inner bailey, and she stopped a moment to watch Rhys. As the commander had said, he was sparring with a group of soldiers, wearing full chainmail armour. And yet he moved as if he were unfettered by the weight. Three men opposed him, and he used both a sword and a shield to deflect their blows.

Lianna stepped closer and chose a place upon the stone stairs that led to the battlements. Rhys fought like a demon, lashing out at the men, his sword biting through their wooden shields. He poured his efforts into the fight, and Lianna's skin warmed at the sight of his strength. He moved swiftly, attacking their defences and winning.

And when the sparring was over, his face gleamed with sweat. She imagined him removing the armour, revealing his hardened muscles. The urge to touch him was strong, and it was only with great effort that she retreated from the training grounds.

He had a way of tempting her, and she pressed back the desire rising. From behind her, she heard footsteps. When she turned, she saw Rhys approaching her. His face held annoyance, and to his sister, he said, 'Leave us, Joan.'

The young woman obeyed, and Lianna suddenly sensed the caged anger rising within him. His blue eyes stared hard at her, as if he were angry for the interruption. 'What did you want, Lianna?'

She was fascinated by the brute strength of her husband. In her mind, she imagined him lifting her up and carrying her away, like a conquest of battle. The idea interested her more than it should.

'You fought well,' she said softly. 'I wanted to watch.'

'You were a distraction I didn't need.' His anger radiated from him, and though she ought to be bothered by his harsh words, it occurred to her that he might be feeling frustration.

'I will order a bath for you, if you want,' she offered. 'It might ease your aches.' Her pulse quickened at the thought of washing Rhys.

'I have no need of it.' He strode past her, and his abrupt dismissal should have angered her.

Yet, he had been unable to ignore her presence, and the thought pleased her. She had her own battle to fight, and she refused to surrender until she won his forgiveness.

His wife's presence unnerved him. Just as she'd done at Eiloch, she had begun giving orders here. She had sent extra rations to his soldiers, and he had overheard the men praising her. Whether she knew it or not, Lianna MacKinnon had gained their affection, and they would now obey her orders without question.

Rhys did not join her at the noon meal but simply took extra food from the kitchens. He suspected she would attempt to share his bed tonight, and he had not yet decided what to do. While his body welcomed the idea of lying with her, he had not forgotten the way she had shied away from his touch.

He retreated above stairs to his chamber and was startled to find a tub of water waiting for him inside. Once again, she had ignored his wishes. But when he touched the water, he found that it was still hot.

'Do you want my help?' a female voice asked.

He spun, unsheathing his dagger out of instinct. Then he relaxed his grip when he saw Lianna emerge from behind the door.

'No.' He sheathed the dagger again and opened the door. 'You can leave me now. Joan will share her chamber with you.'

She paled and went towards the door. But instead of leaving, she closed it behind her. 'I am not going away, Rhys.'

'You will if I command it.'

She crossed the room and stood before him. 'I travelled a long distance to be with you.'

'Because it is your duty to be here?' he questioned. He removed his gauntlets and then reached for his coif. The heavy chainmail was a punishing weight, but it was a reminder of the battles they still might face.

'I came to apologise,' she said. 'Not out of duty.'

She took the armour and set it aside neatly, kneeling before him to help with his boots. He removed his hauberk, then the linen undertunic. She averted her gaze, and he reminded her, 'You may go, Lianna. I have no need of your help now.'

'Get into the tub,' she ordered, 'and I will tend to your bath.'

Rhys wanted to deny her, to force her to leave. And yet, the thought of hot water upon his skin was a welcome idea. So be it. He stood before her, waiting until he had captured her gaze. And then he stripped away his remaining armour and underclothing until he stood naked before her.

She didn't move from her place, but her face flushed at the sight of him. He stepped into the tub, suppressing a groan of satisfaction. It *did* feel good to ease the pain of training with the hot bath.

Lianna went to fetch a linen cloth and soap. He watched as she returned and dipped the cloth in the water, lathering the soap in it. Then she brought the cloth to his back and began washing him.

'Use your hands,' he ordered.

She did, and from the moment her fingers glided over his skin, he grew erect within the water. She rubbed his skin, and then she began massaging his shoulders. Her touch affected him strongly, and frustration tightened inside.

'I spent time walking through the grounds today,' she said. Her hands moved to his chest, rubbing in slow circles.

'And what did you see?'

She described a broken wall and the masons who had begun fixing it. Then his mind drifted away while she spoke of the soldiers and their defences. Rhys lay back in the tub, and she helped him wash his hair. When he sat up, water dripped over his face and down his neck. She was leaning over the tub, and her face was flushed from the heat of the water.

'Why did you follow me?' he demanded. 'I want the truth.'

She bit her lip and lowered her gaze. 'There were many reasons. But I did not want you to go. My place is at your side.'

'For over a fortnight at Eiloch, you lay beside me and did not want my touch,' he accused. 'Because you were forced to lie with me.'

She frowned at that. 'I was never forced.'

Rhys rose from the tub, water spilling over his naked skin. He made no effort to hide his arousal, and just as he'd expected, Lianna appeared uneasy about it. She gave him a linen drying cloth, and he commanded, 'Dry me off.'

She moved in closer and obeyed, wiping the water away. He cupped the back of her neck, and when she bent lower to dry his legs, he felt her breath against his shaft. His need grew fierce, and he clenched his hands to keep from touching her.

Rhys refused to let himself fall beneath her spell. She would not seduce him, leaving him powerless. Right now, he intended to show her just who was in command. Though she might have drawn the bath, hoping to lure him into her bed, he would not let her use him in that way.

After she had finished drying him off, Lianna stood and began folding the cloth into neat squares.

'You pulled away from me the last time I touched you,' he murmured. 'Will you pull away now?'

She did shudder when his hand moved over the curve of her breast. But she admitted, 'I was sensitive to your touch. You startled me.'

'Why did you prepare this bath?' he asked. 'Did you think I would succumb to temptation and let you seduce me again?'

She shook her head. 'I only thought you would find it soothing after your training.'

'Then you do not want me at all, do you?' He let his hand trail from her nape down to her spine.

She swallowed hard. 'Rhys, don't play games with me. I will do what I can to be the Norman wife you should have had.'

He didn't understand her at all. 'You think to change yourself?'

She shrugged. 'I don't ken if that's possible, but I will try.' She rested her hands upon his shoulders, sliding them down his arms.

His suspicions darkened, for that wasn't Lianna's

way at all. She was a Scot and had always spurned Norman ways. 'Why?'

'Because you are the husband I want,' she whispered. 'And I believe we can build a good marriage between us.'

Though her words were the right ones, he could not surrender his disbelief. If that were true, what had changed her mind? Or was she only saying what he wanted to hear? He couldn't understand her reasons for returning to Montbrooke. But if she *did* want a better marriage, there was one way to find out if she was telling the truth.

'Remove your gown,' he ordered.

For a moment, she appeared shocked at his orders. He waited for her to refuse him, the way she had during the past few weeks. But instead, Lianna faced him, her expression holding an uncertain emotion.

She was wearing a *bliaud* that laced up the front, and she stood before him, loosening the bindings. She peeled back the gown with its tightly fitted sleeves, until she was clad only in her shift. The sight of her curves evoked a strong desire, but he wanted to know her purpose in coming to Montbrooke.

He reached for her shift and pulled it away, revealing her bare skin. Her breasts were fuller than he'd remembered, and the nipples puckered in the cool air.

'Lie down on my bed,' he commanded. 'Open your legs to me.'

Her expression turned startled, her cheeks flushed with colour. Yet she obeyed him, lying down naked upon the coverlet, though he could tell that she was feeling shy.

Rhys had no intention of joining with her. He

wanted to drive her into madness until she admitted her reasons for travelling this far.

He knelt at the edge of the bed, pulling her closer until her legs rested upon his shoulders. For a moment he waited, watching as the gooseflesh rose upon her skin. This position made her vulnerable, and he sensed her nervousness. He rested his cheek against her inner thigh, and when he breathed against her, she shuddered.

'Rhys, what do you want from me?'

'I want answers.' Without warning, he touched his tongue to her intimately. Lianna cried out in shock and arched her back. His anger and frustration drove him to torment her in this way. She had journeyed here against his orders, and he didn't know why she had disobeyed him. But no longer would he let her freeze him out. He intended to prove that she *did* want him, despite what she'd claimed to others.

'Am I forcing you against your will?' he demanded.

'N-no,' she breathed.

He licked the seam of her, finding the raised nodule that drove her towards madness. And when he suckled against it, her breath came in ragged gasps. But he could not stop his own rigid response. Her arousal and needs made him long to thrust inside her, taking her until she seized around him in the throes of release.

Rhys drew her to the edge of the climax, using his tongue and his mouth to pleasure her, fully aware of Lianna's yearning. 'Should I stop?'

'Please don't,' she begged.

Rhys continued to taste her, sliding his tongue against her folds and nibbling against the centre of her pleasure. 'Why did you come to Montbrooke?'

She was breathing in rhythm, her body squirming as he drew her closer to the edge. 'I needed to see you.'

'But you had another reason, didn't you?'

She rested her hands upon his hair, lifting her hips as he tasted her intimately. When she said nothing, he reached up to caress her breasts. Though he'd only meant to repeat his question, the barest touch shattered her. Lianna released a keening cry, her hips rising with the tide of her release. Her body trembled violently, and her hands dug into the coverlet as she came apart.

His own body was roaring for fulfilment, but he tightened the bonds of control. He would not give her this now—not when she'd refused to answer his questions. Instead, he simply moved away and pulled the coverlet over his wife's naked body.

Lianna sat up in confusion. 'What about you, Rhys? We haven't finished.'

'We have.' He reached for his braies and chausses, and then withdrew clothing from one of his trunks. She had given him no answers, and her silence irritated him. He didn't at all believe that she had come here to be a Norman wife. Lianna remained loyal to Scotland and always would. His mood hardened at the awareness that he'd deluded himself into imagining she had feelings for him. And when her kinsmen had accused her of switching sides, she'd admitted her own truth—that she had been forced into their union and into his bed.

It abraded his pride that she would think that. And he had needed to prove to her that he would never, ever force her into his bed...he would only tempt her.

Lianna sat up, clutching the coverlet to her body. 'Why did you do this?' she demanded. 'Were you trying to punish me?'

He eyed her flushed skin and met her gaze evenly. 'I hardly think you were punished just now, Lianna.' But despite her claim that they were not finished, he wondered if she truly wanted him. After all this time apart, he had his doubts.

Rhys finished dressing himself and prepared to leave. It was still afternoon, and he had other duties that required his attention.

Lianna kept the coverlet wrapped around her body and stood from the bed. 'You're not leaving, are you?'

'I am.' He was glad to see that he'd evoked a response from her at last. 'Besides, you never answered my question about why you travelled here. I don't believe it was only about wanting to be my wife.'

'You are right,' she admitted. 'I had another reason.' She tried to walk towards him, but the coverlet was tucked beneath the mattress and would not budge. Then she muttered a curse and let it fall, striding towards him naked.

He could not help but be aroused by the sight in front of him. Her red hair spilled over her breasts, and her skin was rosy from his earlier touch.

'You asked me why I came this distance,' she said, reaching for his hand. Then she brought it to just below her stomach, where he felt a hardened bump, barely visible. His veins seemed to flood with ice, and he stared at her in disbelief.

'I came to tell you that I am with child,' she said. 'And I do not want to be abandoned at Eiloch when I give birth.'

* * *

If she had struck him in the heart with an arrow, her husband could not have appeared more surprised. Lianna had the satisfaction of his gaping expression and his loss for words.

He kept his hand upon her womb, and she added, 'That was why I pulled away when you touched my breasts. They were so sensitive, it hurt.'

'When did you first learn of this?' Though his words sounded demanding, there was a tone of concern within them.

'I suspected it a month ago, but now I am certain. The baby will be born in the spring.'

If I survive the birth, she thought, but didn't say it. She was trying not to think of her mother. It was easier to force back the fear, pretending it wasn't real.

Her husband still appeared perplexed by her confession, and Lianna decided to get dressed again. She reached for her shift and then donned her gown. All the while, Rhys was staring at her, saying nothing. She had rather hoped he might be happy about the child, but he appeared more confused than anything else.

'You do not seem pleased by this,' she said.

He shrugged and seemed to shake off his reverie. 'I am surprised, but I suppose it was inevitable.'

And there it was, the shield closing down again. Of all the things he could have said, it was the last thing she'd imagined. She pulled her laces tight, her anger growing hotter. 'Is that the only thing you can say?'

Was he not pleased about the child? The slightest movement of the babe, rather like a butterfly's touch, was a fragile gift to her heart. She loved this child already, though the thought of giving birth frightened her. But instead of dwelling on the possibility of death, she could only live each day and pray that both of them would survive.

'You caught me unawares,' Rhys said. 'I did not think it would happen so soon.'

She wanted to throw a shoe at him. This was a child, a flesh and blood being, conceived in their marriage bed. And yet, he showed no happiness at all, no joy at an heir. His response was not at all what she'd expected.

Instead, she finished dressing and tightened the command over her hurt feelings. If he intended to behave as if it were of little consequence, so be it.

Lianna followed the spiral stairs down towards the Great Hall, but Rhys did not follow. Her heart felt brittle, as if the slightest emotion might shatter it. She pushed her way through the people, nearly running into Joan. The young woman was taken aback, and her face held sympathy. 'Are you all right, Lianna?'

The kind words made her burst into tears. Humiliation washed over her, but she let Rhys's sister guide her outside towards the garden where she could weep in private. It seemed that the pregnancy caused all manner of emotions to spill over, no matter how she tried to contain them. Joan embraced her, rubbing her back while Lianna sobbed out the story. When she had finished, she pulled back and saw the rueful smile on Joan's face.

'That sounds just like my brother. He must have been utterly stunned by your news.' Her eyes held amusement, and she added, 'But I am very pleased for you both. A new baby is such a blessing.'

Lianna wasn't so certain, but she didn't say so. She rested her hand upon the swelling at her womb, feeling so uncertain. 'Rhys doesn't seem to think so.'

Joan squeezed her hand. 'My brother is a fool. Don't worry. In time, he will grow accustomed to the idea.'

'I hope so.' She dried her tears and tried to think of what she could do to make herself useful. She needed a task to occupy her time, preferably one that involved sorting supplies. The mindless task was what she needed to push back the hurt within her heart.

Joan walked back with her, and she cast a sidelong glance at Rhys's sister. Lianna felt a slight sense of guilt that she had never tried to become better acquainted with the woman. 'May I ask you a question?'

'Of course,' Joan responded, slowing her pace.

'Why do you only wear white? I never see you in any other colour.' Lianna wasn't certain if the question would offend her, but she did wonder.

Joan's expression dimmed. 'It's my own protection against evil spirits.' She reached for the iron cross she wore and added, 'And the fairies.'

Lianna blinked a moment. 'Forgive me, but you don't seem like...'

'Like a woman who believes in fairies?' Joan finished. 'I wasn't once. But I am cursed, so I do whatever I can to overcome the shadows.'

From the look in her troubled eyes, Lianna could see that the woman believed it. There was a sadness in her face, and she ventured, 'What sort of curse?'

The young woman's mouth tightened. 'Suffice it to say, I shall never marry. I will not bring the curse upon any other man.'

'Were you married before?' She had heard no one speak of Joan's husband, but the woman seemed adamant about avoiding marriage.

'I was betrothed. Twice.' Her words came out clipped, and before Lianna could say another word, Joan insisted, 'I don't wish to speak of it again.'

They had reached the *donjon*, and Lianna touched the woman's shoulder out of sympathy. 'Thank you for walking with me. And I'm sorry if I brought up painful memories.'

'It's not your fault,' Joan answered.

She paused near the entrance, preparing to leave when Lianna asked, 'I would like to find a task to keep from being idle. I saw the storage chamber earlier and wondered if I might sort through your supplies.'

Joan appeared uncertain but then shrugged. 'I suppose there's no harm in organising our winter stores. But bring a cloak to stay warm,' she advised, 'and keep the door raised.' She ordered a servant to raise up the trapdoor and sent another maid to fetch a woollen cloak.

Once Lianna had settled it across her shoulders, she climbed down the ladder leading into the storage chamber. Joan gave her an oil lamp to carry with her, and it lit up the dim space enough to see the contents of the space.

It was indeed cool below the ground, but as Lianna turned and saw baskets and barrels in disarray, she braved a smile. She would sort through the mess and bring order where there was none.

This was her special talent, and after the frustration of her conversation with Rhys, she needed a means of occupying her time. The barrels were too heavy for her to move, so she concentrated her efforts on the smaller baskets and cloth-wrapped bundles.

Her hair kept falling in her face, so she braided it loosely and tucked it away, opening one box and then another to sort them by the contents. She organised the herbs together, then the dried meats, then the bags of grain. The work was difficult, but she found satisfaction in sorting neat rows of baskets.

She had nearly finished her work, when the trapdoor abruptly closed. The gust of air from the motion extinguished her oil lamp. Lianna let out a curse, guessing that someone had forgotten she was inside. She reached out to the wall, using it to guide her back towards the ladder. She stumbled over one of the barrels and caught her balance before she could fall.

In the darkness, she found the ladder and climbed up, trying to shove open the trapdoor. But it was too heavy for her and would not open. A sense of uneasiness passed over her, but she knocked against the wood and called out for someone to open the door.

Over and over, she called out, but no one could hear her shouting. It must be the noon meal now, and possibly the din of all the people made it impossible to hear her.

But surely Joan had not forgotten.

Lianna continued to knock against the wood, even using her shoulder to try to lift the door. But it was useless.

She climbed down the ladder, gathering the cloak around her for warmth. Eventually, someone would notice she was gone. For now, she was wasting her breath trying to be heard through the crowds of people talking in the Great Hall. She didn't believe she was trapped in this chamber out of malice; more likely someone had seen it open and had closed it during the meal. They would come for her soon enough.

She settled down on the floor with her back against one of the barrels. The air was frigid, and she shivered, trying to keep warm.

The cloak helped, and in time, she found herself becoming weary. She lay down and curled up, resting her hand upon her unborn baby. Her body was aching, as if her very skin had been stretched tightly across her stomach.

In time, the trapdoor opened and a voice called out, 'Lianna?' It was Rhys, and she said a silent prayer of thanks that he had found her.

She opened her eyes and sat up. 'I am here.'

'Don't move,' he warned. 'I am coming down to help you.'

She squinted when a light flared in the darkness. Her husband was descending the ladder, and she had never been more grateful to be found.

'I suppose they forgot I was in here,' she said lightly. 'Did Joan tell you where I was?'

'She did.' Her husband stood beside the ladder, and the expression on his face was dark and grim. 'Come here, and I will help you out.'

She started to rise, but a vicious pain stabbed her gut, and she faltered. 'Give me a moment. It hurts to stand.'

She rolled to her side, her knees curled up beneath her. 'Could you help me up, Rhys?'

He moved closer, but the look on his face was like nothing she had ever seen before. Each step appeared to be a torment. 'Are you all right?' she asked.

But he gave no answer. She tried to stand, but although the stretching pain had abated, a dizziness washed over her. She gripped the edge of the barrel, closing her eyes as she caught her balance.

Her husband had still taken only a single step towards her. She steadied herself, wondering what it was that bothered him so. Then she walked to him and took his hands in hers. They were freezing, and his stare was hard, like a shield of ice.

'Why did you come down to this place?' he demanded. 'Or were you locked in?'

'I came to sort through the supplies and was not strong enough to lift up the door,' she said.

'It was locked,' he countered.

The fury in his voice revealed his own anxiety for her sake. 'It was likely a mistake, Rhys. I doubt if anyone did it on purpose.' But there was something more within his tone, making her wonder aloud, 'Were you ever locked inside here?'

'Many times,' he answered. 'And I want to go now.'

She drew her arms around his waist. 'Who did that to you, Rhys?'

He held her for a moment, breathing against her hair. 'My stepmother Analise. When I was only four and ten, she...punished me.'

Lianna tightened her grip around him, holding him close. 'Will you tell me what happened?'

'Not here,' he started to say, but she did not want to set the conversation aside. Not when he was giving her a glimpse of his past.

'It's only a storage chamber,' she said quietly. 'Perhaps if you have bad memories of being locked away, we should confront them.' She lifted her face to meet his. 'Or if you would rather leave, I will go with you.'

He let out a slow breath, hesitating. 'I tell my soldiers to confront their fears. I suppose I should do the same.'

'So long as we are not locked inside this place together,' she teased. Then she reached up to touch his cheek. 'Unless you want to be.'

She noted a flare of interest in his blue eyes. Then he turned back. 'You spent a lot of time organising this space.'

'I did. It should be easier for your servants to find what they need now.'

He gave a nod, but she could tell that he had no interest in the supplies. Instead of describing what she'd done, she rested her cheek against his chest. 'Why did your stepmother punish you, Rhys?'

'Because I refused to let her touch me. And I refused to lie with her. I could not imagine such a sin.'

She could feel the rigid tension in his body, the tight control over his emotions. In spite of his stepmother's unwanted advances, he had remained strong. It had taken great courage to stand up to her as a young adolescent.

'And she locked you in here when you refused?'

'She did. And she warned me that because I had disobeyed her, Warrick would also be punished.' He kept her in his embrace, as if trying to protect her. 'We both hated Analise. It was she who murdered her own daughter and blamed my brother for it. She claimed that he dropped the baby, but I believed Warrick when he told me the truth. Our father will never accept it, nor will he forgive my brother for what happened.'

'That's terrible,' she murmured. But it did explain the animosity between father and son.

'She warned Warrick never to tell anyone, or she would hurt me. When she locked me away in this place, it was also a warning to him. But he did not listen to her. I pray she is rotting in hell right now. She died from a fall on horseback, and it serves her right.' He stroked back her hair, and yet, she could feel the chill in his skin.

He had bared the wounds of the past to her, and she wanted to lead him out of the darkness that haunted him. No young boy should have been mistreated so, and she rested her cheek against his heart. 'Rhys, I am sorry for what she did. It was wrong.'

He gripped her in a tight embrace, and now she was beginning to understand his anger. He was a man who had grown up with no love from his parents—only a connection with his brother and sister. He had a fierce need to be in command, after being a victim as a child.

He had tempted her earlier today, driving her wild with need and asserting his control. But instead of joining with her, reinforcing their marriage bond, he had pulled back, refusing to take his own pleasure. He was a man filled with suspicion and years of past wounds. Now, she realised what a mistake it had been, waiting for him to touch her.

Though he would never say it, Rhys was a man who needed love. He needed to understand that she *did* care for him, and she had returned to prove it to him.

'Come with me,' she bade him.

'Wait.' He drew his hands down to her waist,

touching the soft swell of her womb. 'I am sorry I did not help you up when you asked me earlier. Are you all right now?'

'I will be fine. Sometimes it hurts when my skin stretches. And I get dizzy at times.' She covered his hands with her own and added, 'Rhys, are you not happy about this baby?'

In answer, he embraced her so tightly, it was as if he wanted to fuse his skin into hers. 'I am. And yet, it fills me with fear and the need to protect both of you. I cannot let anything happen.'

Her own feelings mirrored his, for she knew the dangers of childbirth. And yet, she felt her spirits lift at his words. She kissed his cheek, and Rhys turned her face to lower his mouth to hers. His kiss revealed a tenderness and yearning that tempted her to stay together in this space. But she could not ask that of him, knowing the harsh memories he'd endured. Instead, she led him towards the ladder. Once they were out of the storage chamber, he lowered the door again and secured it. She took his hand, but he started to pull back.

'I should return to my men.'

'Not yet.' She drew his face down to hers and murmured in his ear, 'I travelled this far to tell you of our child, but also because I wanted you to ken that you are the husband I desire.' She kissed his earlobe, noting how his fingers dug into her waist. 'You are going to follow me to our chamber. And now, it is my turn to give you pleasure.'

Chapter Twelve

They barely made it inside Rhys's bedchamber before he kissed her again. Lianna felt the raging needs of her husband, and he ripped the laces free, lowering her gown to her waist. Once again, he was taking command, as if trying to exorcise his demons. His mouth closed over her nipple, and she went liquid between her legs, craving his body inside hers.

But this was not about mindless lovemaking. She wanted him to know the feelings locked away inside her heart.

'Don't ever leave me again,' she said against his mouth, kissing him. 'We belong together.'

He started to reach for her skirts, but she stopped him. 'No, Rhys. You had your turn before. Now it's my turn to love you.'

He went motionless, his blue eyes staring into hers. For a moment, she could not tell if she had made him angry.

She removed her gown, standing naked before him. 'I made a mistake at Eiloch, thinking that you would never want my touch, after I misspoke to Iona. But I want you to ken that I *do* want you. And if you will allow it, I am going to pleasure you until you can no longer bear it.'

At that, his eyes smouldered with lust. In silent answer, her husband removed his clothing and walked towards the bed. He sat down, and when she drew close, he reached for her waist. 'Will the baby be all right?'

She nodded. Then she stood between his legs, resting her hands on his shoulders. 'If there is anything you do not want me to do, you need only say the word and I will stop.' She wanted him to know that this was about her desire to give back to him, not to force him. 'Will you trust me?'

He hesitated. 'What do you intend to do?'

In answer, she pressed him back against the bed, straddling him. When she sat against his rigid erection, he hissed. 'My God, you're wet.'

'Because I want you. And I want to prove to you how very much I desire your touch.' Lianna drew her hands over his chest, feeling the rapid pulse of his heart. She leaned in and kissed his mouth, sliding her tongue inside. His tongue met hers, and she felt him grasp her hips, sliding his shaft against her body.

Her breasts tightened and she guided him inside, feeling the stretch as he invaded her flesh. It was sweet torment, but she held him there without moving. He sat up, and the change in the angle made her tighten her inner walls against his hard erection.

Rhys lifted one breast to his mouth. 'Will this hurt you?'

She shuddered at the sensation of his breath against her nipple. 'I am still sensitive there.'

'What about this?' he asked, moving his thumb

to her hooded flesh. Her body quaked at the sudden caress, and she moved against him, trying to take him deeper.

'I like that,' she said. Slowly, she rose up on her knees, then thrust against him once more. She squeezed him between her thighs and was rewarded when he closed his eyes and dug his fingers into her backside.

'Lianna,' he breathed in wonder.

She began riding him, thrusting gently. He kept the pressure of his thumb between them, and she fixed her gaze upon him. This man had come into her life, disrupting everything. And yet, she could not imagine being without him.

She wanted to tell him that she loved him, but the words would not come. Instead, she tried to show him, by loving him with her body. She learned when to hasten her tempo and when to slow down. Her skin was hot, slick with perspiration as she continued to move upon him.

'Are you all right?' she whispered. 'Does this bother you at all?' She wanted no memories of the past to intrude upon them.

'Only if you stop.' Rhys adjusted the angle between them, and somehow he seemed to sense what she needed. Lianna rode him harder, until she felt the shimmering release breaking forward. She took him hard, accepting him inside her until she felt him shaking.

His breathing was rhythmic, and he groaned when she thrust upon him, over and over, until she felt his release seize him. She let go, surrendering to the tide of her own desire, and he grasped her bottom, penetrating her deeply and spilling his seed.

Rhys gripped her body upon his, and she could not help the aftershocks that claimed her. Then he rolled her to the side, remaining sheathed within her depths.

Lianna rested her palms upon his heart. 'The past is gone, Rhys. There is only now.'

He held her closely, his hand sliding down over her bare spine. 'I won't let anything happen to you, Lianna. Or our baby.'

She tried to smile, but she held back the fear. There were some things he could not guard against, but she said nothing. For now, she wanted him to know that she had forgiven him. And it was enough.

There were moments when Rhys felt as if his life had shifted into a dream. Lianna had transformed herself into a Norman lady, but she still found her own secret ways of winning the hearts of his people. His soldiers adored her, for she sent them gifts of food or flagons of ale. Under her direction, Montbrooke had transformed into a beautiful castle, with immaculate gathering spaces and delicious meals.

But he knew she missed Scotland. It was in her eyes, and in the way she sometimes stared out into the green hills. He had already decided to take her back home before the heavy snows fell. She would want to celebrate the Yuletide with her family.

A light snow was falling from the sky, and he saw Lianna walking across the inner bailey, her *brat* pulled over her red hair. Snowflakes dotted her lashes and face, and as she drew near, he beckoned her closer.

'Good morn to you.' He reached out and brushed the flakes from her cheek. 'You look cold, my wife.'

'It is cold,' she agreed.

He drew his arm around her waist. 'I may need to warm you.'

A flush stole over her pale cheeks, along with a smile. But he saw the shadow beneath it. This pregnancy worried her, and he was well aware of how she tried to hide the pain and sickness. He walked with her towards the keep, but then he grew aware of a rider who had just arrived at the gates.

Lianna turned, and her face blanched. 'That's Brice MacKinnon.' The fear on her face tightened, and she murmured, 'My father…'

'Alastair might have sent him to us,' Rhys said quietly. But he knew she was afraid her father had died. He took her gloved hand in his, squeezing it in silent support. Then he walked with her towards the MacKinnon rider, who was dismounting from his horse.

Brice hurried forward and held out a missive to Rhys. 'Eiloch is under attack.'

Lianna tightened her grip on his hand. 'Is my father all right?'

'He is alive, though still weak from illness,' Brice said. 'We need the aid of your Norman army.' He turned his gaze back to Rhys. 'Alastair has asked you to return and bring soldiers to help drive out the MacDonnells.'

Lianna's face visibly paled at the mention of the men who had attacked her. Rage darkened through Rhys at the thought of what they had done. He moved his palm to the base of her spine in a silent token of reassurance.

'They want vengeance, don't they?' she asked softly. 'Because their men were killed after what they did to me.'

Brice lifted his shoulders in a shrug. 'Possibly. But I suspect it was more likely out of greed. Sían owed them debts from gambling, and Alastair refused to pay them. It was the reason why they tried to ransom you.'

Rhys knew he had to respond swiftly. 'How many men attacked?'

'Two dozen or so. They have set up camp surrounding Eiloch and some have taken over crofters' homes.'

Even if they left today, it would take nearly a fortnight to reach Eiloch. Rhys didn't know what would become of the clan in that time, but it was now clear that he could not leave that fortress undefended. He would have to choose men willing to live in Scotland throughout the year.

'I will assemble men, and we'll leave at dawn.'

Lianna nodded her agreement. 'Brice, go to the kitchens, and the cook will give you food after your journey. In the meantime, I will have our belongings packed.' She started to turn, when Rhys caught her arm. He waited until Brice had departed before he spoke.

'Lianna, you are staying here.'

She stared at him, aghast. 'I will not. Eiloch is my home. Those men have attacked my kinsmen. How can you ask me to stay behind?'

'I'll not risk your life or our child's.' There was no question that she had to stay here among his father's men. It humbled him to realise that she would bear his child, and filled him with a sense of wonder. His wife would bring a son or daughter into the world, and he wanted to be a better father in a way Edward had never been. Now he understood what Ailric had tried to tell him—the love of a wife and child was beyond price. Never could he imagine bringing Lianna and their unborn child into a battle. He needed them safe, where she would be guarded at all times.

Frustration tightened her expression. 'I can ride as well as the others. I won't hinder your pace, despite the babe.'

It was clear that she misunderstood his reasons. Rhys leaned in against her ear. 'I know how ill you've been each morn, Lianna. I see the pain in your eyes, and I know full well that this pregnancy has not been easy on you.' Her body had shown only a few changes, but her weariness was evident. Rhys drew his hand to her womb, feeling the slight bump. 'I cannot endanger you—especially now.'

'No pregnancy is easy,' she argued. 'But I'll not stay here while my people are under attack.'

'You will. You must have faith in me, that I can defend them.' In this, he would not be swayed. He didn't miss the trouble brewing in her eyes, and he added, 'I will send word as soon as we've taken Eiloch. And you may travel back with an escort of my father's men.'

'And what if something happens to you?' she asked. 'Do you think I want to remain here if you are killed?'

'If I am killed, a part of me will live on,' he reminded her, resting his palm upon the slight swelling at her waist. 'I need you to protect our child.'

She broke free of him, and he let her go. Her shoulders were lowered, and he saw her swiping at her eyes. He understood her despair at being left behind, but nothing would convince him to put her in the midst of a battle.

He cared too much about Lianna MacKinnon to ever risk her life.

'Rhys de Laurent is going to murder me,' the Norman soldier muttered. 'When he finds out I brought you to Scotland, he'll use my guts as a noose.'

'I won't let him murder you,' Lianna reassured him. 'As long as we stay out of the way, no one will ken that we are here.'

'Forgive me, my lady, but the moment they see your hair, they will know exactly who you are.'

Lianna had braided her hair and hidden it beneath a *brat*, but she knew the man was right. Her distinctive hair instantly identified her as the MacKinnon's daughter. And for that reason, she was determined to hide herself.

Snow covered the ground, and her fingers were numb with the cold. But she felt a lift within her heart at the sight of the familiar hills. Her people were here, and she would do everything possible to save them from their suffering.

Once they reached the edge of the forest, she raised her hand for them to stop. 'If we go any closer, we'll be seen.' She wanted her guard to find out what was happening. Thus far, she had seen no sign of Rhys or his men. Where were they? She had followed behind them, but it was as if her husband had disappeared.

'Make your way towards Eiloch and find out if Rhys and the others are there,' she told the soldier. It would not surprise her if her husband had managed to slip inside, disguised as a MacKinnon. 'Then come back and tell me what you have learned.'

He appeared wary of her suggestion. 'And who will guard you, my lady? I cannot leave you alone.'

She nodded towards the woods. 'I will remain here, well out of sight.' There was no question of her interfering with her husband's plans. Although Rhys would be angry with her, she belonged here at Eiloch. So long as she remained hidden, there was no harm in being here.

The Norman soldier appeared uneasy by her statement. But she was weary from the travel and was content to stay back. If the fortress had been captured by the MacDonnells, then she would ask him to take her to Ballaloch nearby. She would seek sanctuary with the MacKinloch clan until it was possible to return.

The soldier hesitated, and she reassured him again, 'I will be fine.'

She adjusted the folds of her *brat* around her and chose a place near a tree and a patch of underbrush. 'I promise I will stay out of harm's way.'

He didn't look eager to leave, but in time, he acceded. 'I will return, my lady. If you do not see me within the hour, continue on to Ballaloch.' He was muttering his wish that she should have brought more men. But if she had, it would have drawn attention to their travelling party. She'd wanted her journey to remain secretive, especially so her husband would not know she had come.

'Go,' she told him.

The soldier was wearing chainmail beneath the clothing she had purchased for him when they had arrived in the Highlands. He appeared to be a Scot, and she had cautioned him not to speak, if at all possible. His voice would easily give away his identity.

He left the woods and she kept a close watch over him as he approached Eiloch. From this distance, nothing appeared to be out of the ordinary, but she would not make that assumption until he confirmed that all was well.

She wanted to believe that Rhys's men had retaken command of Eiloch, but she could not surrender her suspicions. His absence was conspicuous, for she had expected to see a full army of Normans surrounding Eiloch.

But there was no one. An ache caught her heart as she feared the worst.

The MacKinnons were afraid to fight. Rhys knew it, but he did not blame them. They feared losing friends and family to the enemy's blade, for the MacDonnells had threatened some of the children as captives.

Rhys had commanded the rest of his army to stagger their camp in small groups, all the way towards Ballaloch. The closest group was half a mile away, and he had arranged signals to alert the rest. He had ordered his commander Desmond to remain by his side, in case his own life was threatened.

Although he could easily have taken Eiloch back by attacking the MacDonnells openly, many of the MacKinnons would have died in the battle, and Lianna would have been devastated by their deaths. Rhys had fought hard enough for her forgiveness, and he would not risk more animosity from her clan.

Strategy would make it easier to take back the fortress with minimal losses. He wanted to reconnoitre, to get a strong sense of his enemy's weaknesses before he sent word to the rest of his men. He hoped that if the MacKinnons saw him among them, he could enlist their help to fight against their common enemy.

The MacDonnells had claimed Alastair's house, and several of the men had taken over crofters' homes. Rhys had hidden himself with Lianna's maid, Orna, pretending to be her son. But the older woman was visibly shaken by the presence of the enemy clan.

'I thought you would return with soldiers,' she chided him. 'Why have you come with only one man? And why have you not attacked?'

He studied her, seeing the fear and anxiety in her eyes. 'I do have more men. But I wanted to find out more about the MacDonnells before I bring them here.'

Orna grimaced. 'Why would you wait? When we're all dead, the MacDonnells won't matter.'

Rhys did not correct her assumptions. Instead, he wanted answers about what had happened. 'This was more than a raid, wasn't it? They intend to stay.'

'Aye, they do. They keep asking about the silver Sían promised them.' The old woman's mouth tightened. 'They've torn Eiloch apart, searching for it.' Her mood darkened, and she added, 'The men who attacked Lianna were MacDonnells. The chief intends to claim everything we have and avenge their deaths.'

Which meant the chief would want Rhys's life. Likely, they had waited at Eiloch in the hopes of killing him. And after stripping Eiloch of everything, it meant the clan members were more likely to hold resentment and turn against him. Staying here was a grave risk, but he needed to find their weaknesses in order to strike swiftly and drive the men out.

It was late afternoon, and Rhys planned to wait until nightfall to return to his men. He had spoken to several of the MacKinnons, Eachann included, and they were willing to join him in the fight. He had ordered the men to attack from within Eiloch, creating a distraction. During the commotion, his men would surround the MacDonnells and retake the fortress.

'Have patience,' he warned Orna. 'I will slip away tonight and gather our forces.'

The older woman appeared uncertain, but she muttered beneath her breath. He started to walk towards the door when he suddenly heard shouting and an uproar of voices outside. Rhys kept his hand upon the dagger at his waist and ordered, 'Stay here,' while he left Orna's house to investigate.

At the centre of the fortress, there were three female captives with sacks covering their heads and faces. One was heavily pregnant, a second one had long dark hair in a braid, and the third was thin, with only the slightest hint of pregnancy. The moment Rhys saw the last woman, his blood ran cold. He didn't need to see her features to know it was his wife standing there.

How had she come to Eiloch? Numbness settled within him as he drew closer. One of the MacDonnells stood beside the women with a long blade in his hand.

He saw Eachann blanch at the sight when he recognised his own wife Janet. Rhys hurried forward and caught the man's arm. It took all his strength to hold him back.

'Don't,' he warned. 'It's what they want.'

But the Scot fought against him. 'They're going to kill all of them. And I'll not stand back like a coward.'

'I need you to fight with me, not against me,' Rhys swore. His mind was reeling with what to do, and all thoughts of careful strategy seemed to disappear like smoke. Like Eachann, he wanted to rush forward and cut down Lianna's captors, keeping her safe. But that would only end up in death for both of them. He had to maintain control, to keep his wits about him, especially now.

A single lock of red hair escaped the sack obscuring Lianna's face, and the people gave an audible gasp as they recognised her.

'Which of the women will live?' the MacDonnell taunted. 'And which will die?' He touched the tip of his blade to Janet, who flinched.

Rhys's hand dug so hard into Eachann's arm, his knuckles whitened. 'I'm going to save all of them. I swear to you.'

But first, he caught the gaze of his commander and nodded for Desmond to leave. It would take time to signal the men for reinforcements.

'Your clan has refused to hand over the silver promised by Sían MacKinnon,' the man said coolly. 'And after all these weeks, you still refuse to give us what is rightfully ours.' A cruel smile stole over his face. 'You stole from us. Not only silver, but three lives.' He moved the blade to Lianna's throat. 'If you will not tell us where the silver is, then we will avenge our dead with three of your women.'

Rhys released Eachann and said softly, 'Trust me.'

The man met his stare as if he didn't want to. But

then he muttered, 'Save her. But if they harm a single hair on her head, I will end your life.'

Rhys walked slowly through the crowd, and the people parted on either side of him. He felt their angry stares like a palpable presence. They blamed him for not defending Eiloch, but that would change, soon enough.

When he reached the prisoners, he said calmly, 'Let the women go.'

The MacDonnell sneered at him. 'And why would I do that?'

'Because I am giving myself over as your hostage,' Rhys said. 'I am Rhys de Laurent, the son and heir of Edward de Laurent, Lord Montbrooke. My life can be ransomed for all the silver you desire.'

The MacDonnell stared at him as if he'd gone daft. To make his point, Rhys switched into the Norman language, knowing Lianna would understand him. 'Are you unharmed, my lady wife?'

'I am,' she answered in the same language. 'They do not understand your words. There are twenty-two men here, armed with daggers, bows, and no swords. They have been searching for the silver Sían stole from me.'

'My soldiers are not far away,' he assured her.

'Stop talking,' the MacDonnell backhanded Lianna, and her face snapped sideways.

Rhys's hand clenched into a fist, and it took all his control not to lunge at the man. He drew his sword and held it out. 'Eachann, go and free the women.'

He tensed, not knowing if the MacDonnell would stand down, but the man lowered his dagger. Eachann removed the hoods from each woman and reached for his wife. But before he could free Janet, Rhys saw the MacDonnell move towards them. He deflected the man's blade before he could strike, and roared, 'Take the women, now!'

Eachann obeyed, dragging them away. The MacDonnell lifted his blade and swung hard, but Rhys defended himself once again. Now that the women were away from the fighting, he concentrated his energy on winning this battle.

Over and over, he struck, only to hear Lianna cry out a warning, 'Rhys, behind you!'

He turned, just as a club struck him across the forehead. Searing pain radiated through him, and he dropped to his knees, fighting to remain conscious.

'Take him,' the MacDonnell said. 'But not for ransom. This Norman killed my son, and the only ransom I want is his head upon a pike.'

Lianna cried out in horror, but Eachann shoved her back, along with Janet and Iona. He was trying to get them to safety, but she could not tear her gaze away from her husband. Four men were holding him back, binding him, while the MacDonnell picked up Rhys's fallen sword.

'A fine weapon,' he remarked. He ran his thumb along the edge until blood gleamed. 'One blow should remove his head.'

Her insides turned to ice, and she pleaded with Eachann, 'Gather the men. Please…you have to save him.'

'He gave himself up for you,' the man said quietly. 'Don't let his sacrifice be in vain.'

Her terror transformed instantly into rage. 'Sacrifice? Do you believe that I will stand by and let them kill my husband for the sake of my own life?' Lianna reached out and seized the dagger from Eachann's waist. 'I will fight for Rhys, and so will you.' She turned to her kinsmen, levelling a dark stare at them. 'All of you.' With a dark glare, she added, 'Were it not for my marriage to Rhys, you would all be starving now. You owe your lives to him, and now he needs our help. Do not dare turn away from him.'

The men appeared taken aback by her demand, but she would not relent. All her life, she had remained in the shadow of her father and brother, never daring to take command. But they owed everything to Rhys. She trusted him and knew that his men would come to help.

'Will you rise up against our enemies? Or will you cower when you are needed the most?'

Her words had the desired effect, and the men straightened, reaching towards their own weapons. Eachann stepped forward and promised, 'We will give him our support, Lianna.' His expression softened as he met his wife's knowing gaze. 'I promise you that.'

He charged towards one of the MacDonnell men and knocked the man to the ground. Before they could stop him, Eachann seized the fallen man's bow and an arrow. He pulled back the bowstring, aiming the arrow towards the MacDonnell chief who had ordered his men to press Rhys's shoulders down against a log, intending to take his head. But Rhys fought against them with all his strength and both men struggled, unable to force him from a standing position.

Precious seconds remained as Eachann took aim with his bow, and Lianna's heart pounded with fear.

He might strike Rhys instead of the MacDonnell holding the sword, if his shot went awry. And the thought was unbearable. She could not imagine living without Rhys de Laurent, the man she had come to love. He was stubborn, proud, and one of the most intelligent men she had ever known. Never in her life had she been so terrified, and her hands shook as she tried to gather control of her emotions.

'Be careful,' she whispered to Eachann, just as the MacDonnell raised the blade. They had only one chance to save Rhys's life.

She prayed with all her heart as Eachann released the bowstring. The arrow flew through the air, across the space…and embedded in the wooden enclosure behind Rhys.

The shot had missed.

Chapter Thirteen

Two men held Rhys by both arms, unable to force him to the ground. And when the MacDonnell's sword came down towards his torso, Rhys pulled with all his strength. A brutal scream cut through the air as the blade sliced through his enemy's arm instead. He spun and ducked as the MacDonnell raised his weapon again.

To his shock, the MacKinnon clansmen charged forward, chaos erupting within Eiloch. Men were armed with spears, others with daggers, as they released a fierce battle cry and attacked. Rhys seized a weapon from one of the MacDonnell men and stabbed the chief, shoving him back as he spun to fight against the others.

At that moment, the first group of Normans charged through the gates. His men poured into the fortress, fully clothed in chainmail armour. All around him, Rhys heard the clang of swords and the cries of men being struck down.

He glanced up and saw a flaming arrow soar into the sky—the next signal the men had been waiting for. One by one, the staggered army would launch burning arrows to alert the group behind them to attack. The MacDonnells would not only be surrounded—they would be pounded with wave after wave of highly trained Norman soldiers.

But even as Rhys gave himself over to instinct, his sword cutting through flesh and bone, he searched for a glimpse of Lianna. He needed to know if his wife was safe.

At last, he saw her standing near Janet and Iona, all three with weapons in their hands. Even Janet, in her advanced pregnancy, wielded a spear, staring at the MacDonnells as if daring them to fight her.

His commander, Desmond, joined him, and they fought side by side along with the MacKinnons. He saw the determination of the clansmen and the subtle confidence in their fighting when they realised that they held the advantage.

It took only minutes for the fight to be over. And when only a handful of MacDonnells remained, Rhys barked out orders for their enemy to be brought to him.

His soldiers surrounded the MacDonnells, and from the rigid cast upon the prisoners' faces, they fully expected to die with the rest of their men. But Rhys wanted to make a point of his own.

'You attacked our men and women, attempting to seize property that was not yours. By all rights, you should die for this raid. But I am leaving your fate in the hands of the MacKinnon chief.' He spoke quietly to Eachann, asking him to summon Alastair.

Then, Rhys studied the faces of the MacKinnons. It did appear that most of their men were unharmed, and several were smiling at their victory, in spite of the bloodshed. But there was more they needed to know. 'The Normans who accompanied me have offered to dwell among you—but not as invaders. We will build homes for them, and they will offer their protection to you for as long as it is needed.'

There were nods among the men, and soon enough, there were murmurs of approval. They would accept Norman soldiers among them, as long as it did not interfere with their lives.

Soon, Alastair emerged from his house, flanked by Eachann and Desmond. The chief appeared weary, and when he saw the fallen MacDonnells, his mouth drew into a line. 'Many have lost their lives this day. But it could have been far worse for us.' He switched into the Norman language and addressed the soldiers. 'I am grateful for your assistance, and we welcome you to stay at Eiloch.'

There were nods of agreement among the people as the chief continued addressing the clan. 'I have been your chief for over twenty years,' he began. 'But time has caught up to me, and it is time that another took my place. Someone who can defend Eiloch and who will protect us from our enemies.'

His attention shifted back to Rhys, and one by one, the clansmen began to chant his name. The uproar of support startled him, but Rhys had already made his own decision. There was someone else who deserved to be chief, far more than himself. Someone who had selflessly taken care of her clan all her life.

He caught a glimpse of Lianna and beckoned for her to come forward. She started to walk calmly, but when she came closer, she broke into a run. Within seconds, she was in his arms. Rhys held her tightly, asking, 'Are you all right?'

'No,' she whispered, embracing him with all her strength. 'I thought I'd lost you.'

Rhys smoothed back her hair to reassure her. 'I am unharmed.'

But still, she would not let go of him. Several of the MacKinnons smiled at the sight of her gripping his waist. Rhys leaned down to her ear. 'I promise I will hold you longer in a moment, my wife. But there is something else I need to say to you.' He extricated her from his embrace, but continued to hold her hand.

He spoke in Gaelic, so that all would understand his words. 'For the past few years, there is a MacKinnon who has put this clan before all else. She knows every one of you, the names of your children, and what your needs are. When our lives were in danger, she brought our men together to fight. And I can think of no better chief to lead our clan than Lianna MacKinnon.'

His wife's face flushed crimson, but he squeezed her fingers in a silent warning not to protest. Janet MacKinnon was the first to lift her arm into the air and cry out, 'To the MacKinnon!'

The echoes and cheers were deafening, and Rhys was glad for her sake. Lianna was the rightful leader and deserved her clan's loyalty. Several men pounded their spears against the ground in a show of support, while others continued to shout, 'The MacKinnon!'

Lianna squeezed his hand and then took a step forward to address her people. Although she paled at being the centre of attention, she steadied herself and began to speak.

'For years, I served my father and then my brother, because I wanted every person in this clan to have all that they needed. I spent my days watching as each of your families changed and grew. And it gave me joy to see homes repaired, to give you food to eat, and to see smiles on the faces of your children.'

She reached out to Rhys and drew him to stand beside her. It now seemed that she had gathered her courage, and her voice held conviction. 'When my father commanded me to wed a Norman lord, I tried in all ways to avoid it. I feared what it would mean for us, and never in my wildest imaginings, did I think to see the day when Norman soldiers would fight our enemies alongside us. But they have. And these men are our allies now, not our captors. And we are not alone.'

He reached out to touch the small of her back, letting her know that he would always stand by her. The men and women were serious now, listening to every word she spoke.

'In the next two days, I ask you to choose six men who will be a part of my council. I will not make decisions on behalf of the MacKinnon clan without listening to your views first.'

It was a wise move, and pride swelled within him at her decision. Rhys reached down beneath her hips and lifted his wife into the air, letting her hear the sound of the people's cheering.

And he knew the decision to choose her had been the right one.

Later that night, Lianna returned to their bedchamber. His wife appeared exhausted, and there was dirt on her face and hands after the long day.

'Do you think the council made the right decision to release the MacDonnell men?' she asked, pulling the ribbon free from her long braid.

'As long as they send one of their boys for fostering,' Rhys agreed. Since there was so little trust remaining between the two clans, Lianna had spoken with several of the MacKinnons, and they had all agreed to take a hostage from the MacDonnells. She would demand one of the sons of the high-ranking men, and as long as peace remained between their clans, the boy would be treated well. One day, the boy might even marry a MacKinnon woman, securing the bonds between the clans.

Lianna used her fingers to unbraid her hair and poured water into a basin. She had never been more beautiful to Rhys than before now. Her courage and strength had led them to victory against their enemies.

'Let me help you,' he commanded, guiding her to sit down. He dipped a clean piece of linen into the warmed water and washed his wife's face. Rivulets of water spilled down her cheeks towards her bodice. He took her hands and drew them into the basin, washing them gently.

Her brown eyes grew heated, and she shivered when his thumbs caressed the centre of her palms.

'I didn't like being left behind,' she murmured.

'I know. But I didn't want anything to happen to you. I would have sent for you afterwards.' And he meant that. A part of him wanted to chide her for disobeying, but he understood that this was her true home.

'These are my people,' she admitted. 'I could not abandon them.'

He went to fetch a comb from her belongings. 'Sit down.' She did, and he began to draw the comb through her hair. She leaned back as he did, and he was careful not to pull against the tangles.

'Seventy-seven times, is that it?'

She turned and smiled at him, taking the comb. 'I ken you must think me foolish. But my mother taught me this.' A sadness drifted across her face, and she added, 'She was always beautiful to me. Her hair was soft, and everything about her was clean. Wherever she went, she was always keeping the house tidy and neat.'

The hollow tone of her voice revealed her grief, and he was beginning to understand that she had fallen into her mother's footsteps.

'I—I tried to do the same after she died. She loved my father, Sían, and me. It was her way of showing she cared, and I thought I could keep her memory alive by holding on to those habits.'

He moved her hair to the side and kissed her nape. Lianna drew her hands to his shoulders. 'She died giving birth to a son when I was eight years old.'

He didn't miss the tremor in her voice, and he moved his hand down to the swelling at her waist. 'Don't be afraid, Lianna.' Though he spoke the words, he knew that there was danger in childbirth. Many women died, and so did the infants. The very thought caught his gut with fear. He made the silent vow that he would protect Lianna and their unborn child in every way possible.

'I cannot help but be afraid. I was there on the day she laboured with my brother. And there was nothing the midwife could do. Th-they cut her open to try to save the baby, but it was too late.'

Tears gleamed in her eyes and spilled over. 'I don't want to die, Rhys. Not like that.'

He held her close, stroking her hair. 'I won't allow it.'

At that, an unexpected smile crept through her tears. 'You speak as if you can command me not to die.'

'And so I do.' He needed to distract her from her fears, to show her how much she meant to him. 'I would walk to Hell and back to keep you with me.'

'I'm not going to Hell.'

But her smile deepened at his words. 'You might. For you have been quite disobedient as of late. I told you to stay at Montbrooke.'

'I was never going to listen to that command, you ken this.'

He supposed he had. Lianna would do anything for her people, and she would never stand aside while they were in danger. 'You prefer to give the commands, is that it?' he asked softly.

Her eyes flared with interest. 'I might. Perhaps I'll tell you the way I want to be touched.'

There had been a time when he had rebelled against the thought of a woman commanding him in the way Analise had tried to. He had always demanded control, never surrendering his will.

But the idea of letting Lianna give commands aroused him deeply. He admired her strength and wanted to see what she would do.

'What is your first command?' he asked, sliding his hand beneath the shoulder of her gown. He needed to touch her bare skin, to quench his thirst for this woman.

'Take off your clothes. Let me see you,' she said quietly. Her brown eyes were fixed upon him, and her skin was flushed with anticipation.

Rhys removed the outer tunic, revealing the heavy chainmail armour he'd worn beneath it. Then at last, he took off the undertunic until he was half-naked before her. She bit her lip slightly, and he reached for the fallen clothing to fold it. She disliked any chamber in disarray, and he wanted to please her.

But she surprised him, saying, 'Leave it be, Rhys. I want to see the rest of you.'

He caught her gaze, slowly unfastening his chausses and braies. Those, too, he left on the floor before he straightened to face her. His heavy erection bobbed, but he let her look her fill. Seeing the fascination in her expression and the unveiled interest only intensified his arousal.

'Lie down,' she commanded. He walked towards the bed and pulled back the coverlet. Then he arranged the pillows and lay back so his shaft rested against his stomach. She went to stand beside the bed. Her red hair held the waves of her braid, and it spilled over her bodice. She let the *brat* fall from her shoulders, and slowly unlaced her gown. It hung against her shoulders, and he was spellbound by the sight of her creamy skin. She lifted the gown away until she stood naked before him.

Her breasts were fuller, rosier than he'd remembered. Her waist held a slight curve, one that made his heart ache at the sight of it.

'Come here,' he bade his wife. 'Let me love you.'

'In time,' she answered. She moved to lie beside him, and he rolled to face her, resting his palm against her backside. She was the most beautiful woman he'd ever seen, and he was grateful that she was his to protect.

'What do you want, Lianna?' he asked.

She took his right hand and guided it between her legs. He gritted his teeth when he discovered that she was already wet for him. 'I want you to pleasure me.'

'All night,' he swore. 'Until you beg me to stop.'

Lianna lifted her leg atop his hip, giving him easier access. He stroked the wet pearl of her, watching as she responded, rising to his call.

She reached out to cup one of her breasts, and offered it to his mouth. 'Kiss me here. But be gentle.'

Rhys obeyed, gently stroking the tip with his tongue. Her reaction was instantaneous, a moan spilling from her lips. He stilled instantly, not wanting to hurt her.

'No, don't stop,' she breathed. 'It feels good…only stronger than I'd imagined.'

He used two fingers to enter her body, caressing her deep within. With his thumb, he circled her nodule, with the gentlest touch.

Her body was trembling, her breathing coming in shorter gasps. And this time when he suckled her breast again, she arched hard, her nails digging into his hair. Her response was almost violent, and seeing her like this only made him want her more.

He was startled when she reached for his erection and guided him inside. He slid home easily, sheathing himself fully. Lianna changed her position, pressing him to his back so she was atop him.

Her eyes were bright with desire, and he drank in the sight of her beautiful body with the swollen nipples and the growing child within her. She remained on her knees, rising and thrusting against him.

When she squeezed her inner walls against his shaft, his hands fisted the sheets, unable to stop the fierce jolt of pleasure that rolled through him. She took charge of him, making love to him.

But it was not about conquest. With each thrust, she was offering herself to him, giving him what he needed most. He sat up to bring them closer, and she wrapped her legs around his waist.

'Is this all right?' she whispered. 'Does it bother you that I am claiming you?'

It didn't. Instead, he felt the rightness of being with this woman, of loving her. There was no sense that she was trying to force him into anything—only that she was trying to please him.

'Do what you will with me,' he murmured against her mouth, kissing her deeply. 'I belong to you, Lianna. And I love you.'

The words transformed her, and Lianna kissed him back, sliding her tongue against his. She had wanted to show her husband how much she needed him, and she had also wanted to take away the harsh memories of Analise. Once before, a woman had given orders, punishing him when he did not obey.

But she had wanted to take command of him in a manner that pleased him. She wanted to love him, to give of herself, until he could no longer bear the intensity of her touch.

'I love you,' she told him, continuing to thrust upon

him. The kiss grew more heated, and he moved in counterpoint, penetrating her deeply. Lianna was fighting for her own control, and when he moved his thumb between them, pressing against her intimate flesh, she felt the release rising within her.

She leaned back, changing the angle so he was rubbing against her as she sat back. But it still was not quite what she needed. He seemed to sense it, and he asked, 'What do you want from me, Lianna?'

'I want you to take command now,' she whispered.

Rhys stopped moving but remained embedded inside her. He leaned forward and kissed one nipple, then the other. The heat and wetness of his mouth echoed in her womb, and she murmured, 'Yes. Like that.'

He changed their position, rolling her to her back. Then he slid his tongue over the erect nipple, softly touching it until she began to shiver with need. Her body was burgeoning against his, needing him.

But he didn't move at all. Instead, his rigid erection pressed against her while he continued his exquisite torment of her breasts.

She raised her knees, shuddering as the feelings gathered into a tight ball, rising higher until suddenly she broke apart. Violent tremors rocked through her, and she gasped with the force of the release. Rhys balanced his weight upon his arms, and she grasped his hips, silently urging him to thrust.

With each stroke, she felt her body merging into his, becoming one. This man was everything to her, and it frightened her to think that she'd nearly lost him.

She met his hips with her own as he drove within her, his body tensing as she squeezed him tightly.

'I love you,' she whispered again. And with the words, he gripped her bottom and thrust inside over and over until he groaned and seized his own release. She felt thoroughly loved, and suddenly she realised that Rhys belonged with her. No matter what happened, he would be at her side and she at his.

They could never know what the future would bring or if her fate would be the same as her mother's. But for now, they could live each day, loving one another, for as long as possible.

Rhys ran his palms down her spine, cupping her bottom as he remained buried inside her. 'Are you all right?'

'I feel loved,' she confessed, smiling softly. 'And whatever happens, wherever we live, I am yours.'

'You *are* loved,' he answered. 'With everything I am, Lianna, I love you. And we will find a way to live here and at Montbrooke. I swear it.'

She kissed him again as he stroked his hands over her body. There had been a time when she would have done anything to avoid marriage to this man.

But he was the best thing that had ever happened to her.

Yuletide

Outside, fat flakes of snow drifted down to the ground. Lianna sat inside her chamber, watching it fall. It was the morning of the solstice, and her people had planned a feast this night to celebrate. Already, her stomach rumbled at the delicious scents coming from outside.

A knock sounded at the door, and when she called

out for the person to enter, her maid Orna arrived, carrying yards of emerald silk. The colour was beautiful, and Lianna rose to greet the older woman. 'What have you brought?'

''Tis a gift from the MacKinnons. They want you to wear it on this day.'

She brightened with joy and agreed. With her maid's help, she donned the gown, and Orna arranged her hair so that it fell across her shoulders. Last, Lianna wore the ruby that her husband had given her, letting it rest at the edge of her bodice. 'It is beautiful,' she said, running her hands over the silk. 'I will have to thank them.'

'Follow me,' Orna said. 'You can tell them yourself.'

Lianna wondered if there was more that her maid hadn't said, but she noticed that the older woman was also dressed in a clean, crimson gown. Curiosity caught her, so she accompanied the old woman down the stairs where she found Rhys waiting for her. He, too, was dressed in new finery. She smiled and greeted him, taking his hand. 'You look handsome, my husband.'

He kissed her cheek. 'You look lovely as well.' Then he nodded towards Orna. 'I was told that the MacKinnons have invited us to their feast. But I thought it would be this evening.'

She shrugged. 'As did I. What are they planning, do you think?'

'I've no idea.' But he guided her outside. The snow had stopped falling, and she was startled to see the clan lined up on both sides of the clearing, creating a pathway for them. All were dressed in finery, and she also saw the Norman soldiers standing among them. One of the MacKinnon girls came forward, her hair tied up in colourful ribbons.

'They are here for your wedding celebration,' came a deep voice from behind them. Lianna turned and saw her father Alastair standing there. He was dressed as befitted a clan chief, with a saffron shirt and hose, as well as a hat adorned with a hawk's feather.

'But we have been married for months now,' Lianna said.

'Not properly,' her father said. 'You are a Scot, and you should be married as one of us.' He nodded towards the people. 'Go on, then. The priest is waiting.'

A sudden swell of emotion caught at her heart, and Rhys squeezed her hand. When she met his gaze, she fought back tears of happiness. The people had remembered her desire to be wedded here, and this was their way of accepting Rhys among them.

She took his arm as he helped her down the stairs, through the snow. The people cheered for them, and she smiled as they walked towards the kirk. Someone had decorated it with holly and greenery for the Yuletide season, and the priest stood outside the door, ready to hear their vows.

A few tears did escape when he began the words in Latin, offering blessings upon her and Rhys. She spoke the vows binding them, and he did the same. All throughout the Mass, she kept her gaze fixed upon her husband's face, her heart filled up with joy.

Afterwards, a deafening roar of approval sounded from the crowd, and Rhys kissed her. He lifted her up so the clan could see the new bride, and she laughed at him. 'It must feel as if you are lifting a fat cow.'

'I am lifting the two most important people in this world,' he said quietly. 'And I am proud to be your husband.'

She touched her forehead to his, whispering words of love. After he lowered her to stand, the clansmen began carrying long trestle tables into Alastair's house. Then came the food—roasted mutton, fish, boiled eggs, beef, cheese, and plenty of ale.

Rhys walked with her back into the house and their table had been raised up on the dais. He guided her to sit at the centre of the table, and Alastair beckoned for two of the servants to come forward. They were carrying a large barrel of wine, and Lianna waited for them to set it down. But Alastair raised a hand, saying, 'We will wait until all the people are inside, to offer our blessings.'

Dozens of clansmen, women, and children entered, taking their places at the long trestle tables. Several children were too excited to sit, and two chased one another until their fathers intervened.

'I sent for our best wine to celebrate the occasion of my daughter's wedding to Rhys de Laurent,' Alastair said. 'This barrel has not been opened for many years.'

There was a gleam in his eyes as he turned to them both. 'It took two men to bring this wine here. And I believe you will understand why it was so heavy when they pour it.' He nodded for the men to open the barrel, and Lianna wondered what the reason was for her father's amusement.

She passed her goblet, but instead of wine, gold and silver coins poured from the opening of the barrel.

The people uttered exclamations of surprise, and

Rhys began to laugh. 'So this was where your brother hid your treasure.'

Lianna picked up several of the coins, and let them fall through her fingers. She could hardly believe that they had been here all along, but a part of her grew thoughtful. Her brother had stolen the coins from her, but he hadn't gambled them away, as she had believed. Instead, he had saved them, along with the rest of his winnings.

He had made many mistakes, but she chose to forgive him. And for her father to find the coins, on this day above all days, made her want to believe the treasure was an unexpected wedding gift from her brother.

She picked up several of the coins and met Rhys's gaze. With a warm smile and a nod of silent understanding between them, they began tossing the fallen coins into the crowd of people, sharing the wealth.

There was laughter among the people as the children scrambled for the coins, and a different barrel of wine was opened to share. Rhys raised his goblet and offered a toast, 'To the MacKinnons!'

'To the bride and groom!' another man answered, and the cheers erupted through the house, filling the space with joy. There would be enough food and wealth to see them through all the years ahead.

And in time, a new life would be born into the world. Lianna rested her palms upon their child, feeling as if there had never been a moment of greater happiness than this.

Epilogue

Four years later

Rhys stood with his brother Warrick and their sister Joan while their father, Edward de Laurent, lay in his bed, his face grey in pallor. They did not know how much time remained, but he knew his father was dying.

The door opened abruptly, and his three-year-old daughter Sorcha came skipping in. Her face was filled with smiles, and her dark hair framed a mischievous face. 'Grandfather, I brought you flowers!' She carried a fist filled with buttercups, and Rhys scooped her up in his arms before she could pounce upon the bed.

'Your grandsire is very tired, Sorcha. Leave him be.'

Seconds later, Lianna hurried through the doorway. 'I am so sorry, Lord Montbrooke. She was too fast for me.' And it was little wonder, given that she was heavily pregnant with another child.

'Both of you may stay,' he said. 'It does not matter.'

Perhaps the little girl brought him memories of his younger days. Rhys let Sorcha sit beside the old man, and she pressed the crushed buttercups into his hand. 'For you,' she insisted. And a faint smile cracked across the man's face.

Then he turned back to Warrick. His expression held regret, and he ventured quietly, 'I have need of your help, if you are willing.'

Over the past four years, there had been a tentative peace between them. Warrick had fought hard to win the heart of the woman he had loved, and now their son, Stephen, had become the pride of his grandfather, while his sister, Mary, was outspoken and fierce. It was no secret that Edward's brittle hatred had cracked apart at the presence of his grandchildren—especially after Rowena had died last winter. He had endless patience, and it did seem that he was trying to atone for his earlier misconceptions. He gave his grandchildren anything and everything they wanted, and in return, there was a fragile truce restored between Warrick and himself.

Edward took a breath. 'I have arranged a marriage for Joan, in Ireland. I would like you and Rhys to accompany her there, to witness the betrothal.'

Joan appeared horrified at the idea. 'No. You cannot ask this of me.'

'It is well past the time you should have been wedded,' he said. 'And I trust Warrick and Rhys to be there on my behalf.'

Joan took a step back. 'Did you forget what happened the last two times I was betrothed?' Her voice came out in a quaver. 'They both died, Father. I am cursed, and no man will ever want to wed me.' She shuddered at the thought. 'And besides that, I am too old.'

Edward shrugged with disinterest. 'You are still breathing, are you not? You may be too old for child-bearing, but this husband will not mind. He has children from his first marriage.'

'But...Ireland?' Joan looked appalled at the prospect. 'You would send me away, to be married to a stranger? One who will probably die, too?'

A tightness stole over Edward's face. 'Your fears are meaningless, Joan. You will do as you are told.'

Rhys saw the panic on his sister's face and intervened. 'Don't be afraid, Joan. I will go with Warrick, and you may meet the man. If he does not suit, the betrothal will not happen.' He caught a glimpse of his wife's face, and Lianna nodded her approval. Then she went to stand at his side and held his hand in silent support.

'We also have an alliance with the King of Laochre, Patrick MacEgan,' Rhys reminded Joan. 'And Warrick holds estates in Ireland now, through his marriage to Rosamund.'

His sister still appeared uneasy. 'I don't want to be married.'

'You will not be alone in Ireland, I promise you.' Warrick came to stand beside her. 'All of us will go, if it will make you feel better.'

But Joan did not seem eager to make the journey. 'No, I would prefer to stay here. I may become a bride of the Church.'

'I will not give your dowry over to a greedy abbot.' Edward grimaced at the thought, and at that, Sorcha hopped down from his bedside, returning to her mother.

Lianna picked their daughter up, and Sorcha nestled her cheek against hers. Then she brightened and smiled at Joan. 'Don't worry. You're going to marry a prince.'

At that, Edward gave a bark of laughter. 'She has no hope of that, sweet girl. But perhaps a nobleman will do.'

Sorcha shook her head. 'You're wrong. It will be a prince, and he will love her very much.'

Rhys didn't bother to correct his daughter, for she was strong-willed and loved to argue. 'We will discuss our travel plans later,' he told Joan. 'But the choice is yours.' He took Sorcha from Lianna's arms, knowing that his wife's back was bothering her.

Then they departed his father's chamber, while Sorcha continued to chatter about Irish princes with castles. Lianna only smiled. 'Orna has been filling her head with stories.'

'So she has.' Rhys brought Sorcha back to their bed and tucked her in for a nap, placing her cat beside her to snuggle. Then he embraced his wife from behind, nuzzling her neck as they waited for their daughter to fall asleep. 'Do you think we should let Joan have her wish to remain unwed?'

Lianna turned around. 'My father arranged a marriage for me, and it turned out to be the greatest gift of my life. Let Joan meet the man and decide for herself.'

Rhys drew his arms around her waist. 'You didn't want me at first. Or have you forgotten?'

She reached up to embrace him. 'Oh, I wanted you

from the first moment I saw you. When I believed you were a handsome Scot, come to carry me off.'

'And when you found that I was a Norman, you were eager to be rid of me,' he teased. He kissed her lightly, loving the way she responded to him.

'I was stubborn,' she confessed. 'But then I grew to love you for the man you are. And I never intend to let you go.'

He claimed her mouth, kissing her until both of them were breathless. 'If I had a thousand years in your arms, Lianna, it would never be enough.'

'But we have every day of the rest of our lives. And I will love you through all of them.'

Rhys held her close, so grateful for the love of this woman. His life had been years of meaningless duty before Lianna MacKinnon had entered it. But now, she had filled up the emptiness, offering him the precious gift of her heart.

And nothing in this world would ever part them.

* * * * *

If you enjoyed this story,
you won't want to miss the first book in
Michelle Willingham's
WARRIORS OF THE NIGHT *series*

FORBIDDEN NIGHT WITH THE WARRIOR

And look for
FORBIDDEN NIGHT WITH THE PRINCE
coming soon!

And, if you're looking for more sexy warriors,
you'll love Michelle Willingham's
WARRIORS OF IRELAND *duet!*

WARRIOR OF ICE
WARRIOR OF FIRE

COMING NEXT MONTH FROM

HARLEQUIN®

HISTORICAL

Available February 20, 2018

All available in print and ebook via Reader Service and online

MISS MURRAY ON THE CATTLE TRAIL (Western)
by Lynna Banning
Cowboy Zachariah Strickland has no choice but to take greenhorn Alexandra Murray with him on his cattle trail. As feelings mount, could it be that Alex belongs in the Wild West—*with* Zach?

FROM GOVERNESS TO COUNTESS (Regency)
Matches Made in Scandal • by Marguerite Kaye
Count Aleksei Derevenko hired governess Allison Galbraith for her skills as a herbalist, not a mistress! But with rumors spreading and Allison's fragile reputation, will the price of their passion be one worth paying?

RESCUED BY THE EARL'S VOWS (Regency)
by Ann Lethbridge
Lord Jaimie Sanford is Lady Tess Ingram's last resort when seeking help to avoid a forced marriage or banishment. However, a convenient arrangement soon becomes more than is strictly proper...

THE WARRIOR'S VIKING BRIDE (Viking)
by Michelle Styles
Celtic warlord Aedan kidnaps and returns warrior maiden Dagmar to her estranged father. When ordered to marry, Dagmar chooses Aeden, expecting him to refuse—but he's intent on making her his bride!

THE TON'S MOST NOTORIOUS RAKE (Regency)
by Sarah Mallory
When Molly Morgan is rescued by handsome Beau Russington, the scandalous rake shakes up her quiet country life. The sparks between them *could* be explosive, if Molly dares to surrender...

LORD RAVENSCAR'S INCONVENIENT BETROTHAL (Regency)
Wild Lords and Innocent Ladies • by Lara Temple
The Marquess of Ravenscar is furious when heiress Lily Wallace refuses him purchase of her property. But when they're scandalously trapped together, there's only one solution: take Lily as his betrothed before desire consumes them completely...

If you are receiving 4 books per month and would like to receive all 6, please call Customer Service at 1-800-873-8635.
